A TINCTURE OF SECRETS AND LIES

WILLIAM SAVAGE

Ridge & Bourne

A TINCTURE OF SECRETS AND LIES

by William Savage

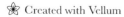 Created with Vellum

For Jenn and my daughters

"The boast of heraldry, the pomp of pow'r,
And all that beauty, all that wealth e'er gave,
Awaits alike th' inevitable hour.
The paths of glory lead but to the grave."

Elegy Written in a Country Churchyard
Thomas Gray (1716–1771)

1

APRIL 13TH, 1793

'I'M AFRAID THERE'S VERY LITTLE MORE THAT I CAN DO, MRS Probert,' Adam Bascom said. 'I've given him something to ease the pain at least. It won't be long now.'

He looked around the wretched hovel in which they lived and wished he could do more for her as well. Without the few shillings each week that her husband had brought in – and his exploits as a poacher — she would be hard pressed to manage on her own.

'Have you asked the Overseers of the Poor to give you out-relief?' he said.

'Aye, that I have. They says I have to wait until my husband is dead before they'll consider it. How they think I'm going to manage until then, God only knows.'

Adam felt in his pocket. He knew there wasn't much money there. It wasn't sensible to carry too much cash when you were out on the roads at night. He took the few coins into his palm and peered at them in the dim light from the tallow candle. Fifteen shillings and fourpence. He gave the old woman fourteen shillings, waving away her expressions of gratitude. He wished he could have given her more. If the Overseers refused her out-relief, she would

1

end up in the workhouse, like many another aged widow before her. That was a fate he wouldn't wish on anyone.

'I'll leave you this bottle of medicine,' he said. 'Give him five drops if you think the pain is getting too bad. The taste is bitter, so you will need to put it into something strong tasting.' He was going to say wine or brandy, but realised she would have neither. 'Strong ale, perhaps.'

'Probert likes his ale, sure enough. Thanks to you, Doctor, I can get him some now.' She jingled the coins she'd tucked in the pocket of her apron. 'Last he'll ever have, probably.'

It was fully dark by the time Adam left. Fancy, his horse, didn't like being out in the dark. To tell the truth, he didn't either. Still, it was only a few miles back to his home in Aylsham. They'd be there in half an hour.

He was never sure afterwards what had startled his horse. Just a vague memory of a loud noise and something white close by. It could have been a barn owl. Whatever it was, it scared Fancy so badly that she must have reared up, throwing her rider into the road. That's what he told himself anyway. He had no real recollection of what happened. One minute they were plodding along, his mind occupied by sad reflections on the wretched state of the labouring poor, the next he was on the ground, fighting for breath against the agonising pain in his arm and side. Then all slid away into blackness.

Barely a mile from where Adam was lying, a man was using his feet to push the body of the young woman he'd just strangled further under the hedge. There wasn't time to bury her properly and he needed to be away from this place. He stood back and tried to imagine he was a casual passer-by. The old cloak he'd brought to cover her blended nicely with the earth and leaves. Unless you bent down and looked carefully underneath the tangle of brambles and gorse that served for a hedge hereabouts, you wouldn't notice anything was there.

God, it was cold on this heathland. Nothing to stop that damned east wind, howling in off the German Ocean. Dark too. He didn't dare risk lighting his lantern again. Someone might notice the light and wonder who was out on the heath so late.

He shook himself, muttering angry words under his breath. There was no need to get so jumpy. All anyone could have seen were a man and girl slipping into that old barn. Nothing sinister about that. He'd enjoyed her for one last time, then come out, one arm around her shoulder, to pull her down and do what needed to be done.

Did she think he would be willing to bury himself in this back-water, while she grew fat and produced a tribe of infants as ignorant and narrow-minded as all the rest? That he would scratch a living and tug his forelock when the squire passed on his grand horse? That was all she and her family were fit for — not him. He had not come here for this. He had another task, another destiny.

That wasn't why he had to kill her though. It was the night when they'd last been lying together in the straw in this same old barn. He'd woken and seen her going through his pack. How she cried when he'd slapped her! Pretended she only wanted to be part of what was so important to him. Promised she'd never do such a thing again. Clung to him. Told him she didn't mind what he was involved in. She'd stick by him, whatever he did, even if he went to prison.

His masters would say he'd brought it on himself. He should have kept his mind on the task before him, not indulged himself in his all-too-frequent vice of womanising. That was why he'd cleared out as quickly as he could, hoping it could end there. He couldn't take the chance of anyone's carelessness revealing his identity. That was far too precious to risk. Those who sent him would be as ruth-less as any English hangman in seeing him pay the price for spoiling their plans. They'd already shown the world that mercy was not something they valued greatly. His best hope had been to leave her and disappear so completely she'd give up hope of finding him. He thought it had worked — until that day in the street.

The silly little bitch had recognised him at once, damn her! Yet even then she could still have saved herself, if she hadn't been so stubborn. Too stupid to let things be! Once she'd managed to make contact again, he knew he'd never be able to shake her off. She had to be silenced. It was the only answer. He had never been the kind to shrink from what needed to be done, however unpleasant it might be.

In the end, killing her had proved shockingly easy. A secret meeting, hastily arranged, a leather strap pulled tight around her throat and it was over. She'd hardly struggled. Now her body was hidden in the dense undergrowth by this hedge. With luck, it might not be discovered until there was nothing to see but bones. If it was found before then, so what? She'd laughed a good many times over that idiot of a local farmer's son who had been pushed by her father into asking if he could walk out with her. If people blamed her death on anyone, it would be him.

Time to head for Norwich. The critical moment, the time for invasion, was approaching and he needed to be in the right place to do what he'd been sent to do. There could be no more mistakes.

He didn't look back.

2

LATER — MUCH LATER — ADAM LEARNED THAT HANNAH, HIS parlourmaid, had been the first to notice the strange noises at the front door. Bumping and scraping, a rattle like the easterly wind made when it blew hard over the German Ocean. Yet that night the air was calm and what breeze there was came from the west. When the girl summoned the courage to open the door to investigate, she found her master fallen in a heap on the doorstep, either dead or unconscious, with the horse, Fancy, standing beside him.

First, she ran to call Mrs Brigstone, the housekeeper, and her son William and Molly, the kitchen maid. Between the four of them, they managed to half carry, half drag Adam inside and stretch him out in the hallway. William fetched a lantern and stumbled in the darkness of the street to the house and shop where Mr Lassimer, the apothecary, lived. All the way he muttered a prayer to himself, 'Please God, let him be at home. Please let him be at home.' The two of them hurried back together, pausing only for the apothecary to snatch up the bag he took when calling on patients.

After the fall, Dr Bascom must have managed to pull himself up one-handed by holding on to a stirrup. Once he was on his feet, Fancy, his horse, led him home. In the state he was in, he could no longer have known where he was or which direction to take. Without the horse, he would have died where he lay or stumbled into a ditch to perish alone.

Of Peter's arrival and the efforts to get him undressed from his travelling clothes and into bed, Adam retained no recollection beyond a vague sense of well-known voices and a relaxation of his fear. He had few memories of his journey home either. Vague images of houses and streets as they entered Aylsham. Fancy refusing to take him further. Hands lifting him from the ground, then setting him down again. Someone saying, 'he's burning with fever.' Nonsense. He'd rarely been so cold. Being lifted again and carried somewhere.

After that, nothing but darkness and indistinct sounds. Once a familiar voice urging him to stay with them — whatever that meant. In the background, the sound of a woman sobbing. Someone urging her to leave if she couldn't control herself. A man's voice, one he knew, saying he had done everything possible; the rest lay in the hands of providence. Once, such a sense of repose as he had never known, so all he wished was to let go and sink into the blessed peacefulness for ever.

It was not to be. A different voice, perhaps a spirit or an angel. Either way, this being stroked his hand, bent over him and whispered something that cut through the fog of his battered mind.

'No! No! You cannot leave me. One such loss is enough; a second would destroy me. Can you understand me, Adam? I forbid you to die. I forbid it. Oh God, don't take him from me!'

A soft touch on his brow that he knew was a kiss.

Adam didn't die, though Peter told him later he had come closer to death than any man should, save at the end. Even after the fever broke, he lay inert and senseless as his body recovered its strength and stability. People forced him to drink and washed his body, though he could not acknowledge their presence. Instead, his mind would fill on a sudden with vivid images, so that he moaned and wept.

Lying on the ground with his horse, Fancy, nuzzling his face. The darkness of the sky and an owl calling from somewhere nearby.

A wonderful sense of comfort, marred only by the coldness of the rain falling onto his cheek. He must have stayed like that for some time, until a nagging from his mind urged him to start moving again, to go home. Several times he attempted to get up and failed. It seemed there were hours of pain and effort, until he could stand — but only if he held on tightly to Fancy's stirrup. Without the horse by him, he would never have managed it.

He must have stumbled along, leaning on the horse, for the next thing he remembered was being outside his own door, drenched to the skin yet so hot that sweat mingled with the rain that ran into his eyes. That was where his strength ran out. He fell against the door. Tried to call out. Then darkness swept over him and all faded into nothingness.

He returned to a voice in the swirling blackness. A voice he recognised. To open his eyes was beyond his strength, let alone giving a reply, but he could make out what was said. Peter Lassimer.

'Has he shown any sign of returning to his wits, Mrs Bascom? It is five days now. His strength must be nearly at an end, for he has eaten nothing and drunk but the few drops you have been able to dribble between his lips.'

Now his mother.

'It is hard to say, Mr Lassimer. From time to time he seems about to wake, for he tosses and turns, often moaning and weeping. Then he sinks back into whatever darkness surrounds him. To be plain with you, I fear as much for his mind as his body. I said as much to Lady Alice when she came last —'

That was the moment when, with a near inhuman effort, Adam opened his eyes and forced a single word from between cracked lips.

'Thirsty.'

The effect was overwhelming. His mother snatched him into her arms, tears flooding down her face. She seemed to be trying to suffocate him with kisses. Past her head, Adam could see Peter, grinning like a perfect fool and jangling a small bell as if he would raise the dead.

Hannah the maid ran into the room, white-faced and gasping, to be sent post-haste to tell Mrs Brigstone, the housekeeper, to send up a cup of the rich beef tea she had kept ready for this moment. Peter was gently disentangling Adam from his mother's grip and peering into his face.

'Welcome back, my friend,' he said. 'Welcome back. We were beginning to despair of you. Still, no matter. You are awake and, if I am any judge, as near to sanity as I have ever seen you.'

3

SOON AFTER DAWN, MISS SOPHIA LASALLE PAUSED IN THE DOORWAY of Adam's room. She could hear people moving about in the kitchen below, but the rest of the house had that stillness that betokens the earliest hours of the day. The bedroom before her was spacious, well-lit and furnished with elegance. Several landscapes reminiscent of those by Claude Lorraine hung on the walls, along with two fine mirrors in gilded frames. There were Chinese vases on the mantel, either side of a carriage clock in a case dark enough to be of ebony with gilded mounts and decorations. Even the mantelpiece itself was made of pale, figured marble — or of some plaster or similar material painted to appear of that stone. Not the normal bedroom of a bachelor, not even a wealthy one. Even so, something about it — a certain lack of any but the essential furniture, the plainness of the bed curtains — indicated the absence of the feminine. She had reconciled herself to the knowledge that the ordering of this house would never be hers. A foolish, girlish dream. She would be unlikely to marry anyone, let alone a wealthy man like Dr Bascom.

Still in the doorway, she looked across the room to where he lay in his bed, propped up on several pillows. He seemed to be asleep.

Then you noticed the heavy bandages on one arm, lying stiff on the coverlet. The pallor of the face, with its darkened eye sockets and the dark fuzz of beard on the cheeks.

She heard a floorboard creak behind her and turned, expecting to see Mrs Bascom or Hannah, the maid. It was the apothecary.

'You are about early this morning, Miss LaSalle.'

'As I have been for several mornings past, Mr Lassimer. It has become my habit to check on the doctor at the start of the day.'

'You have also spent many night-time hours in this room, as I understand,' Peter said. 'Dr Bascom could not have hoped for more devoted nursing than you and his mother have supplied. I am sorry if I startled you just now. Hannah let me in through the back door. I crept up to the room as silently as I could. I hoped my patient was asleep and do not wish to disturb him. Dr Bascom needs rest more than anything. His fever has passed, but he is weak and exhausted. He lay so long between life and death I had come close to despair.'

Peter was about to move up to the bed when a slight noise caught his attention. Adam was not asleep. He was peering at the visitors in the doorway.

'Miss LaSalle? Lassimer?'

'You should be asleep. How are you feeling? It's a miracle you're alive at all.'

'I don't feel very alive. My head aches, my side and arm hurts. I cannot recall much of what happened between leaving old Probert's cottage to come home and waking up in this bed. How did I get like this?'

'As far as we can tell, you fell from your horse.'

'It feels more as if the horse fell on me.'

'Maybe she did, Doctor.' Sophia tried to keep her tone light. 'All we know is that your maid found you lying on the doorstep with the horse standing next to you. Where you fell and how you got home is a mystery.'

'My horse?'

'Well enough, your groom tells us.'

'I think I owe her my life. From what little I do recall, it was by walking beside her that I came home again. She knew where to go. I barely knew how to set one foot in front of the other. How did you get here, Miss LaSalle?'

'William came to tell your mother what had befallen you and she insisted in returning with him at once. I came to help her with looking to your needs. This is the fourth day since we came.'

'You could not have had better nursing, Bascom,' Peter said. 'This young lady and your mother have divided the hours between them. You have never been without someone watching over you.'

'Was I so very sick, Lassimer?'

'When you were found outside the door, you were soaked to the skin, shivering and delirious. It wasn't surprising you developed a most malignant fever. Five days you lay here senseless, until your fever broke last night.'

'Why is my arm wrapped up? Why can't I move it? My chest is stiff too, I can hardly breathe.'

'A fine physician you are! Can you not diagnose your own hurts? Your left arm is broken in two places. Your left collarbone is broken. You have one, possibly two cracked or broken ribs and severe bruising to your chest. You also have many cuts and scratches to your face, neck and shoulder and the large lump on the back of your head. I've done all I can for you. Nature must do the rest. That requires you to allow your body time and peace to recover. You are not to even to try to get up for at least another week. After that, you may rise for a few hours each day and sit in a chair.'

He raised his hands to stop Adam speaking.

'No, no. I know what I am doing. Besides, I assure you that if you try to get out of bed you will find it far more difficult and painful than you think.'

'But —'

'You have been closer to dying than any person I have ever known, Bascom, yet you survived. What saved you? I would like to say my unmatched skill, but to tell the truth I have no idea. The devoted nursing of Miss LaSalle and your mother must have helped, but I dare say even they had their doubts. Maybe we all despaired of you. All, that is, save for Lady Fouchard. I've never known a woman so determined on the outcome she wanted. Whether she prayed to God or sent him his orders, I cannot tell. Whatever she did clearly worked. Behold, you are alive and on what I believe to be the road to recovery. A long road it will be though.'

'Lady Fouchard has been here?'

'Several times in the past three days, Doctor,' Sophia told him. 'Your mother sent William to tell her of your situation, knowing she would be concerned about you. Yet even she did not expect her ladyship to be so assiduous in visiting your bedside. Mr Scudamore and his sister have also been here.'

Adam said nothing to that. What did so many visits mean? What had prompted her to come in person too? He gave up. There was no doubt Lady Alice Fouchard knew her own mind. She always did. A memory struck him. Had it been Lady Alice who told him so fiercely that he must not die?

'What now?' he asked, breaking the silence after several minutes had passed.

'I will go down and call Hannah to tell Cook to prepare you something suitable to build up your strength. Poor Hannah. She and Molly must be worn out with attending to all our needs. Will you stay for something to eat or drink, Mr Lassimer?'

'I thank you, Miss LaSalle, but I must be on my way to supervise the opening of my shop. I have more patients to visit as well. I only came to see if last night's improvement had been maintained.'

'What I meant was what must I do now, Lassimer, other than to stay in bed for a few days.'

'I have told your mother. You must have complete rest for at least two more weeks. Then, depending on your progress, you may go downstairs. In due time, you may take short walks into the garden. Travel, or strong exertion of any kind, is forbidden for at least six weeks after you are up and about. Horse riding for much longer. Indeed, given this propensity to fall off, you would do well to confine yourself to a carriage in future.'

'Weeks stuck in this house! You cannot mean that, Lassimer. I will die of boredom. What about my practice?'

'Your practice will manage very well without you. It has done so before, while you were away solving your mysteries, or whatever you call them. Do you want to risk your fever returning? Hush now, here is your mother coming. I assure you she will backup what I say.'

Adam looked across at his mother as she entered the room. It was like being a child again. She showed the same business-like manner, the frown she used to conceal her concern and the same crisp, no-nonsense tone of voice.

'Do as Mr Lassimer says, Adam. Let there be no argument. I have promised Lady Alice that you will follow the treatment he has prescribed and do so without complaint. I will not be forsworn.'

Adam struggled to sit up against the pillows.

'Lie still,' his mother said. 'Lady Fouchard is not here at present, though she has been a constant visitor. She is as worried about you as all of us. It would be a poor return to Sophia and myself for our sleepless nights if you were to endanger yourself now.'

'I fear, Mrs Bascom, our patient appears more concerned for the good of his practice than the feelings of Lady Fouchard and our worries.'

'Your practice will manage well enough without you, Adam,' his mother said. 'Let us hear no more of such nonsense. Besides, you are a wealthy man. You need not wander around the countryside at night, especially to treat the poor.'

'It is my duty to help such unfortunates, Mother. No matter if they cannot pay me. I may not need their money, but they surely need what help I can bring to them.'

'You have a greater duty to your family and friends. I'm sure Mr Lassimer will look after any who need urgent treatment.' She swept onwards without bothering to ask whether he would or not. 'Alice, Lady Fouchard, has visited us to enquire after your welfare three days in succession while you were unconscious. You would not believe the politeness and condescension of her manner towards us all. She is such an elegant lady too, who wears only the best and most fashionable clothes.'

'Then I must shave before she comes again,' Adam said. 'I imagine I look like a brigand or a pirate. Call for some water, soap and my razor, Lassimer, and help me to get up.'

'You look more like a vagabond to me,' his friend said. 'How many more times must I say you must not leave your bed? If you try, you will fall down and hurt yourself further.'

'I will ask her not to come today,' his mother said. 'William can go with a note explaining that you have at last come to yourself, but need complete rest. If you behave yourself, I will suggest she visits you tomorrow. If a few hairs on your face concern you so much, I will send a maid to tell the local barber to come early tomorrow morning to shave you.'

'Don't worry, Mrs Bascom,' Peter said. 'I saw Mr Charles Scudamore riding up a few moments ago. Doubtless he will carry news of the doctor's state to his aunt and explain when she can next pay him a visit. My, my, Bascom, you are becoming far too excited at the prospect of seeing that young widow again.'

Adam glared at the apothecary. That only produced a burst of laughter.

'Behave yourself, sir.' Mrs Bascom would not allow Peter to speak with such levity towards a member of the aristocracy. 'It is right that my son should prepare himself correctly for her ladyship's visit. It is extremely kind of her to come at all. Now listen to me, Adam. Now you are out of danger, I'm planning to spend a few days at Trundon Hall with your brother. Sophia will come with me, of course. Mr Lassimer here will supervise your progress and, through his good offices, I have engaged a nurse to attend to your daily needs.'

'I'm sure my servants. . .'

'They have their own duties, Adam, and none of them are skilled in medical matters. Besides, it was Lady Alice herself who suggested I should do this.'

'It is a foolish person who ignores a suggestion from Lady Alice, as I hear,' Peter muttered, just loud enough for Adam to catch his words.

Mrs Bascom either missed what he said or chose to ignore any further disrespect towards the upper classes.

'Do you require anything to eat or to drink?' she asked Adam. 'If not, we will leave you to sleep. I will attend to whatever Mr Scudamore wants.'

Nevertheless, Charles came in a few minutes later. He had been allowed in for five minutes at the most, he said, but only because he had come at his aunt's request. It still seemed odd to Adam to hear him use that word of Lady Alice, since he and Ruth, his twin, were but a year or two younger than her. Charles's father was Lady Alice's eldest brother and there were nearly twenty years between those two siblings.

'My aunt will be delighted that you have regained consciousness,' he said. 'Expect to see her yourself tomorrow, soon after noon. Her dressmaker is coming at ten o'clock, so she will not arrive before then — unless she is so eager to see you she bundles the poor woman out of the house at record speed. Now I must go. I'm glad to have good tidings to bear her about your recovery. The other news I carry will cause great upset. A young woman, the daughter of the blacksmith in Melton Constable, has been most foully murdered. Her father is a skilled craftsman and was a favourite of Lady Alice's late husband. Sir Daniel employed him often on the estate, so he became well-known to all of us.'

'Who can have done this dreadful deed?'

'No one knows. Perhaps some vagabond. At present, suspicion rests against the young man who was courting her. He cannot be found, I am told.'

'Do you know how she was killed?'

'Strangled. A passing labourer found her body pushed underneath a hedge not far from her home. . . Bascom, Bascom! I know that expression. Your mother will have my hide if she thinks I have set you off worrying about yet another crime. You can do nothing in this case, especially confined to your room. I wish I had not mentioned it.'

'I'm glad you did, Scudamore. I may need to rest my body, but my mind definitely needs exercise. Can you tell me anymore?'

'No, I'm glad to say.'

Was the murderer some wandering beggar? People often seized on that idea only because they could come up with none better. After Charles had gone, Adam cursed himself for forgetting to ask at what time of day the murder had taken place. He should also have enquired whether there had been an assault on the young lady's person or if she had been robbed. Would Charles have mentioned such details? The suitor could not be found. That was suspicious, but it might not signify that he had caused her death. . .

Adam was busy turning these problems over in his mind when he fell asleep.

4

APRIL 22ND, 1793

WHY HAD HE WOKEN CONFUSED AND MUDDLED THIS MORNING? HOW much laudanum had Lassimer given him to help him sleep? He would have to put a stop to that. Better to lie awake in discomfort than find his mind so disarrayed.

You do not come as close to death as Adam had done and return untouched. Even he was only dimly aware how much his mind had been forever altered. He had been within a hair's breadth of dying before he had truly lived; and that was a mistake you could not risk making a second time. Eventually, those about him would also notice the change, calling it a greater firmness of purpose, or a stronger determination to follow his own inclinations, whatever the rest of the world might think or say. These were only symptoms of the real transformation that had come over him. What had shifted in those days and hours when he wavered between this world and the next was more like the movement of a glass lens in a telescope. The hazy, uncertain view of his future he had previously been content to accept had snapped into focus. He was still uncertain about getting what he craved, but one desire at least was now sharp-edged and incontrovertible. What he wanted most in this world, what he was determined to have if he could — despite all his denials — was the love of Alice, Lady Fouchard. As soon as a suitable opportunity arose, he would ask her to marry him.

Adam shifted again, trying to find how far he could move before the pain started. Not far. Still, there was no doubt he was feeling a little better. He had asked for a cup of chocolate this morning instead of the endless beef broth they had been feeding him. His mother had overruled him in that. Tomorrow would be different.

He raised his right hand and stroked his cheeks. It was surprising what an effect such a small matter as being shaved could make. The barber had agreed to come every other morning until he could manage for himself. When that would be, he didn't know. Progress in other ways was not quite as he wanted. He had insisted on rising to use the chamber pot, only to find he couldn't stand without clinging to the bedpost, while the effort had left him exhausted for more than an hour afterwards.

He frowned. That nurse was also coming today. Peter had told him so.

He was sure he needed no nurse, but his mother was insistent and Peter backed her up. At least it would mean his mother and Miss LaSalle could make their visit to Trundon Hall. He was grateful for their presence, but his mother did insist on treating him as her little boy. Miss LaSalle's sudden reserve towards him also made him feel uncomfortable. What could he have done to her?

Peter came soon after ten, examined his patient and pronounced progress satisfactory. For some reason, he then seemed reluctant to leave. Instead, he moved to the window to look down into the garden.

'I had not realised you are such a favourite of the nobility — aside from Lady Fouchard, of course. Lord Townsend has been enquiring after your health.'

That gave Adam a jolt so that he tried to turn to look at his friend. His sharp cry caused Peter to hurry back to the bedside.

'If you try to change position as violently as that, you'll hurt yourself.'

'You startled me. Did you say Lord Townsend? Viscount Townsend, Deputy Lord Lieutenant of the County?'

'He sent his man of business to my shop this morning for that express purpose.'

'But I have never made the acquaintance of Lord Townsend.'

'It seems the noble lord knows of you and is concerned for your welfare. According to his messenger, he was enquiring both on his own behalf and for others well known to you at the King's Court. What have you been doing on those trips to London?'

'Not visiting the Court, I assure you.'

'I am beginning to think you are quite the man of mystery, Bascom. I assumed your trips were to visit a lady.'

If Peter was fishing, he did not know how close he had come to making a catch. Adam kept his face as blank as possible.

'I had business there, as I told you.'

'No matter.' A shrewd look at the same time. 'I gave the messenger the information he required and he will doubtless relate it to his master. Now, I must be on my way. I will be back this afternoon, eager to hear what you will tell me about your meeting with her ladyship. You had better be careful, Bascom. I am certain she has her eye on you.'

'Stuff and nonsense, as usual. You let your imagination run away with you. Her position in society is far above my own.'

'That will not stop her. She is a widow and may make her own decisions about marriage.'

'There has been no talk of marriage.'

'None yet perhaps—'

'Go away, Lassimer. You weary me with your nonsense.'

After his friend left, Adam could not help his mind running wild. Did he know what her ladyship felt about him? His own growing feelings maybe, but hers …? Best not think about it. Then Viscount Townsend asking about him. What could that be about? Had his brother said something? As Deputy Lord Lieutenant, Viscount Townsend would be bound to have dealings with all the local magistrates. Even so, why express more than the conventional sympathy demanded by politeness?

His mother had placed a small bell by his bedside so he could summon a servant if he needed one. He rang it and Molly, his kitchen maid, came. That surprised him, so he asked her where everyone else was. She chose to take him literally.

'Hannah is gone to Mr Lassimer's shop to collect more medicines, Master. Cook and Mrs Brigstone are in the kitchen. I don't rightly know where William is. I'm here, answering your bell. Your mother and Miss LaSalle went out half-an-hour ago. They said it was to buy gifts for Mrs Bascom's grandchildren. I'm sure they'll return well before Lady Fouchard is due.'

Adam was sure too. The presence of a member of the aristocracy in the house caused his mother immense pleasure. She would not miss a moment of it. Sir Daniel, Lady Alice Fouchard's late husband, had been a wealthy baronet. Her ladyship, as the great-granddaughter of an earl, was an aristocrat in her own right. If Lady Alice did 'have her eye on' Adam, Mrs Bascom would be delirious with joy. The same would not apply to Giles Bascom, Adam's elder brother. Giles may have inherited the family estates, such as they were, but they had not brought him wealth. He was still struggling to pay off the mortgages their feckless father had taken out. Adam knew his brother was already jealous of his success and growing wealth. There was a coldness in their relationship that had not been there before. Marrying a rich widow would be a severe test of their relationship.

Adam pulled himself up. He was getting as bad as Peter. All speculation! He closed his eyes and tried to sleep, but he was far too nervous about what to say to Lady Fouchard.

The visit did not turn out as he expected. Her ladyship swept into the room, accompanied by Adam's mother and Miss Ruth Scudamore. She seated herself and dismissed the others with the curt demand she be allowed to speak with the doctor in private. Once they had gone out, she burst into tears.

'What a fright you gave me! I thought you were going to die. It is but six months since I buried a beloved husband. To have to grieve afresh for a dear, dear friend. It would be too much. I do not think I could bear it. You must never, never do such a thing again.'

Adam was so dumbfounded he became incoherent. 'Your ladyship. . . Lady Alice. . . I never meant to. . . just an accident. . . you must know how deep my regard is for you. . . to have hurt you breaks my heart. . .'

'Hush, my dear Doctor. Remember I am still in mourning.' She bent forward and touched a finger to his lips.

'But not to say what is in my heart. . .'

'Be patient until I have fulfilled my duty. I know you loved my late husband too. Neither of us would wish to sully his memory. Until I am finished with mourning, we must both hold ourselves in check. Give me but a moment to compose myself, Doctor. Now ring that little bell by your bed and tell your maid to ask my niece to join us. I had to have some private speech with you. Even so, it would not be proper to be alone together for too long — even if you are, so Mr Lassimer tells me, almost immobile.'

'It was kind of Miss Scudamore to join you.'

'She is concerned for your health, Doctor. Yet that is not the principal reason why she wished to accompany me. It is to cast her eyes over your mother's companion, Miss LaSalle. Ruth believes her brother is developing a certain *tendresse* towards that young lady. She wishes to decide whether she approves or not.'

Could that be the case? Miss LaSalle was of the right age, tolerably pretty and accomplished. She definitely had a sharp mind — and sometimes a tongue to match it. Could Scudamore have developed warm feelings for her? Yet was it so strange? There was a time when he himself might have inclined in her direction, had he not known how much his mother would have disapproved.

Lady Alice was still talking. 'We are also on our way to undertake a most melancholy duty. Mr Wormald is the blacksmith in Melton Constable and an excellent craftsman in metalwork. My late husband employed him often. Now his eldest daughter, Betsy, has been killed — murdered. He and his wife are beside themselves with grief. Ruth and I go to give him what comfort we may, but I fear it will be little enough. If you had not been confined to your room, I would have asked you to do what you could to discover who the murderer might be.'

Hannah came in and Adam sent her to fetch Miss Scudamore. It gave him a moment to think.

'My lady, it is true my body is hurt. I have also promised to obey Mr Lassimer's instructions and rest. My mind, however, is unaffected and craves activity. If you wish me to seek the killer of this young woman, I will do it — at least as far as I can under the circumstances. If I but had someone to go about for me and ask questions, I would indeed be of help.'

Ruth entered into the room while Adam was speaking and hastened to answer this request. 'My brother would do it. I know that he would. It will do him good to have something definite to do. He is an idle fellow. He's supposed to be looking for a suitable place to establish his legal practice. Yet he displays little diligence in that direction. Instead, he finds constant excuses to come to this house. The reason for that is not far to seek.'

She brought a chair and set it down with a bang beside her aunt's. 'I will also assist you myself, Doctor, so far as I am able. I did not know Betsy Wormald, but no woman deserves to die as she did. If I can help bring the killer to the gallows, where he belongs, you have only to ask.'

Adam hadn't thought of the Scudamore twins. There is the start of my team of investigators, he said to himself. Yet what these two members of the upper gentry will be able to do amongst the working people of Melton Constable I cannot imagine. Still, I need not limit myself to them. I'm sure Peter will help when he can. Then there are my servants…

Lady Alice was looking at her niece with an expression compounded in equal parts of surprise and amusement.

'You are right,' she said after a moment. 'My nephew needs some definite employment. This will do better than most. He can continue to look for a location for his practice at the same time. Do not be too hard on him, Ruth, in the matter of his frequent visits to this house. He too is concerned for the doctor's welfare. Besides, I sent him myself on more than one occasion.'

Ruth's expression and half-suppressed exclamation showed what she thought of that.

'I will tell Mr Wormald that you have agreed to look into this matter, Doctor,' Lady Alice went on. 'As the opportunity arises, I will try to discover further details about the poor girl's death.' She turned and looked at her niece, her eyes sparkling with mischief.

'I will send Charles here to tell you what I have discovered and to receive his orders. Now, Ruth, we must be on our way. I will come again in two or three days if I may, Doctor. Ruth will be with me again, so you may set out her instructions in detail at that time. I am far from sure if it is her brother or she herself who most needs proper employment.'

She rose and took her leave, though Adam could have sworn she winked at him as she went out. No, it could not be. She must have had something in her eye. Well brought-up ladies did not wink at anyone.

5

ADAM'S ELDER BROTHER, GILES, CAME EARLY NEXT MORNING, FULL of complaints. Amelia, his wife, tried to turn the conversation to more cheerful matters, but her husband was having none of it.

'I am so overburdened I wish I had never agreed to become a justice of the peace,' Giles moaned. 'It's bad enough having to spend so much of my time dealing with local matters. Now fear of invasion by the French has brought me yet greater burdens.'

In truth, Giles loved the importance being a magistrate gave him and made constant reference to his status. Along with hunting and shooting, it was how he most liked to spend his time. He was especially eager to remind his upstart younger brother of his official position. Adam might be richer, cleverer and better connected, but only he, Giles, held office under the Crown. Adam winced when he recalled what Peter had told him about Viscount Townsend's enquiry. If only Giles wasn't so fixated on his position as the elder brother, they might be easier with one another.

'The damned militia are bad enough,' he droned. 'Now people are raising volunteer troops to defend the coasts. The men who join are exempt from serving in the militia. That means double the units — and commanders, of course — with no greater number of men

24

serving. Most of these volunteer units are completely untrained or disciplined. Instead of looking to military matters, their colonels amuse themselves designing fancy uniforms. I tell you, Brother, they terrify the locals far more than they will ever frighten the French. Only recently, a troop practising to fire their cannon blew a hole in the side of it. Another troop doing the same thing managed to kill their own officer! It's madness!'

On and on he went. Troops from the Pembrokeshire militia were stationed at Holt. Their bright uniforms and strange accents had turned the heads of the many local girls, so there were constant cases of bastardy to deal with. He was expected to force the man to marry the woman expecting his child, or pay for their upkeep. If they did not, the cost of their children would fall on the parish. Whatever he did, most of these fellows would return to their homes in Wales in due course and leave their local 'wives' anyway. The ratepayers were already complaining about the extra demands, which were bound to drive up the Poor rates.

If that wasn't enough, the smugglers along his part of the coast were also causing concern. The Revenue men kept pressing him to help them, but these so-called free-traders operated in large, well-organised gangs. What resources did he have that would be up to the task? So many men had been taken to serve in the militia or pressed into the Navy, the fishing villages were filled with old men, women and children. And it wasn't just the smugglers. French priva-teers had become a constant menace off the coast, seizing ships for ransom or taking them back to France. Despite the flags they flew, many privateers were crewed by Englishmen. The lure of easy money, he supposed.

Adam nodded and attempted to make sympathetic comments, but none of this was new. Soldiers and sailors had always seduced local girls, then left them and their bastard children to be supported by the parish. The north coast of Norfolk had been infested with smugglers for decades. Adam knew of several local gentlemen whose wine cellars would be a great deal emptier were it not for the wine and spirits brought in by the 'night owls'. Privateers and pirates had preyed on shipping in the German Ocean since time out of mind. His eyelids began to droop. The sound of his brother's voice was sending him to sleep. Fortunately, Amelia was keeping watch and was more interested in Adam's welfare than her husband's monologue. She had doubtless been subjected to it many times.

'We must not tire your brother out, my dear,' she said to her husband. 'I'm sure he sympathises with your problems, but he is in no position to render you any assistance. Besides, it's time we were on our way. Look, here comes the nurse with a bowl of broth.'

Despite his earlier misgivings, Adam had found himself warming to Mrs Munnings, the lady Peter had found to act as his nurse. She was a widow, of course, and an attractive one. Peter would not have known her otherwise. Yet she had other qualities Adam found far more important. She was quiet, competent and did not fuss over him. She got on well with the other members of the household. Best of all, she was attentive to his true needs. For example, the bowl she carried now did not contain the inevitable beef broth. It was a helping of warm, creamy chocolate.

'Mr Lassimer is coming to see you shortly,' she told Adam. 'I gather he is not in a good mood today, so you had best be careful not to upset him. I hoped to persuade him to allow you to spend an hour or so sitting in a chair, but I will leave that for the moment.'

'Do you know what has upset him?'

'I do not. William, your groom, told me. He has been paying court to one of Mr Lassimer's maids. Her master caught them chattering together this morning and chased William away with curses and threats. That's quite unlike Mr Lassimer, as you know well. He usually has the sunniest of dispositions.'

Adam's curiosity got the better of him and he ventured a delicate question.

'Have you known Mr Lassimer long, Mrs Munnings?'

The lady looked at him for a moment, then burst out laughing. 'That's not the real question in your mind, Doctor, is it? No, I have not known him for a long time, only since my husband died a little over twelve months ago. Mr Lassimer's unique way of bringing comfort to a grieving widow proved very effective in my case, as it has for many others, I hear. Does that satisfy your curiosity?'

Adam's blush brought another burst of laughter.

'Here is the man himself. The doctor has proved a model patient, Mr Lassimer. He is already a good deal brighter than when I arrived yesterday.'

'I see he now has you telling lies for him, Mrs Munnings. Model patient he could never be. About his progress, I will make up my own mind, thank you.'

Adam felt so annoyed on Mrs Munnings's behalf that he gave in to the temptation to rebuke his friend.

'What on earth is the matter with you today, Lassimer? There is no need for such bad temper. Did some lady turn you away from her door last night?'

'Don't be coarse, Bascom!'

There must indeed be something amiss. 'What has upset you, my friend? First you are rude to Mrs Munnings and then you snap at me. Out with it! You know my curiosity will not allow me to let up until you have confessed all.'

Peter took little more urging to explain. A quack calling himself Professor Panacea had pasted flyers about the nearby town of Holt, announcing a lecture on 'The Secret Principles of Abundant Health'. The address was to take place in two days' time in the great room at The Three Feathers Inn. He would also be selling bottles of his Universal Elixir, guaranteed to strengthen the body and the mind against all ills.

'He means to steal my business, the devil! I'm told that he's a most persuasive speaker. He's already gathered a large following in Norwich.'

'I suppose he may tempt a few people round about,' Adam said, 'but he'll soon be on his way. These travelling quacks rarely stay long in any one place. To do so risks people finding out what they sell is worthless.'

'Not this one. He seems attached to Norwich and the towns to the north. I was told that he was in Fakenham two days ago and in Swaffham before that. Last month, he went no further afield than Dereham and King's Lynn before returning to Norwich.'

Adam was curious. That was certainly unusual behaviour. All

such quacks expected the legitimate local medical men to object to their presence. They generally moved on before someone accused them of being common vagabonds and brought them before the magistrates.

'If he has been in Norwich for so long, why has the mayor not taken action against him?'

'This one is not like other quacks. Yes, he sells patent medicine, but what he advertises are scientific lectures. He even claims to be skilled in medical matters. His followers say he trained as a physician somewhere abroad — I'm not sure where — and later became a respected teacher in Paris. When the mobs of san culottes began hauling the wealthy off to the guillotine, he was forced to flee for his life, ending up in Switzerland or Bavaria — or somewhere like that. Now he's chosen to seek his fortune in England, like so many other Frenchmen nowadays. London was not to his taste, it seems, so he moved north and established himself in Norwich.'

How very odd. If he were a physician, why not set himself up in practice as such? Why take to the road selling quack remedies? There was something puzzling about this man. Adam tucked the problem away in the back of his mind to return to later. For the moment, there were more important mysteries to deal with.

He was certain Peter would have heard of the murder of Betsy Wormald. The apothecary's shop seethed with gossip, so that Peter knew everything that occurred for miles around within hours of it happening. Past cases had convinced Adam he should always pay attention to such gossip, however unlikely. A nugget of gold might be hidden amongst the trash. The only way to find it was to search through everything.

'You've heard of the murder of the blacksmith's daughter at Melton Constable?'

'I wondered how long it would take for you to nose that out.' Peter's good humour was returning.

'It seems the blacksmith is known to Lady Alice. She has asked me to see if I can help find his daughter's murderer.'

'From your bed? Listen, Bascom. If you think I am going to allow you to wander —'

'As I told her ladyship, I may need to rest my body, but my mind craves employment. All I need are a few people who can go about asking questions for me —'

'You need not think I have time to roam the countryside at your beck and call. I have a business to run.'

'Have I suggested any such thing? It merely occurred to me how much gossip makes its way into your shop. I felt sure you must have heard some further details of the murder. Have you?'

'I might have.'

'Stop playing hard to get, Lassimer. You're going to tell me, so you might as well do it right away.'

'You know that her father's an important man in the Independent Chapel in that village? A very upright, God-fearing fellow with a strict moral code, by all accounts. However, his daughter Betsy, so the rumour goes, was somewhat more free-and-easy in her outlook, particularly after a troop of the militia was quartered in the village. According to several people, she talked of little but life in the big city. Her dream was to dress in fine clothes and be seen on the arm of some fellow in a fine military uniform.'

'That's true of many girls.'

'This one's father wanted her to marry a farmer's son well known to the family. That's the person now suspected of killing her.'

'Why would he do such a thing?'

'According to the medical examination requested by the coroner, Betsy Wormald was expecting a child.'

'That isn't so unusual in rural communities either. Many a young woman goes to the altar pregnant. Provided the man marries her, no one takes much notice.'

'This case is a little different. For a start, the girl's father has puritanical ideas about men and women. He would have seen they didn't have any opportunities to be alone together. The young man suspected of the murder wasn't an ardent lover either. It's said her father pushed him into asking Betsy to walk out with him. Another thing. The fellow has been going back and forth to Ipswich for most of the past six months or so. Why I do not know. For all these reasons, it seems unlikely he could be the father. People are saying he must have discovered her condition and attacked her in a fit of jealous rage; then fled when he realised he had put an end to her life.'

It was a plausible enough story. If Betsy had hardly walked out with this young man, there was little chance for them to spend enough time together alone to account for her condition. Besides, no one suggested the fellow had yet asked her to marry him. If he didn't wish to bring up another man's child — and most did not — he need only walk away. Why should the thought of her lying with another cause him to choke the life from her, if his suite had been lukewarm from the start? He might not even have run away, as rumour claimed. Once she told him of her condition, he might simply have returned to Ipswich. There would be no reason for him to remain in the area any longer.

Peter had no more gossip to offer so Adam didn't detain him. He wanted time alone to consider all he had heard so far. It was not to be. Within minutes of Peter leaving him, Adam fell fast asleep.

6

WORD HAD SPREAD QUICKLY THAT THE DOCTOR HAD SUFFERED AN accident and come near to death. Over the next day or so, several of Adam's wealthy patients sent servants to enquire after his wellbeing. Adam suspected most were far more concerned they would lose access to his services for a time. Unfortunately, his practice would be bound to suffer, just when it had grown to a most flourishing state. There was little he could do either. Peter would help where he could, but many of the local gentry believed apothecaries were fit only to treat their servants.

A more welcome visitor was Mr Jempson, the elderly merchant whom Adam had once rescued from highway robbers, who called to express his concern and offer best wishes for a speedy recovery. His house in Aylsham was close to Adam's, yet the two of them met only rarely. Mr Jempson claimed to have handed over the running of his shipping interests to managers, yet he was often away supervising his various businesses in King's Lynn and Great Yarmouth. Since he was also highly respected amongst the Quaker communities of Norfolk, they added to the demands on his time with matters concerning the sect. His only child, a daughter, was now married and living in Norwich. Visiting her and her husband took him away from Aylsham as well.

Mr Jempson didn't stay long, so Adam had returned to fretting over the problems facing him in keeping his practice afloat by the time Mrs Munnings came in to check the splints on his arm and bathe his various cuts and scrapes. Adam did not protest. He had come to look forward to her gentle ministrations. There was something undeniably luxurious about lying in bed while soft hands busied themselves about you. Mrs Munnings was most deft in her movements and rarely caused him the slightest pain.

'You are a most able nurse, Mrs Munnings. I admit I was apprehensive when my mother told me you were coming. I know now I need not have been.'

'Most women soon become skilled at nursing, Doctor. When sickness or injury strikes a household, it is the womenfolk who are expected to attend to it.'

'I suppose so. Yet I cannot believe many are as skilled as you, especially at adjusting bandages and splints.'

'My late husband was a surgeon. Many times, I helped him in his work. He was also something of a perfectionist, so meeting his standards was a struggle at first. Eventually, even he admitted I was almost as skilled at bandaging a wound as he was.'

'How do you manage now he's dead?'

'I have a small annuity and my needs are few, Doctor. Mr Lassimer is also kind enough to recommend me from time to time, as he has in your case.'

'As I will too, Mrs Munnings. You may be assured of that.'

'Thank you kindly, Sir. I had thought of becoming a midwife, but many women now prefer a physician and man-midwife at their lying-in.'

'During the process of labour and birth perhaps. Yet the need for care does not end when the child is born. The poor generally rely on their mothers or grandmothers. The rich know that theirs would be horrified at such menial duties.'

'I do not move amongst the rich, Doctor.'

'But I do, even though, like most physicians, I also devote some of my time gratis to those who cannot pay me. Yes, Hannah?'

'Captain Mimms has called, Master. He asks if he may spend a little time with you.'

'Send him up as soon as Mrs Munnings has finished.'

The nurse bent her head to continue her task, but Adam had not finished with his questions. It occurred to him he didn't even know where Mrs Munnings lived. For the moment, she had been provided with an unused bedroom on the top floor, near to the one occupied by Mrs Brigstone, his housekeeper. Where was her real home? Was it in Aylsham?

It turned out she lived in Briston, some five or six miles distant.

'That is close to Melton Constable, is it not? Do you know the blacksmith there?'

'Mr Wormald? The one whose silly daughter, Betsy, has been murdered?'

'Why do you call her silly?'

'That's what she was, poor girl. She yearned to have some joy and pleasure in her life, but her father denied her such frivolities. A most gloomy man, Doctor. Very much a Christian of the old, puritan school and a strict member of the Independent Chapel. It was obvious he expected her to move from obedient daughter to obedient wife with nothing in between.'

'She had other ideas?'

'Ideas were all they were, as everyone thought. Providence might have blessed her with good looks, but it denied her much in the way of brains. If she had been clever, she would have found ways to evade the future her father planned for her. As it was, she spent as much of her time as she could daydreaming and reading novels she hid from her father.'

'What of her mother in all this?'

'The poor soul died a good time ago. The girls' father raised them as best he could, I suppose, but he was not a man to show affection or understand the needs of young women. For him, the only acceptable ways of spending your time were work and prayer. He did teach them both to read and write, but his idea of proper reading matter was more or less restricted to the Bible. Betsy used to beg the loan of novels from some of the other girls in the village, since her father wouldn't allow them in the house. Then she smuggled the books up to the room she shared with her sister and they read them at night by the light of stolen candle-ends.'

'You heard she was found to be with child?'

'Everyone heard in a matter of hours. I doubt many were surprised. Matthew Wormald might have believed Betsy was the perfect, chaste Christian daughter, but few others did.'

'She was wild?'

'Not wild, young, silly and romantic; eager for adventure. I can well imagine any man she imagined was like the heroes in her novels would find she put up little resistance. It is often that way with girls whose families are excessively strict. The only way they can think to express their need to be themselves is to defy whatever their fathers stand for.'

'Wasn't there supposed to be a suitor in this case?'

'That would be Joseph Carse. He was her father's choice, not hers. If she had ever married him, it would have been an act of desperation. The boy is a very milksop, even if he is likely to inherit a good business. I doubt he will keep it long when he does. If I say he should have been born a girl, Doctor, you will understand what I mean, I'm sure.'

'Like that? And him a farmer's son too?'

'Yes — and the despair of his father. Besides Joseph, he has only daughters, any one of whom would be more able to run that farm than their brother. Show Joseph a cow and you'd need to remind him which end the milk comes from. Face him with a bull — nay, a bull calf — and he'd run away. Farming is much too raw and dirty for his tastes.'

'He's been much away from the village, as I hear.'

'His uncle has an ironmonger's business in Ipswich and no heirs to leave it to. That was a good part of the reason why Matthew Wormald settled on him. That and the fact that young Carse is another member of the same sect. It would not have occurred to him that his daughter should have any choice in the matter of a husband. Joseph has been working on his uncle to recognise his suitability as an heir, so folks say. When I heard he had returned to press his suit on Betsy Wormald, I could not prevent myself from laughing. Believe me, Doctor, such a feeble, precious fellow would never be able to attract a healthy young woman. As for putting Betsy with child, he would be more likely to faint at the sight of a naked woman than rise to the occasion.'

'If others think as you do, why is he even suspected? Perhaps it is because he cannot be found and that is taken to show guilt? It seems a weak argument.'

'I agree. I doubt any who know him believe he has anything to do with Betsy's death. If he has truly run away — which I for one do not credit — I suspect it is through cowardice. My own view is that he has returned to Ipswich with all the speed he can muster. If he thinks this rumour may reach his uncle, he will want to be on hand to scotch it at once, in case it puts paid to his hopes of a fat inheritance. No more questions now. I have finished and you should not keep your visitor waiting.'

Captain Mimms did not appear at once after Mrs Munnings left, so that Adam wondered what might have delayed him. He ought to have realised Briston lies not far from Holt, where the captain lived, and he and Mrs Munnings were acquainted. Mimms might be advanced in years but, like most sailors, he rarely missed a chance to flirt with a pretty woman.

'Glad to see Charlotte Munnings is looking after you, Doctor,' the captain said when he came in. 'Fine woman. Uncommonly handsome too. I knew her before her husband did. Missed my chance there, more's the pity. I knew her husband too, of course. Before he set up in Briston, he'd been a naval surgeon. It was a tragedy when he died. Far too young, like you are. You gave us all a fright.'

'I frightened myself.'

'What happened?'

'To tell the truth, Captain, I recall little enough of events that night. That I reached home at all was mostly thanks to my horse.'

'Were you attacked? Footpads? Highway robbers?'

'Not so far as I recall. I am not an accomplished rider, Captain. If my horse stumbled or shied, I would be very likely to fall off. I usually travel in my chaise, but I knew the roadway to Probert's house is too narrow to admit anything other than a horse. Why do you ask about footpads?'

'The countryside roundabout is full of unrest nowadays, Doctor. Food prices are high and wages low — when work is available, that is. Too many of the poor are in dire want. Our workhouse in Holt is full and the Overseers tell me they have never faced so many requests for out-relief. The fear of invasion has but added to the problems. The Impress Service, the press gangs, are active in all the fishing villages as well as the ports. Mercantile sailors are given a certificate of exemption, but a good many have been taken all the same. Landsmen are of little use to the navy, Doctor, save to fetch and carry. What they want are seamen who can go aloft and tell a halyard from a shroud.'

'My brother Giles has been here complaining about much the same things.'

'He's a magistrate, ain't he? I pity him, to be honest. He'll be caught between local people complaining that the farmers and millers refuse to sell them grain and the millers demanding protection from hungry mobs. The trouble is the farmers can get better prices in London, or by selling to the government, than by selling locally. There have been several food riots already where mobs seized the wagons carrying grain to the coast and attacked the mills. They force those they attack to hand over their grain, then they sell what they have seized at a price they deem acceptable. Afterwards, they hand the money over to the miller or farmer, thus convincing themselves what they do is not theft.'

'I doubt the law agrees.'

'Indeed not. Those damned smugglers have grown far too bold as well. You can't blame the poor for assisting them. Poor families help the gangs unload their goods or lend them their horses and carts for the night. That way they can earn more in one night than they can get in a week's legitimate work. If they don't co-operate, their horses are taken anyway and they get nothing. If they complain to the Preventive Service, their wretched cottages are burned down. Informers are found somewhere with their throats cut. The gentry fuss and fume, but I know for a fact many rely on the free traders for their tobacco, their wine and their brandy, while their wives happily deck themselves out in French lace.'

Adam knew it was true. Even clergymen turned a blind eye to the use of the church tower or some convenient tomb as a storage place. In return, they would find packages of tea or tobacco and small barrels of spirits left on the vicarage doorstep.

'The artisans and weavers used to be immune to poverty around here, but this war has ruined the textile trade,' Mimms went on. 'What few orders there are go to the new mills in the north, which can make the cloth more cheaply, if not so well. Our weavers, spinners and dyers are angry. They blame those in power for provoking an unnecessary conflict and the merchants for failing to win enough fresh orders from countries beyond French influence. That's why these radical groups can meet more or less openly in the towns to discuss their grand notions of republics and revolutions and the rights of man. The writings of that cursed traitor Tom Paine may be bought at their meetings for a few pennies, while other pamphlets are smuggled in from printers in The Netherlands or France. Those who can read buy them, then gather others together and read them aloud. Sedition, I call it, plain and simple.'

'Would they act on what they read?'

'Not by themselves. If some leader came forward to give them direction, I would not answer for what might happen. These are dangerous times, Doctor. Many are becoming desperate and desperate men do desperate things.'

How desperate would soon become clear.

Charles Scudamore was Adam's last visitor that day. He arrived shortly before three o'clock in the afternoon with a message from Lady Alice. She and his sister had been to visit Mr Wormald, the blacksmith, he said. They had found the poor man so distressed that they hesitated to press him with any questions or stay long. Instead, they arranged for Ruth to return in a day or so with a gift of vegetables and fruits from the garden at Mossterton Hall. Susan Wormald, Betsy's younger sister, was trying to take her place in charge of the household. She would be grateful for fresh supplies and it might give Ruth a chance to speak to her in private.

Adam was impressed by Lady Alice's quick thinking. The younger sister might well have been party to her sibling's secrets, but she would be most unlikely to mention them in the presence of their father. If Ruth could strike up a relationship, he might gain much useful information.

Charles also professed himself eager to help Adam in any way he could, claiming he had not needed the urging of his sister or his aunt. If he might be excused for a day or so while he escorted Adam's mother and Miss LaSalle to Trundon Hall, he would place himself fully at the doctor's disposal.

'I am told there is much unrest around here, so it would not be safe for the two ladies to travel with only a groom for escort,' Charles explained. 'I will see them to Trundon Hall in safety and return at once. By the way, I have also offered to escort them back to their house in Norwich when they are ready.'

There's more, Adam thought.

'I was wondering, Doctor. Is there anything useful I could do for you in Norwich?'

'Aren't you supposed to be looking for somewhere to set up in practice in Holt or Aylsham?'

'Yes, of course I am. But I imagine that this murder business should take precedence. Holt will still be there when it is all finished.'

'So it will,' Adam said, speaking in his driest tone. 'There is one matter that could be undertaken in Norwich, I suppose. I was going to leave it until after we had made better progress on the matter of the murdered girl. It might occupy you for a day or so. After that, don't look to me for an excuse if your aunt decides you have been idling away your time.'

Charles grinned. 'Unlike you, Doctor, I am an excellent rider. To slip away from Holt to Norwich for a day would cause me little difficulty. In truth, I have already found a suitable property. If I delay signing a lease, it is because my dear aunt will expect me to start legal work as soon as I have somewhere to hang up my shingle. It's not that I am lazy. I simply have a different view about the priorities of life. Now I must return home or I will be late for dinner. I'll come back tomorrow and you can tell me what progress you have made. I seem to have been at your house a great deal recently, don't I?'

'So you have, so you have,' Adam said. He was beginning to have a good idea of the reason why.

After Charles had left, Adam rang the bell, hoping Hannah might come. Mrs Munnings came instead, so he pretended he'd wanted to speak to his housekeeper to be assured all was well within the household. Then, when Mrs Munnings offered to fetch her, he dismissed that idea.

'Tomorrow will do,' he said. 'I find myself feeling rather tired after so many visitors. If I had a cup of chocolate it might help me to sleep.'

Mrs Munnings said she would fetch one for him, but he told her to send Hannah instead, claiming it was because he would not have Mrs Munnings acting as his servant. In truth, he wanted to get Hannah into the room on her own. She was an inveterate gossip and there were things he wanted to know, especially about events over the past week or so. It would take little to get her talking.

That proved to be the case. An innocent comment, that he could barely remember much of the time when his illness was at its height, provoked a flood of words.

'It was ever so exciting, Master. I mean, it must have been terrible for you, but you say you can't remember it, so it won't matter, will it? I heard a noise at the door and there you were lying on the doorstep. After that, the whole household was roused. Everyone was running about, not knowing what to do for the best. Not me though. I sent William to call Mr Lassimer straightaway. He grabbed up his bag and they came running back together. It was they what managed to get you upstairs and into bed. It was wonderful to see Mr Lassimer take charge. He told us all to go down to the kitchen, blow up the fires and heat pans of water, while Mrs Brigstone was to fetch extra blankets and pillows and William was to take your horse to its stable, feed and water it and see if it was hurt. After that, he was to go to The Black Boys Inn to hire a chaise at first light to take him into Norwich as fast as it would go. There, he was to tell your mother what had happened and fetch her here, if she would come.

'He must have got a fresh horse in Norwich, because he was back before noon the next day, Mrs Bascom and Miss LaSalle with him. They both looked as white as sheets and came upstairs as soon as they arrived. The next thing, William was down in the kitchen, talking to his mother. Guess what? Mr Lassimer had told him to saddle your horse and ride to Mossterton Hall to tell Lady Alice about your accident.

'There were even more comings and goings after that. William came back riding on top of a fine coach with Lady Alice and that nice Mr Scudamore inside. Lady Alice talked for some time with Mr Lassimer and your mother, while Mr Scudamore and Miss LaSalle watched over you. After that, her ladyship and Mr Scudamore came every day. We were all so frightened for you, Master, and overjoyed when Mr Lassimer told us the fever had broken and we could have hope again.'

So that was how Miss LaSalle and Charles had met. An unconventional introduction, but none the less successful for that.

Hannah was still talking. Once she started, it was hard to persuade her to stop. 'Is it right that Mr Scudamore is looking for somewhere to live in Holt, or here in Aylsham, Master? He's a lawyer, ain't he? Is he thinking of setting himself up in business round here? If it's true, he'd be a rare asset to our community, for he's a fine, handsome young gentleman. I saw him walking with Miss LaSalle yesterday when she went to take some air. She'll miss him when she goes to Trundon Hall. Even more so when she and your mother return to Norwich.'

'I expect he'll be around,' Adam said. 'She won't be rid of him as easily as all that – assuming she wants to be, which I rather doubt. Thank you, Hannah, I'll drink the chocolate and leave the cup by the side of my bed. You needn't return for the moment. I'm going to try to sleep for a while, so please don't disturb me.'

He had dropped off to sleep when Hannah came back. She was full of apologies, but her eyes were shining with pleasure and excitement.

'It's one of those men come here again, Master. The ones who ride the huge black horses and have the king's coat of arms on their saddlecloths. Ever so grand they look. Handsome too. Well, this one is. He's brought a letter for you all the way from London, he says. I know you told me not to disturb you, but I thought you might want to have it at once.'

Adam reassured her that she had been quite right to bring him the message straight away. He felt nervous as he broke the seal, for it had to be from Wicken. What might that lofty government official want of him this time?

Sir Percival Wicken (when had he been knighted, Adam wondered?), Principal Secretary at the Cabinet Office, began by offering Adam his best wishes for a speedy recovery. He had asked his good friend, Lord Townsend, he wrote, to enquire about Adam's progress and had been delighted to receive a positive report. Adam should know that he had many friends in London. Even His Majesty had asked to be kept informed.

How the devil did His Majesty come to be aware of his existence? Adam was used to Wicken conveying unexpected news, but he could hardly see how his state of health could be of any interest to the monarch. He received a royal pension, it was true, but he assumed that was arranged by the government. A good many sinecures and pensions were handed out in the name of His Majesty King George III. He could surely not be keeping track of them all himself.

Setting that problem aside, he turned back to the letter. The next part shook him even more. Wicken wrote that a certain 'newly minted young physician, fresh from Glasgow University', would shortly present himself at Adam's house. If Adam was willing, the young man would act as his assistant and locum during his period of recovery. He suggested that Adam should pay him £50 a year salary, plus ten percent of the fees he charged. Wicken had even arranged suitable accommodation for him in the town.

'It will be invaluable experience for him,' Wicken wrote, 'and he tells me he is eager to study under such an eminent physician as yourself. I know you must be worried about your practice, so I hope that this will set your mind at rest. Young Dr Henshaw's father has been known to me for many years. He assures me his son is conscientious in his work and received high praise from several of his professors at Glasgow.'

Shaking his head over the speed of Wicken's response, as well as his kindness, Adam read on. The next part convinced him Sir Percival Wicken had access to sources of information that were close to being supernatural.

Wicken wrote that he was sure Adam would be bored and in need of some problem to occupy his mind. Perhaps he could think about this? How and why might a respected Swiss natural philosopher, chemist and apothecary of middle years disappear? Someone whom Wicken described as 'our person in Geneva' reported that such a person had been travelling in France, where he got caught up in the troubles there. The revolutionary government treated him with suspicion and put him in prison. After a while, his captors relented and hustled him out of France into the Low Countries. There Wicken's men lost track of him. It was possible he was in England, but far from certain. Any ideas that Dr Bascom might have on the best means to find him would be received with gratitude. The man's family were worried about him.

Adam was sure they were — if they existed. When something like this interested Wicken, it was most unlikely to be a simple matter of assisting an anxious family. He was not taken in either by Wicken's casual reference to the man being in England. He took that to mean he was certain the fellow had crossed the Channel, but was unable to find him. Wicken must have a reason to believe his quarry wasn't in London, but somewhere closer to where Adam lived. That meant Norwich.

Wicken had done him a great kindness in sending Dr Henshaw, so he could hardly refuse his help, such as it was, on this matter.

Besides, Wicken wasn't a fool. He knew Adam was incapacitated at present, so it must be his brains he wanted, not his ability to go about searching. As it happened, Adam was already aware of someone who matched at least some aspects of the description of the missing Swiss apothecary. Well, Charles had been looking for suitable occupation in Norwich and this would fit the bill. The young lawyer would be far better engaged on this investigation than he would in trying to deal with village blacksmiths and the like. If Adam's guess turned out to be correct, Peter would be delighted at the outcome.

Adam smiled to himself, re-folded the letter and set it on the cupboard beside his bed. Then he closed his eyes and resumed his interrupted sleep.

7

ADAM'S DAYS WERE BEGINNING TO SETTLE INTO A ROUTINE. AFTER breakfast, Mrs Munnings dressed his wounds and helped him wash his hands and face. Every other day, the local barber came early to shave him. His breakfast would arrive at around nine o'clock, with his favourite morning drink of warm chocolate. He still felt considerable discomfort, but the bruises were beginning to fade and the cuts and scrapes to heal. Only his broken bones remained painful, especially if he moved too quickly. Aside from that, he was on the mend. Most mornings, he left his bed, put on a day gown, and took a seat in a chair by the window to eat his breakfast.

He found the view into the garden especially pleasing. Some of the apple and pear trees were coming into flower. The other plants too had lost their bedraggled, winter look and were showing flushes of bright green growth. When the sun was shining, as it was this morning, he could not help feeling more cheerful as he looked out, even if, so far, Spring had been a disappointment. Too many cold winds from the east. Too many frosty nights. East winds also brought drought. The crops would be suffering, Adam was sure, and poor harvests must mean still more unrest. Perhaps May would bring more seasonable weather.

For the second day, Adam had gone to sleep thinking about Wicken's missing Swiss scholar and woken up puzzling over the same problem. First, why was Wicken so interested in this man's disappearance? He did nothing without a reason. The statement that he was involved only on behalf of the man's family was ludicrous. Second, Adam was certain Wicken's letter showed he believed the man was somewhere in England. Why did this fellow not declare his identity? He was Swiss, not French. The French had put him in prison. Might he not have expected at least toleration in this country, if not a warm welcome?

Adam went on turning these thoughts round and round in his mind, but to no avail. Fortunately, Hannah came to announce Mr Jempson had arrived and asked if Adam would be willing to see him. Adam was, particularly now that he was seated in a chair rather than lying in his bed.

The elderly Quaker was dressed in his normal sober garb, his broad-brimmed hat still on his head. Adam had heard Quakers kept their hats on even in church. Why did they do that? It couldn't be as a sign of disrespect, since they were amongst the most pious and devout of people, practising what they believed on a daily basis. Indeed, because their principles demanded absolute honesty — that every promise be fulfilled to the letter — Quakers were trusted unreservedly, especially in business and money matters. Most of the bankers in the county were members of Quaker families. He must ask Jempson about the hat business sometime.

Mr Jempson expressed genuine delight at seeing Adam out of bed. 'My daughter will be so pleased when I tell her,' he said. 'I've been in Norwich for a day or two, visiting her and she expressed the deepest concern for thee, Doctor. Indeed, she insisted that I call on my way home to convey the warmest good wishes for a speedy recovery from herself and her husband.'

Hannah brought coffee and the two men discussed matters of little consequence in the way good friends do. Mr Jempson reported Elizabeth, his daughter, was very happy in her marriage and the couple were expecting their first child in a few months. Adam offered his congratulations and best wishes for the birth. Thus, they prattled on in a similar vein until Mr Jempson made a comment which caused Adam's mind to spring to attention.

'While I was in Norwich, I decided to have a look at this Professor Panacea everyone is talking about. He was giving an afternoon lecture in The Assembly House. I don't recall the precise title, but the burden was that the road to good health lies in strengthening the body to eradicate the causes of illness. Physicians and apothecaries, he said, focused only on symptoms of disease. Indeed, they are only called in when people have already fallen sick. His own experience, gained during many years of treating the gentry and nobility of half of Europe, convinced him this was fruitless. A case of trying to shut the stable door after the horse had already bolted. Disease must be stopped from arising. Once a person was sick, it was too late.'

Adam was itching to argue several points, but restrained himself. It was more important to hear what Panacea was telling people than register his disagreement.

'It all sounded very plausible,' Mr Jempson continued. 'Of course, by the end he was selling people some patent medicine he called a Universal Elixir. Take enough of that and you would become so strong you would never be ill again.'

'That's typical of these quacks,' Adam said. 'They promise marvels, then hasten on their way before people realise they've been fooled. By the way, did the man sound foreign?'

'I would say so, though he spoke almost perfect English. A little too perfect, if you understand me. It was as if he was speaking his lines in a play. He paused before he said, "shut the stable door after the horse had already bolted", as if he was getting the words exactly right in his head before coming out with them.'

'What does he look like? Tall, short, young, old? A friend of mine has been asking about him.' That was true, in a way. A poor truth, but not a direct lie.

'On the tall side. There's nothing remarkable about his appearance. Between thirty and forty years old. Dark haired. Well dressed. A little like an older version of yourself. What was noticeable was his total confidence in addressing a large audience. I suppose he must have done it many times.'

'Interesting. Did you get the impression he knew what he was talking about?'

'He is without doubt a powerful orator. By the end of his lecture, many of the people present were willing to buy anything. They weren't poor and uneducated folk either. Most were tradesmen and shopkeepers, with a smattering of merchants — even a few of the gentry. He charged a shilling entrance fee too. No poor person could afford as much. He spoke with fluency and chose his words with care. Did he know his subject fully? He is an educated man without doubt. Whether he has proper medical training, I am in no position to judge. Plausible, even influential, but . . .'

'You have some doubts about him?'

'Something makes me uneasy. He seems far too polished, too sure of himself. He speaks with authority, yes, but without any reservations whatsoever. I have known many men of wisdom and knowledge, both theological and scientific. Norwich has no lack of them, for many learned men have been associated with the Octagon Chapel. Some have propounded unusual, even unsettling ideas. Yet all have been quick to admit their ignorance, as well as talk about their discoveries. Without exception, they have confessed they remained unsure about some matters. This man did not.'

Adam knew what he meant. Those with the most genuine grasp of the subject were usually least willing to be dogmatic.

'There is another thing,' Mr Jempson said. 'From time to time he made comments that were almost of a political nature. For example, he likened a man suffering from frequent headaches to a country oppressed by a tyrant. Laudanum, he said, could render this bodily tyrant impotent for a time, but he would always return. The only cure was a total reformation of the system. Later, he described his approach as providing the revolution everyone is waiting for.'

'I see what you mean.'

'There is a great deal of unrest throughout this county at the moment, Doctor. Factions — even groups of ordinary people — meet to discuss radical and republican ideas. The contagion from

France has spread far and wide. Membership of these groups, these 'Corresponding Societies', is greatest amongst artisans and skilled craftsmen, I believe, much like Professor Panacea's audience. Such men often talk wildly, for they desire change and a better chance to influence those who govern this land. Yet, at heart, I am sure most are good Englishmen, who will draw back from the kind of destruction and tyranny that is gripping our neighbour across the Channel. It is reform they hanker for, not revolution.'

'I hope you are right.'

'So do I. The trouble comes from the hotheads who seize control and drag everyone else along with them, regardless of what it may cost. They're the dangerous ones who must be stopped. Something about Panacea reminded me of that kind of person. No, that is not quite right. What I have in mind is not the charismatic leader who marches into battle at the head of his troops, but the clever, unscrupulous schemer working behind the scenes. The one who uses his power over others to send them to die in the canon fire, while he sits somewhere safe from harm and prepares to gather up the spoils.'

So, Panacea was likely foreign, well used to public speaking, but maybe not the learned Swiss professor Wicken was seeking. Mr Jempson was a thoughtful man, clever too, whose judgement could be trusted. His suggestion that Panacea lacked the humility displayed by genuine scholars rang true. Adam was glad he hadn't rushed to write to Wicken too quickly. Still, he could still not be certain this Panacea was no more than the usual type of quack. He needed someone with a sound medical training to attend one of Panacea's lectures. Only such a person could resolve whether or not what Panacea had to say was more than hot air.

After Mr Jempson had left, Adam decided to set the matter of Panacea aside for a while and return to the problem of the murdered girl. He could still not see where to start. The local people might be focused on Joseph Carse, but he was almost sure they were wrong. The trouble was he could offer no other plausible alternative beyond a random killing; and that was as much as to shrug his shoulders and give up. He wasn't ready for that.

He had arranged for Mrs Munnings to return to her home in Briston for part of the weekend, since anyone could see she was tired and in need of some time to herself. The two of them had agreed she would check Adam's bandages and bathe his wounds as usual on Saturday morning, then leave to return on Sunday evening. Best of all, from Adam's point of view anyway, she had also promised to use her time at home to seek out the local gossip about the blacksmith and his daughters.

Since Charles was not coming until eleven o'clock on Saturday to escort Adam's mother and Miss LaSalle to Trundon Hall, Saturday night and Sunday morning would be the only times Adam would need to cope without a nurse. Mrs Munnings was positive his servants could see to basic wants for that long. William would help him into bed and out next morning to sit in the chair. Peter would be bound to drop in as well.

What had Charles Scudamore been doing back at Mossterton Hall? He should have given him more specific instructions, but he was far too used to doing things on his own. How irksome it was to have to wait for people to visit. He wanted to ask his brother, Giles, whether any new groups of smugglers had been noticed along the coast between Blakeney and Weybourne. Thanks to his injuries, instead of rushing over to Gressington, the best he could do was write a letter and ask his mother to deliver it. Heaven knows when Giles would get around to writing a reply. In his current mood, he might well regard Adam's question as an unnecessary imposition on his time and ignore it for several days. Adam couldn't even go to Holt and ask Captain Mimms instead; nor had he any idea when the good Captain might pay him another visit. He could send William with a note, but that wouldn't do. What he needed was the chance to hear the tone of the reply, to judge the certainty behind it and ask further questions if necessary. No letter could accomplish that much.

In the end, Adam was forced to settle for his least favourite option — patience. His mind churned with half-formed ideas and fragments of theories, for so many things about this murder didn't make sense. All he'd got were random bits and pieces of information. So far, he was unable to fit them together into any kind of coherent pattern.

Be patient, he told himself. This is like making a diagnosis. If you settle on any answer too soon, you rapidly find yourself using any fresh information merely to support it. That was an excellent way to get things wrong. You needed to keep collecting information; to doubt everything you thought you knew, until the evidence was too overwhelming to deny. In this case, he didn't have anywhere near that much evidence.

Adam closed his eyes and tried to concentrate, but the nagging pain in his arm and side was getting worse and worse. There was no sense in struggling any longer. Time to call Mrs Munnings to help him back to bed. While he slept, maybe his mind would come up with something useful. It was worth a try.

8

APRIL 30TH, 1793

Peter Lassimer had not intended to go to Holt that morning. Indeed, he had not planned to go anywhere. He had a great deal to do in his shop and there were patients he should visit, bills he should write out and fresh supplies of dried herbs and various compounds he should order.

The cause of his sudden change of mind had arrived in his shop towards the end of the previous day. Mrs Cartwright was a stout, plain-spoken countrywoman, well past middle-age but still active and alert for everything that went on. Talking to her was not something to be undertaken when you were in a hurry to do something else. She demanded ample time to deliver herself of everything she thought interesting in the local gossip that was life itself, now her husband was dead and her children were busy with their own affairs. Still, letting her talk was usually worth it. You felt afterwards as if you had read a compendious newspaper full of local events and tittle-tattle of every kind. Where she got her information, Peter didn't know, but her news almost always turned out to be correct. It also arrived well before it reached him from any other source. Peter and his business thrived on idle chatter. People flocked to his store for the gossip alone, then felt they couldn't leave without buying something as an excuse for being there in the first place.

The previous day, Mrs Cartwright had told Peter 'that professor or doctor, or whatever he is, that everyone is talking about in Norwich' was to be in Holt. He was giving an address — or a lecture or whatever you called it — the very next day in the large room at the Three Feathers Inn. Sensing an opportunity to see off this hated rival, Peter made a spur-of-the-moment decision to set all else aside and attend in person.

The journey to Holt had hardened his resolve. He meant to show the man up for the charlatan he was. Let the wretch see if he could deal with questions from a person with genuine medical training. He'd soon be caught out and unmasked. A good dose of public embarrassment and ridicule would put paid to any threat he posed to Peter's business.

The road from Aylsham had been busy with carts and pack-horses, so Peter arrived barely five minutes before the lecture was about to begin. Handing his horse to one of the grooms to be fed and watered, he made his way inside, paid his money — an act that set his teeth on edge — and looked around for somewhere to sit. It was obvious at once that a good many other people thought listening to Professor Panacea was going to be worthwhile. The room was so crowded he had to be content with perching on a bench at the back.

Now seated, he looked around. At least three-quarters of the space was filled with benches for the audience. In front of those, separated by a gap of no more than six feet, was a low platform with a wooden lectern in the centre and, behind the lectern, he could see twelve chairs arranged in a half circle.

This was odd. There were none of the trappings that quacks of this type usually deemed essential. No cloths painted with Kabbalistic signs; no stuffed, exotic animals hanging from the ceiling; no heavy aroma of incense or spices. The only scent that came to his nostrils was the one you would expect where fifty or sixty people were crammed together in a room that was a little too small for them.

Exactly on time, the man who called himself Professor Panacea came in and took up position behind the lectern. A dozen younger men followed him. Peter judged all were under the age of thirty and were probably a mixture of artisans and persons of a similar class. Most were tall, strapping young fellows. They might have been the professor's pupils, but they looked far more like his bodyguards.

Was this fellow truly a medical man? He didn't dress like most quacks, that was for sure. They wore flowing, multi-coloured robes, strange hats and had the long beards people associated with wizards. Panacea was clean-shaven and dressed in a sober suit of elegant cut, ordinary blue, worsted stockings and the kind of shoes Peter himself might have worn. No hat and no wig. You would take him for a local merchant or a small-town lawyer. Not quite a gentleman from his dress, but not an artisan or a shopkeeper either.

The buzz of conversation in the room died down and the lecture began. It was very much what Peter had expected. The man produced a series of generalisations and platitudes, mostly on the subject of avoiding illness by living and eating in the right ways. What the apothecary had not expected was the power and authority with which Panacea delivered these empty nostrums. There was something about the man that compelled your attention. If what he said was straightforward common sense, the way he said it turned his words into a series of revelations.

The professor must have spoken for some twenty minutes or so, no more. He used no notes. He performed no magic tricks and produced no illusions. Magic there was in that room, but it lay in his voice and his power over the audience. At the end, he swapped to the mannerisms and tricks of every huckster. His Universal Elixir as the ultimate defence against sicknesses of every kind, he told the crowd. Throughout Europe, thousands from shopkeepers to crowned heads swore by its power to keep them safe from infections, miasmas and the fetid air that brought the typhus and the quaternary fever. Even here, he managed to invest his exaggerated assertions and dubious claims with compelling authority. It was a brilliant performance.

At the end, more than half the people present stood and

pressed forward to buy the professor's elixir. Two of the young men seated behind the professor also rose, left the room for a short time and returned with a table, which they set at the front of the platform. Another two who had followed them out returned with a large wooden crate of bottles. The audience surrounded them, hands reaching out to offer the two shillings which was the price of each bottle. Peter estimated four or five pounds were added to the professor's coffers in the same number of minutes.

When the selling was over, the professor invited questions from the audience. This was Peter's cue and he rose to his feet once.

'May I ask, sir, if you would attribute a serious condition such as Locomotor Ataxia or Tabes Mesenterica to the same general cause of pervasive bodily weakness? Would your Universal Elixir be immediately efficacious in cases such as those?'

He had taken Panacea off-guard. For a moment, the man stared at Peter, completely at a loss, but his recovery proved swift and complete.

'Aha!' he called out. 'I perceive we have a member of the medical profession amongst us. You see what he does, ladies and gentlemen? He attempts to blind us by speaking gibberish, or Latin, or whatever it was. That is the way these fellows work. Their authority proceeds but from two causes. The incomprehensible words they spout and the vast fees they charge. Is that not so? I ask you, ladies and gentlemen, is that not so?'

'Aye, 'tis so indeed,' one called out. 'You speak truly, by God,' another shouted. Many people called for Peter to be silent. Some even pulled at his sleeves, trying to force him down upon the bench again but Professor Panacea was not finished. He saw he had his enemy on the run and closed in to finish him off.

'Do I do that, ladies and gentlemen? Do I seek to confuse you with medical terms? Do I establish my authority by speaking in strange tongues? Have I not explained everything to you in words that everyone present can understand?'

The audience erupted in shouts of support. At the same moment, Peter felt himself seized from behind and lifted off his feet.

Two of the young men who sat behind Panacea had slipped around the room and come up at him, one on either side.

'That's enough!' one of them hissed. 'It's time you left, my friend.'

Peter tried to struggle, but they held him fast and dragged him towards the door.

'I paid my entrance fee like everyone else,' he protested. 'I'm entitled to stay until the lecture is over.'

'It is over . . . for you,' one man replied. 'You're a disruptive influence. The place for those is in the gutter.'

Suiting their actions to the words, the two carried Peter into the street and threw him down in the dirt and the filth. As they turned away, the one who had spoken aimed a vicious kick which landed in Peter's ribs. It knocked all the wind out of him, so that he was unable to rise for several moments.

'Here, sir. Let me help you to your feet again.' The landlord of the inn had seen what was happening and had hurried to offer what help he could. 'You have a horse in the stables?'

Peter indicated that he did. He was far too winded to speak. Instead, he nodded his head and pointed towards the back of the inn.

'The groom will recall which one. I'll call him right away. Best you are on your horse and clear of here as soon as possible. I've heard before that The Disciples can turn nasty, if they're provoked. Now I've seen it with my own eyes. You can be assured I'll not let them rent a room in my inn again.'

'The Disciples?' Peter hadn't enough breath to say more.

'That's what people call those fellows. They go everywhere with Professor Panacea, but if they're disciples, I'm a Dutchman. I've kept an inn for more than twenty years, so I know a group of bully-boys when I see one.'

'Why would a travelling quack need to take a band of ruffians around with him?'

'The Professor is no ordinary quack, believe me. What he is, I've no idea, but I'm convinced all this is an act he puts on. Now, here is your horse, good sir. Let me help you up. Your coat is filthy, but you'll have to deal with that when you get to your home. It's too risky for you to stay here any longer. Are you sure you can ride?'

Peter assured the man he could, thanked him for his kindness and urged his horse away, out of the marketplace and down the road towards Edgefield. He had the answer to his question, though it had cost him both humiliation and a beating.

Professor Panacea was not a scholar, a physician or an apothecary. It was plain he hadn't understood the terms which Peter had used and that ruled out any sort of medical training. More significant, Peter was certain he hadn't known whether the words were Latin or in some other language. No scholar would make such a mistake. But then, what kind of scholar who travelled the countryside giving lectures would be accompanied by a band of ruffians ready to turn to violence? To put a stop to Panacea's activities was beyond his powers. He would report events to Bascom and hope he could make some sense of them.

Another thought came to him; one that cheered him a little. Word of how he had been treated must reach Aylsham very soon. When it did, he was sure several ladies of his acquaintance would be moved to offer him solace — hopefully of a most delightful kind.

9

MAY 1ST, 1793

MRS MUNNINGS CAME INTO ADAM'S ROOM NEXT MORNING TO TELL him Mr Charles Scudamore was already waiting downstairs. Adam turned his head, looked at the clock on the mantelpiece and saw that it was ten minutes before nine. Adam couldn't suppress a smile. It was very unlike Charles to be up and about so early.

'We'd better let him come up, Mrs Munnings.'

'But I haven't had time to assist you to sit in your chair, Doctor, let alone prepare you to receive visitors. Could he not wait a little?'

Adam waved those objections aside. She could do all that after Charles had left. 'Are my mother and Miss LaSalle stirring yet?'

'Mrs Brigstone told me they had asked for breakfast to be taken to them at a quarter past nine. I understand William is to have the chaise waiting at the door at a quarter before ten o'clock.'

'You'd better ring for Hannah. I'll tell her to send Mr Scud-amore up at once.'

When Charles came in, Adam couldn't resist teasing him about his early arrival. Charles had the grace to blush, though he protested it was none of his choosing. Mrs Bascom had told him she wished to make an early start.

'Perhaps not this early,' Adam said. 'Do you have another reason for such uncharacteristic eagerness? Never mind. Since you're here, take a seat and listen to me. I have an important task for you. I need you to make careful enquiries in the villages along the coast to establish if there has been any change in the activities of the smuggling gang that operates around there.'

'But —'

'I know. None of the local people will talk about the smugglers, let alone to a stranger and a gentleman. It would be a waste of time for you to attempt to question labourers, fishermen and the like. I need you to contact the tenant farmers whose fields run along the coast and for three or four miles inland. It will also be worth your while to talk to as many as possible of the landowners in the same area. Start with those with whom you, or Lady Alice, have an acquaintance. Don't expect any of these people to offer you details. They either won't know them or will be too wary of the gangs to divulge what little they do. All I am trying to do at this stage is narrow down the area in which I suspect a new group is operating. Oh! I nearly forgot. Make sure you talk to the clergy whose parishes lie there. Their curates too, if you can track them down, and their wives. The clergy move a great deal amongst the fishermen and labourers. They may well have picked up rumours.'

'How far along the coast do you wish me to go with these enquiries?'

'Between Cromer and Wells-next-the-Sea, I suppose. If that's too large a task, concentrate on the area five miles either side of Weybourne. Right! You'd better go. Tell Hannah to let my mother – and Miss LaSalle, of course – know that you're here. They'll be having breakfast in their rooms by now. I expect my cook can find some for you too. When you get to Trundon Hall, start your enquiries with my brother. I don't have time to write him a letter before you leave, but I've told you what I need to know.'

'There's something I almost forgot to mention,' Charles said. 'My sister and aunt will soon be on their way here. I came ahead, but I know they ordered the carriage for a quarter to ten. I imagine they'll arrive around an hour later.'

Charles bustled out, full of purpose, leaving Adam wondering what to do first. Should he call Mrs Munnings back to help him rise and put on a clean day gown? Should he send Hannah to make certain the barber was coming to shave him, as he had promised? There should be time to make all ready, but only if there were no further interruptions.

In the end, Adam was frustrated on all counts. Peter Lassimer came into the room, limping from the effects of the rough treatment he had suffered in Holt the day before and Mrs Munnings with him. Then Hannah entered, neatly avoided Peter's hand as usual, and announced that the barber was waiting downstairs and a Dr Henshaw had called to see her master.

'Are you intending to stay long, Lassimer?' Adam said. His irritation showed in his voice. 'You can see how busy I am. Lady Alice will be here at eleven and I have much to do before then.'

'Heaven forfend that you should not be washed, shaved and primped before her ladyship arrives, Bascom! Now, to more important business. Mrs Munnings has told me your cuts and scrapes are healing well and your arm is giving you less pain. All that is as it should be. Indeed, I would be on my way at once, if I did not have important information for you.'

'Can the barber shave me while you're telling me your news?'

'Get your maid to send him up then. He might as well hear what I have to tell you as well. What has happened to me will be all around the town before noon and will afford a great deal of amusement, I'm sure.'

'I can see that you're hurt, my friend, for your face is bruised. You were also limping as you came in. I find nothing amusing in that. How came you by these injuries? Did you imitate me by falling off your horse?'

'No,' Peter said, then went on to relate the events of the day before in Holt. When, part way through, the barber came in, Adam waved for him to wait until Peter had finished his story.

The more Peter told him, the more sombre Adam became. Throughout the whole tale, he asked no questions and made no comments. Indeed, he said nothing afterwards until the barber had finished shaving him, patted his face dry and had gathered up his things and left the room. All the time, his expression grew more forbidding.

'I can see I have underestimated the seriousness of what this Professor Panacea is doing,' he said at length. 'The amount of danger that's involved too. I have been unforgivably complacent. Even if I had known you intended to attend one of his meetings, I could not have warned you. I am heartily sorry you were hurt, Lassimer. If it gives you any consolation, I promise you that you have achieved a great deal. It's clear this is not the Swiss scholar that Sir Percival Wicken —'

'Sir Percival?'

'Indeed. I don't know when he received the honour, but I swear that is now his title. As I was saying, there was nothing about Professor Panacea before that pointed to him being other than he appears — a travelling quack healer. Now we know better. He is not a scholar or a medical man, but he's definitely more than an ordinary quack. They do not have ruffians about them who attack any who question or heckle. The problem now is to find out what the fellow is really doing. It's not simply selling patent nostrums, believe me. Call Mrs Munnings back, would you? You can both help me dress and get out of this bed.'

A travelling quack with a bodyguard of bully-boys. What in deuce might that mean? Panacea was drawing the crowds and doubtless making a good deal of money. Did he fear being robbed? No, there must be more to it than that. Whatever Panacea's real purpose was, Adam was resolved to find out, even though Peter's experience had proved great care would be necessary. Adam was glad Peter had gone to Holt on his own initiative. If he had sent the apothecary to do what he did, he would have felt himself to blame. Not that he could have known . . .

'I see you're away inside your head, Bascom,' Peter said. 'Well, I will leave you now. I expect you'll wish to deal with your other visitor as soon as Mrs Munnings here has rendered you fit to receive her ladyship.'

'My other visitor?'

'This Dr Henshaw. The poor man is still waiting downstairs. Who the devil is he, by the way?'

'Sir Percival sent him to me. He's a young, newly-qualified physician, here to help maintain my practice while I am unable to leave this house.'

Peter laughed. 'I declare that man looks after you with greater devotion than most mothers show towards their children. Why you're so important to him, I cannot imagine.'

'Neither can I,' Adam said. 'I didn't ask him to do this. He wrote and told me the man was coming. He's even found him somewhere to lodge while he is here.'

'First Sir Percival — I must remember that — asks Lord Townsend to enquire about you when, by all rights, he shouldn't yet be aware you were injured. Then he finds you an assistant who will act as your locum, makes all the necessary arrangements and sends you a letter announcing what he's done. All that in less time than it would have taken the noble lord to send him the information he asked for. How does he do it?'

'I have long since given up wondering how Wicken gets his information. If I were not a confirmed rationalist, I would believe he has a scryer's crystal ball. Perhaps he can communicate using crows and jackdaws — or ravens from the Tower.'

They both laughed at that. A messenger, riding hard and changing horses every ten miles or so, could travel from Norwich to London in twelve hours. Still, neither could believe that Wicken deployed a whole team of such men to deliver him reports on Adam's activities. His sources of knowledge remained a mystery however they considered them.

Adam noticed that, as Peter turned to leave, he managed to rest his hand for a long moment on Mrs Munnings's rump. The man was incorrigible! He also observed that the lady failed to protest. He knew she had been one of Lassimer's harem of attractive widows. Was there still something going on between them?

'When you go downstairs, Lassimer,' he called after the apothecary, 'please ask Hannah to send this Dr Henshaw up to me in five minutes. I must bid him welcome, though I'll not detain him long. If

I may, I'll send him to call on you at your shop after we have spoken. It's important the two of you should get to know one another and be able to work together.'

Mrs Munnings dressed Adam in his best day-gown, settled him into his chair and bustled off about her own business. She passed Hannah and Dr Henshaw in the doorway.

Dr Harrison Henshaw proved to be an eager, personable young man, somewhat overawed to be in the presence of Dr Bascom at last. Several times he assured Adam he was most eager to learn and would devote himself without reserve to his duties. It was all a little overwhelming. Wicken must have exaggerated a good deal in telling him what to expect. He must also have put the fear of God into him should he not give complete satisfaction. Adam hoped this protégé would soon feel more at ease. At least then he might be less effusive in his protestations of conscientiousness.

Finally, with Dr Henshaw welcomed and dispatched to see the apothecary, Adam was able to sit back and compose himself as best he could to await her ladyship's arrival.

10

THE SAME DAY

SOON AFTER THE CLOCK STRUCK ELEVEN, ADAM HEARD SOMEONE answering a knock at the front door. There followed a buzz of voices in the hallway. He readied himself to greet his visitors. Five minutes passed, then ten, but nobody came. Was he imagining it, or could he still hear voices below? It was almost twenty minutes past eleven before Hannah finally showed Lady Alice and Miss Ruth Scudamore into his room.

Seeing Lady Alice caused Adam a marked shortness of breath. She had, to Adam's mind, never looked lovelier, despite being dressed in the black-and-white of half-mourning. Her clothes were elegant and modest in the fashionable classical style; her hair was caught up in a neat chignon beneath a small hat trimmed with fine lace; and she wore no jewels, save a necklace of jet pieces interspersed with small balls of gold filigree. Yet, despite this simplicity, she looked magnificent — a vision of beauty and refinement. Poor Ruth was quite outclassed.

'We have been talking with Mrs Munnings,' Lady Alice told him. 'She tells me you are progressing well; your bruises are fading and your cuts are almost healed. Now I am here, I can see there is some colour in your face again.'

'Good morning, my lady,' Adam managed to reply. He was still finding it hard to stop staring at her like a love-sick boy of eighteen. 'As always, I am delighted to see you. Please take a seat. Hannah will bring us some tea shortly.'

How ridiculous his voice sounded, so high-pitched and weak. Adam cleared his throat and coughed, trying to return all to normal. Damn! Was he trembling? He was! Quick, think of something guaranteed to quench desire, he told himself. Imagine the rector's eldest daughter. The poor girl was scrawny, ill-dressed and ill-favoured, with a perpetual drip at the end of her nose. Define the correct usage of the ablative absolute, gerund and gerundive in Latin. Recite the names of the bones of the arm and hand.

'You sound breathless, Doctor. Mrs Munnings made no mention of such a condition.'

'It is nothing, I assure you, my lady. The damage to my ribs does not allow me to take a full breath. Even so, I have hopes that the condition will not last long. Mr Lassimer now believes my ribs are cracked, not broken. If so, they will heal quite quickly.'

That was better. That sounded more like his normal voice. He must pull himself together. He wasn't a callow youth to be overcome by lascivious thoughts and random erections. If only he could prevent himself from imagining how it would feel to kiss the flawless skin on that beautiful neck; to press his hand against the thin bodice and feel the firm, warm breasts underneath . . .

'Do you think you are as well as you imagine, Doctor?' Lady Alice said, her voice full of concern. 'There are beads of perspiration on your brow.'

'I assure you they are of no significance, my lady. Please don't be concerned. It is a little warm in here and I have not long risen from my bed. I was able to sit in this chair for most of yesterday and suffered no ill effects. Ah, here is Hannah with the tea.' Thank God for that!

The three of them exchanged the usual small talk while they sipped the fragrant liquid. Gradually, Adam's excitement subsided and he was able to pay full attention to the conversation. By the time Lady Alice set down her cup and began to tell him of her visit to the blacksmith at Melton Constable, he was almost his usual self.

'I fear our time there produced little or nothing useful,' she said. 'Mr Wormald was so distressed it would have been cruel to press him to answer any detailed questions. Miss Betsy Wormald's younger sister was not in any better state, was she, Ruth?'

Ruth agreed it would have been hopeless to try to draw her aside and talk about her sister's life. Both father and daughter seemed overawed by the presence of members of the gentry in their house. They were so concerned to avoid any embarrassment that she and her aunt had stayed for less than fifteen minutes.

Adam was disappointed, but not surprised. He knew the information he needed could only be found by questioning working people. Unfortunately, those available to help him were almost all gentry or people of the middling sort, who would never be at ease with artisans and the common people. Even he had few links to them. Those whose ailments he treated gratis were still uneasy in his presence. He needed to find less prosperous persons to act as his eyes and ears.

Lady Alice interrupted this train of thought. 'Ruth has hit upon a better way of finding some of the information you need, Doctor. Please tell Dr Bascom what you intend, Ruth. I'm sure he will approve.'

Ruth liked few things better than an audience. 'Like you, Doctor,' she began, 'I knew attempting to talk with artisans and tradesmen could never be productive. This is what I intend to do instead. While we were in Melton Constable, I suggested to my aunt we should call on Reverend Oliver Marshall, the rector. I reasoned he must be aware of most of what happens within his parish. He would also be used to conversing with his social superiors. He was indeed quite at ease in conversing with us, yet we found his knowledge of the happenings in his parish surprisingly limited. He must be one of those parsons who never speak with the mass of their parishioners save from the pulpit on Sundays. However, Providence rewarded our efforts by providing an unexpected bonus. The rector has four daughters, two married and two still spinsters living at home. The unmarried ones are twins, like my brother and I. Identical twins in their case, so similar in appearance it's impossible to tell which is which.

'Since they were at home, their father summoned them to meet my aunt. After that, we — the twins and I — left him to talk with her ladyship and went into the garden, where, by telling them that I was a twin too, we established an immediate rapport. Within five minutes, they were chattering as if we had been friends all our lives. Better still, Miss Charlotte and Miss Jessica proved to be inveterate gossips. There was not time for a long visit on this occasion, so I have arranged to return to visit them on my own. I have high hopes they will prove to be bounteous sources of information.'

Adam's congratulations were genuine. This might prove a significant step forward. It would also be a good use of Ruth Scudamore's time.

'Are you any further forward in understanding this poor girl's death?' Lady Alice asked him.

'Only a little,' Adam said. 'I do not have enough information even to guess at the identity of the murderer. The few pieces of evidence I have are more useful at indicating who did not kill Betsy than who did. For example, the young man I was told was courting her was, by all later accounts, not an ardent suitor. He may not have been a genuine suitor at all. He was her father's choice for a husband and I would guess had little interest in marriage to her — or anyone else. He definitely doesn't sound the kind of fellow who would turn to violence if Betsy confessed to being pregnant by another. A milksop, my informant called him, interested in securing an inheritance from a wealthy uncle and very little else.'

'You don't believe it was a crime of passion? He didn't kill her in a jealous rage?'

'I don't believe anything, my lady. Without more information, I can form no firm views of any kind. All I can rely upon is a certain intuition.'

'What does this intuition tell you, Doctor?'

'That this crime is more complicated than it appears. I also suspect there are people involved we do not yet know about. I

cannot prove any of this, yet cannot shake myself free of a premoni-
tion that we are not yet done with violence.'

'The series of events are clear enough to me,' Ruth said. 'Betsy
told her paramour — either that one or another — she was
expecting a child by another man. He grew furious at her unfaithful-
ness, grabbed her by the throat and choked the life out of her.
Horrified at what he had done, he then made a feeble attempt to
hide the body. Why should it be any more complicated? Hasn't this
supposed suitor, Joseph Carse, made off somewhere? Isn't that a
most powerful argument for his guilt?'

'It would seem so, yet I am far from sure. Young Mr Carse has
been living in Ipswich. I am told he made some half-hearted offer of
marriage, but found himself rejected out of hand. If he did not wish
to make a further attempt to win the young lady's hand — and I
doubt he had even wanted to do so the first time — he probably
decided to return there. It may appear unusual that he didn't tell the
young lady's father he was leaving, but I don't feel we can read
much into that. If he was still in the area when the death was
discovered, he would have realised at once he must be suspected.
Maybe he thought it prudent to make off in case the villagers
decided to take justice into their own hands. He might equally well
have left before the body was found. Either way, why should he tell
anyone in Melton Constable what he intended to do? He didn't live
there. As a visitor, he had no reason to explain his movements to
anyone.'

'So, on that basis you believe his absence is innocent?' Ruth did
not sound at all convinced.

'As I told your aunt, I do not believe anything. All I am
suggesting is that, in his case, to be missing is no proof of guilt.
Local opinion has jumped to the solution you outline because it is
the most obvious answer. A crime of passion. It may be one, but I
see no actual evidence —'

'— and your intuition suggests otherwise.' Lady Alice interrupted him. 'Is there another solution in which passion is not
involved?'

'That is going too far, my lady. Passion may very well be

involved, yet still only a part of the answer. I am beginning to think this murder may be part of some larger and more complex criminal activity. Please don't ask me to be more specific at the moment. My mind is a jumble of ill-understood facts and half-formed conclusions. I cannot even explain things clearly to myself.'

'Very well, Doctor,' Lady Alice said. 'I will not press you further. Let me turn to another matter. Have you found suitable employment for my nephew?'

'I have indeed, your ladyship. I have charged him with seeking out and questioning landowners, yeoman farmers and clergyman whose holdings and parishes lie along the coast between Cromer and Wells-next-the-Sea. That area of the coast is a notorious haunt of smugglers. There are few habitations and large areas of marsh, wasteland and heath to provide concealment. There are also enough beaches to offer a choice of suitable spots to land contraband. He is trying to discover if there have been any changes or additions to the normal pattern of smuggling. Something that might suggest a new gang is operating in the area.'

'Has this something to do with Betsy Wormald's murder? It seems so unlikely.'

'Not directly, I grant you. I should have explained that there are several matters which are causing me disquiet.'

He summarised the activities of Professor Panacea; his unwillingness to leave Norwich and his clear interest in towns bordering the northern coast. Next, he referred to the search for the missing Swiss scholar. In this case, he did not mention Wicken directly, referring only to 'a friend in London'. Lastly, he moved to the rough treatment handed out to Peter at Panacea's lecture in Holt. The ladies exclaimed in indignation when he reached that point. For poor Mr Lassimer to be thrown into the street. It was insupportable.

When at length he had finished, the three of them discussed what could account for Panacea's behaviour, but could reach no conclusions before Lady Alice announced it was time to leave so that the doctor could rest.

'Before I go, Doctor, there is another small matter on which I would like some information,' she said. 'It has nothing to do with murders, patent medicines or even smuggling. My niece is convinced her brother is paying too much attention to your mother's lady companion, Miss LaSalle. To say that she does not approve is an understatement. Her actual words, at one point, were that he is demeaning himself — and her — by taking an interest in a person who is no more than a servant. Can you tell me anything about the lady's family background, Doctor? How did she come to be your mother's companion?'

Adam was deeply irritated on Sophia's behalf. What right had Ruth to assume this superior attitude?

'Miss LaSalle's late father was a gentleman with an estate in the south of the county,' he told them, with more heat in his voice than he had intended. 'None of us would ever consider her to be a servant.'

If he were to tell the absolute truth, he couldn't answer for his brother Giles. His attitudes were best described as somewhat old-fashioned — if you were being kind, that is. He decided in this case Giles didn't matter.

'The circumstances that caused her to become my mother's companion are these. Her father was a poor manager of money who regularly spent beyond his means. He and his wife also produced a large family, most of whom survived childhood. Miss LaSalle has three brothers, I believe, and several elder sisters. It thus became clear to her that, as the youngest, she could not hope to receive a sufficient dowry to make a suitable marriage. To make matters worse, her father died at the early age of fifty-five, leaving his affairs in disarray and the estate heavily mortgaged. Her eldest brother is at his wits' end trying to cope with the mess, I believe.

'Miss LaSalle therefore had to face some unpleasant choices. Lacking a dowry, she could not hope to marry into a family appro-priate to her background, but she didn't relish the idea of marrying beneath her either. If she did not marry, she must live a life of genteel poverty, dependent on what resources her brothers could spare for her. At that point, an acquaintance of my mother heard of her plight. Knowing my mother was seeking someone to be her companion, this lady suggested Miss LaSalle. My mother took to the idea at once. She could share her house with a lady whose background would make her suitable as a friend as well as a companion. She would also gain an intelligent, well-educated person to go with her into company without embarrassment. Miss LaSalle accepted the proposition. To my certain knowledge, neither has regretted it for an instant. Does that answer your question, my lady?'

'It does indeed, Doctor. I'm now embarrassed I was made to ask it in the first place.' She turned to Ruth and spoke with unusual sharpness. 'You cannot keep your brother with you for the rest of your life, Ruth. He is bound to marry and must follow his own path. Nor does it become you to jump to the conclusion you did. Let me hear no more such nonsense from you or I will send you back to your father in disgrace. I mean it. You should be grateful you are not in a similar situation. My brother will, I am sure, provide you with a more than adequate dowry. But will any young man be willing to take on the Herculean task of turning you into a wife with whom he might live in comfort? At present, I very much doubt it.'

With that fierce rebuke, Lady Alice dismissed Ruth from her attention. Then, bidding Adam farewell in the kindest terms, she walked swiftly from the room. Ruth nodded to Adam and hurried after her aunt, holding a handkerchief to her eyes. He guessed it would be a long time before she dared speak slightingly of Miss LaSalle again in her ladyship's presence.

11

MAY 3RD, 1793

THE RELATIVE NORMALITY THAT HAD RETURNED FOLLOWING BETSY Wormald's death was shattered two days later by another murder.

The barber brought the news. He'd lived in Aylsham all his life and liked to believe he knew everything that happened for several miles around. As he lathered Adam's cheeks, he rattled on, nineteen to the dozen, adding what detail he could — and mixing it with triple the amount of rumour and speculation. The victim, he said, was the son of the carpenter at Cawston. A lad of eighteen or nineteen. Wild too, folk said. Part of a group of lads of the same age who were always up to no good. Their heads were full of wild ideas, so they'd cheek the squire and play tricks on the vicar. Hard drinkers, most of them too. They'd go to the local tavern until the landlord threw them out. Often as not they'd stagger home after midnight making enough noise to wake the whole village. Sometimes, one or more of these lads would get so drunk his friends would have to carry him — or leave him on the side of the road when they couldn't be bothered to take him further. Then he'd have to bed down in a barn somewhere or sleep under the hedge.

When he could get a word in edgeways, Adam asked him who had found the body.

'His poor father. The boy must have got as far as the back gate and been killed there. What a terrible shock it must have given the man to find his son dead outside his own home.'

'How was he killed?'

'Some says this and some says that, but most agree he was strangled. I did hear it looked as if he'd been soundly beaten first. What's right I can't say. You can imagine the rumours and gossip that's flying around. People are frightened. That's two murders in little more than a week. Do you think they're linked somehow?'

'Cawston,' Adam mused. 'It's not very far from Melton Constable, is it? Do you know if this lad ever went there?'

'Can't rightly say, sir. Not very likely though. Each village has its own carpenter. They don't like others trying to steal their trade, any more than I would. There's definitely a carpenter in Melton Constable.'

'So, he'd stay pretty much in his own village?'

'There and some of the villages roundabout. Might come to Aylsham or go to Holt of a market day, I suppose.'

Mrs Munnings couldn't add anything more, but she told Adam she had a married sister who lived between Reepham and Cawston. She'd send her a message by the carrier and ask if she knew anything. Adam had to be content with that.

Killed outside his own house? Possibly. Beaten there first? That was unlikely, since it would have made a good deal of noise, what with the poor lad crying out in pain and the noise of the kicks and blows. Adam suspected both beating and murder had happened somewhere else, before the body was brought and left outside the place where he had lived. That suggested two things: the murderer knew the victim beforehand and he wanted the body found as quickly as possible. Why? That was harder to fathom.

It wasn't long before Peter arrived, disappointed to discover others had brought the news before him. Straightway, Adam asked him if he knew anything of the family of the dead lad. Peter visited patients in a wide area around Aylsham, so it was likely he'd been to Cawston on many occasions.

'I've met the carpenter,' he said. 'They don't have an apothecary in Cawston, so people there have to come to Aylsham or go to Holt or Reepham. Most of them come to me at Aylsham. People always go where they see the treatment is best.' Peter could never resist the chance to 'puff' his own business.

'Have you met the son, the one who's been killed?'

'I can't say I have. His father's a good workman. A steady kind of chap, not spectacular in what he does, but reliable. His wife came to me once or twice too. She's everything you would expect of the family of a solid, local tradesman. There's nothing odd about them, so far as I've seen.'

'I've been trying to discover if the dead fellow had any connection with Melton Constable.'

'You think he might be the father of that poor girl's child? I suppose it's possible. He might have met her at one of the local fairs, or somewhere like that.'

'Do you know which towns in this area Professor Panacea has given lectures in recently?'

'Now where are you going? Holt, of course. Fakenham, I believe, North Walsham . . . Reepham.'

'Not Aylsham?'

'No, definitely not.'

'I wonder why that should be? Everywhere round about, but not Aylsham.'

'How can you imagine this killing — or the one at Melton Constable — has anything to do with that awful quack? For heaven's sake, Bascom! The way your mind works is a constant mystery to me.'

'Do you know anything about groups of people, anywhere around here, who meet to talk sedition and revolution? Read one another sections from the writings of that firebrand Thomas Paine? That kind of thing. I'd heard that there were some.'

'What are you on about now? How has that got anything to do with Panacea or the murders?'

'Have you?'

'I did hear there was such a group in North Walsham. One in

Holt too, some say. Fakenham seems a likely place, but I get little news from that area.'

'Not here in Aylsham?'

'Not so far as I know.'

Adam said nothing. His face became blank, his gaze fixed on a small picture on the wall opposite.

'You're doing well, Bascom,' Peter said. 'Aside from your arm, you should be good as new within another week or so. The arm will take longer, of course. I'll have a word with Mrs Munnings. Tomorrow she can help you dress yourself and you can go downstairs for a while. Not for too long at first; maybe just an hour or so. I'm sure you'd like a change of scenery from this bedroom . . . Bascom? . . . Bascom? . . . Bascom? Did you hear what I said?'

Nothing. Adam hadn't moved. Recognising the inevitable, Peter turned with a sigh and left the room. He'd ask Mrs Munnings to explain to Adam when he came back from wherever he'd gone. Until then, it was useless to speak to him.

Adam remained deep in thought for most of the rest of that morning. It was after two o'clock and he had dropped off to sleep in the chair when he was woken by Mrs Brigstone, his housekeeper.

'Master! Master! I am so sorry to have to wake you, but I know you'll want to hear about this right away. You see, the milk-seller didn't come this morning as he usually does —'

'You woke me to say that the milk-seller didn't call today?'

'Oh dear! This isn't coming out right at all. What I wanted to tell you is that there's been yet another murder!'

Adam's mind was still fuddled with sleep, so it took him a moment to realise what she had said. When it finally registered, he was all attention.

'Who? Where?'

'That's what I was trying to tell you, Master. When the milk-seller hadn't been by noon, then by one, I sent Molly, the kitchen maid, out to see if she could discover what had delayed him. She's just now come back with this terrible news. Everyone in the town is talking about it.'

Adam reached out and took his housekeeper by the arm. 'Calm yourself, Mrs Brigstone. Take it slowly. Tell me everything from the beginning.'

It took him some time, but he got the story straight in the end. The milk-seller's daughter had been found dead late that morning, her body hidden under a hedge in the lane that ran up to the back of their house. According to the gossip, this poor girl too had been strangled. She was seventeen.

'They say she was found about fifty yards from their house, wearing only her nightdress. It must be this maniac, Master. She must have gone to meet him. Nobody with any sense goes outside in the middle of the night, not even to the privy. That's what you have a chamber pot for.'

'Tell me, where did she live?'

'It's a smallholding somewhere along the road between here and Cawston. Not much of a place, as I heard. Hardly enough land to keep a few cows.'

So, the killing of the carpenter's son hadn't been the end of it. Who else might meet the same fate before it was over? But why these two? How on earth could they have got muddled up in whatever was causing these killings? What if it was indeed a maniac? If it had only been the two young women, he would have thought that a real possibility. As it was, the killing of the man made this explanation unlikely; and even maniacs rarely killed without some reason, however perverted. If what Mrs Brigstone had heard was correct, the girl must have gone out to meet someone. Who? Some man who had taken a fancy to her? She was wearing only her nightgown, so she could well have been expecting to make love to him in an outhouse or a convenient barn. Was this the same fellow who had killed Betsy Wormald? It was hard to imagine two separate men had taken it into their heads to murder the girl they were with, or that two girls had met the same fate for giving themselves to more than one man at the same time. It made no sense!

Adam wasn't to be left in peace long to turn these things over in his mind. Hannah came into the room soon after, with Mr Jempson right behind her.

'Hast thou heard, Doctor? Another person murdered. What evil is this about in our county? I was coming here when I heard the news. Indeed, I was on my way to tell thee of something which may have a bearing on what has happened.'

Adam invited the elderly Quaker to take a seat. Hannah was about to go to the kitchen to ask Cook to make coffee, but Mr Jempson declined any refreshment. He had no time for the normal pleasantries, he said. He would explain what had brought him to the doctor's house, then be on his way.

'Yesterday, late in the afternoon,' he began, 'my housemaid asked to see me. She was upset, my housekeeper said, so I agreed at once. The girl's somewhat excitable, so when she came in I could get no sense from her for several minutes. After she'd calmed down, she told me she'd been out on an errand when a man stopped her in the street and asked her from whom people in Aylsham bought their milk. It seemed an odd question, but she had no reason not to give him a truthful answer. Next, he asked if she knew where the milk-seller lived. As it happened, she didn't. Well, not beyond knowing that it was somewhere outside the town. At the time, she thought these questions were very odd for a man to ask. He didn't look like a servant. More like a journeyman or a weaver.

'There was also something about him that made her feel uncomfortable, so she tried to go on about her business. That was when he took her arm. She told me he squeezed it very hard, enough to hurt her. By this time, she was terrified, of course, expecting him to try to drag her off somewhere and assault her. Instead, he bent his head close to her ear and told her to listen to him carefully. She was to let all her friends know that anyone who repeated gossip from a silly young woman would live to regret it. Those were his exact words.

'She had no idea what he was talking about, of course. Still, she would have agreed to remember anything to get away from him, so she said she'd pass his words on. He seemed happy with that and let her go. She had the good sense at that point to run home at once to tell me what had happened. It didn't seem quite important enough to bother thee with so late yesterday, which was why I left it until this morning. Dost thou think that was the murderer?'

'It may have been. It's certainly very peculiar. Could she describe this man?'

'I asked her the same thing. She said she'd been too frightened to pay close attention to his appearance. All she could tell me was that he was an active-looking fellow with dark hair and one cheek marked by the smallpox.'

'Do you know if your maid knew the milk-seller's daughter?'

'I don't, but it seems unlikely. She may have met the girl if she had come to the house with milk, but I doubt it. The kitchen staff would deal with people like that, not a housemaid.'

Adam agreed. The servants in a house observed a strict hierarchy – stricter than any followed by those who employed them. Still, that gave him an idea. When Mr Jempson had left, he would ask Mrs Brigstone to send his own kitchen maid to see him. She might have known the dead girl.

'I am sure you've already thought of this, Mr Jempson, but you should tell all your female servants to be most careful when they go outside. None of them should go out late in the day or after dark. This man has seen the maid who spoke with you, so she may be particularly at risk.'

'That is why I have decided to send her at once to Norwich to stay with my daughter and her husband for a while. My groom was getting the carriage ready when I came here. I will go with her to explain to my daughter what this is all about. I have no doubt that she will take her in.'

'That is a wise precaution, sir. I keep hoping each killing will be the last one, but I cannot be sure. Maybe this will cheer the girl somewhat. Tell her that what she heard the man say to her may be particularly important in getting to the bottom of this business.'

'I will tell her that, Doctor. Now I must go, for the carriage will be ready. I said a few moments ago that evil is abroad in this place and I meant it. This is the work of Satan, if anything is. Send word at once if there is any way that I can help thee find this wicked man and I will do it. My blessing go with thee, Doctor, and that of all good men. What thou art about in this case is, without doubt, God's work.'

Molly, Adam's kitchen maid was as much bewildered by the killing of the milk-seller's daughter as upset. She kept repeating that there was no harm in the girl. She was sure the murderer must be a madman, merely intent on killing. Bit by bit, under Adam's gentle probing, she grew calmer and began to talk about the girl and what little she knew of her life. It took a while to get her to admit to speaking with her, let alone sharing gossip or secrets. Servants were not encouraged to gossip with those who came to the house. Though Mrs Brigstone was less stern than many housekeepers, she kept a strict eye on the junior members of the household. It was important to make sure they didn't waste their time when they should be working.

Adam persisted through false starts and attempted diversions into irrelevant matters. He endured frequent complaints against the harshness of fate in ending a young girl's life so early. By the end, what he obtained was, he judged, worth all those inconveniences and more.

Jane, the milk-seller's daughter, was always after the men, Molly told him. She wasn't what you'd call wanton so much as lusty. She knew she had what men wanted, wasn't too delicate to use it and enjoyed the attention it brought her. Aside from that, she was a prize chatterbox, eager to share news of anything in her life that went beyond the ordinary. A few weeks ago, for example, she'd been bursting to tell everyone that she'd taken up with a new young man from a neighbouring village. To hear her tell the tale, the lad was everything a woman could desire — strong, handsome and, best of all, virile. As his chosen companion, Jane thought she should be the envy of every woman for miles around. Not long after, there was more news. He would be able, before long, to leave the dull environs of his parents' cottage, she told everyone, and show the world his true worth. People wanted to know what was going to bring about this transformation, but she wouldn't say then. Either that or he wouldn't tell her.

It couldn't have been long before something else happened to increase her excitement. He still wouldn't give her any details. It was too secret. She had to be content with his assurance that a great change was going to come about before many more weeks had passed. Naturally he swore her to secrecy once again and she promised not to breathe a word to anyone.

To have such a piece of knowledge and remain silent tested Jane's frail will-power to the limit. When, only a few days ago, her lover told her the time for the change in their fortunes had almost come, the effort of keeping it all locked within her became almost intolerable. The final straw seemed to have been his promise that, once he had achieved the fame and fortune that awaited him, he would marry her and they would start a new life in America.

It was too much. Now she had told everyone she met of the glorious future before her, swearing each of her hearers to silence. The silly girl must have known in small towns and villages a runaway horse was a major excitement and any oath not to pass on gossip was written in water. What she had said was soon the topic of numberless conversations.

Did Molly know who the young man was? Not by name. All she knew was that he was the son of a local tradesman. Jane said he described his father as a victim. A victim of what? Of 'the outdated laws that serve to keep the rich in undeserved luxury'. The kind who bow to the squire and the parson and convince themselves their lowly status is the unchangeable will of God. That was what he had told her.

Where did he live? She didn't know that either – only that it was somewhere in or near Cawston, she thought. Or was it Saxthorpe? To be honest, she'd grown so tired of the girl's continual chatter that she'd barely listened towards the end.

Of a sudden, she recalled something else. It was a name the girl had mentioned many times. Something like 'Pain'. Was it James Pain? No, that wasn't right. Henry? John? She had it. It was Tom. Tom Pain. That must be her young man's name. For several weeks past, she had gone on and on about listening to what he said about the world. It was clear she held him in awe, so he must be the one.

Adam tried to appear cheerful. He wanted Molly to think what she was telling him was nothing of great importance; trifles of local gossip to fill in a few gaps. After she had left and he was on his own, the grim expression on his face told a different story. He was certain now two young people had lost their lives because neither could keep a secret. If that secret was worth killing to protect, it had to be something of unusual importance. What that might be was still beyond his grasp.

Were all the murders done by the same person? Maybe. It looked that way. Yet it seemed unlikely Betsy Wormald had been involved with either of the later victims. Melton Constable was a good distance from Cawston, especially if your normal mode of travelling was on foot. If she had needed milk, there would be sellers much nearer. Besides, rural families rarely bought milk in that way. If they had a bit of land — or access to any of the shrinking areas of common land — they kept one or two cows. If not, they begged a drop from a neighbour. Perhaps in return for a few eggs or a little basket of fresh peas from their cottage garden. The wealthy had plenty of cattle to supply their needs. It was only urban folk, cut off from other supplies, who bought milk — and only the better-off at that. Try as he might, he could not find a single reason to account for all three killings. What if they were not the work of one man? That did not satisfy him either. He could not shake himself free of a near certainty that they were part of the same pattern.

12

MAY 4TH, 1793

When Charles came to see him the next day, Adam was eager for whatever news he could bring. He'd spent a good part of the early hours trying to set the jumble of ideas, impressions and possibilities that crowded his mind into order. There was a pattern behind what was happening; he was convinced of that. Sadly, it was not yet in his grasp. Maybe what Charles had to tell him might bring much-needed clarity.

Something was wrong. The young man who sat opposite Adam was not the Charles Scudamore he expected. This one had mislaid his ebullience, his usual carefree attitude and his sense of fun. This Mr Scudamore was the careworn lawyer, young in years, but saddened by experience of a world filled with more reasons for disillusion than hope.

'Before you proceed with your news,' Adam said, 'you'd best tell me what is weighing you down.'

A deep sigh.

'Out with it, Scudamore. Your face alone is enough to bring about a relapse on my part. Even if you have gathered no news of any use, it cannot be worth such a state of distress.'

Slowly, in bits and pieces with many sighs and exclamations of woe, the story emerged. Lady Alice had called Ruth and Charles to her morning room and imparted the terrible news that she was leaving Mossterton Hall for good. They would soon need to seek out fresh accommodation or return to London. Without saying a word to anyone, she had been in negotiation with Sir Daniel's heir to the baronetcy and estate. As Adam knew, the Mossterton estate was entailed and must pass to the closest living descendant of the Fouchard who had bought it 150 years before. Lady Alice did not own it. She only had the right under her late husband's Will to live there for the rest of her life, unless she married again, of course. Then it must pass to the heir at once. In the meantime, she could draw sufficient from its revenues to maintain the property, the estate lands and herself.

Now, with Sir Daniel's heir eager to take possession, she had decided not to insist on that right any longer. In return for the payment of a lump sum equal to her original dowry, plus an annuity from the estate, she would agree to leave the property and hand over full control. There was even a date set for her to vacate the hall. Michaelmas. Five months' time.

Adam was speechless. Why should she leave now? Where would she go? Would he still be able to visit her? Might he never see her again? Worst of all, had someone proposed marriage to her? Had she accepted?

For several minutes, the two men sat facing one another in silence, each absorbed in thoughts of the coming disaster.

Adam was the first who managed to speak. 'Do you know where your aunt will go? What does she intend to do from this time onwards? What will she live on?'

'She's very rich, you know. This annuity she's agreed won't matter much, I shouldn't think. It's more for the sake of reminding the wretched heir she didn't need to let him have the estate at all during her lifetime. Since he's older than she is, that could well have meant he'd never take it into his hands. Unless she married, of course.'

'Is she . . . is she thinking of doing that?' Adam could scarcely bring himself to mention the possibility. Yet why should she not remarry? She was still young and handsome — to his eyes the most beautiful woman he had ever known. Didn't she deserve to live a new life with a husband and family? Very rich, Charles had said. That implied a rich man for a husband. She had far too much sense to fall for some worthless fellow interested only in her money . . . didn't she?

'Not that I know,' Charles replied. 'But then, I didn't know she was arranging this bargain either. She had the gall to say that making me leave Mossterton might convince me to stop wasting my time and set myself up in practice as I had promised. There's worse, too.'

'What could be worse than Lady Alice moving away? My God! I can't bear to think of it.'

Those weren't the words that were meant to come out. Fortunately, Charles seemed not to notice.

'What's worse is that my sister appears determined to stay with me, wherever I decide to live. The trouble is she won't have any place to go other than back to our parents. Neither she nor they would relish that idea, I can tell you. Now I feel I'm trapped and in no position to refuse.'

'I thought you loved your sister?'

'I do. It's just . . . you've seen her. She can be so . . . bossy . . . so certain she's always right about everything. I'm convinced she'll try to keep me to herself forever.'

'Won't each of you wish to marry?'

'I do . . . I mean I will . . . someday. Look. Not to put too fine a point on it, who would want to marry Ruth?'

'She's attractive in her person, talented, clever —'

'Argumentative, domineering, high-handed, intractable —'

'Come, come, Scudamore. You are much too hard on the poor lady.'

'You've never had to live with her, Doctor. Here's but one example. She's been making the most confounded fuss about my supposed 'attentions' to Miss LaSalle. According to her, the lady is far beneath me in station, has not a guinea to her name and is nothing more than a servant. Is that fair? I ask you, Doctor, is it anything other than a wish to set me against any woman to whom I might seem attracted?'

'I can assure you it is not fair, Scudamore. Yet we all say unfair things about others on occasion, mostly from ignorance. She hardly knows Miss LaSalle and can have no grounds for saying what she has. Most likely she is simply feeling left out. Lady Alice told me the two of you were inseparable. Is that still the case? I think not. Whichever of you first showed signs of wishing to establish an independent life, the other was bound to feel rejected. Your sister is angry with Miss LaSalle because she has claimed much of the attention you used to give to her. It could happen with any siblings who have been close. Even more so with twins.'

There the subject was left, for neither had the heart to take it further. Too many emotions and fears might be brought to the surface.

The little that Charles had learned in his travels up and down the coast was soon shared. There did seem to be something unusual going on, but he hadn't managed to find anything more specific than rumours and guesses. The smuggling gangs were ruthless with anyone suspected of turning informer. More than one person had told him curious outsiders — no problem understanding who they meant — would do well to mind their own business. If not, they would quickly find themselves in serious danger. In the end, he had given up.

All he could offer Adam was an impression that any new smuggling activity was concentrated on the coastline between Cley and Weybourne. Several people warned him the area had become dangerous and it was best not to fall foul of the smuggling gang along that stretch of coast. There had been several pitched battles between the smugglers and the Preventive men, with casualties on both sides.

'I'm sorry, Doctor. I know it must seem a poor effort, but I tried my best, truly I did. I'm just not clever enough to be of any use to you in this business.'

'Nonsense! When I set you this task, I hadn't grasped the danger. There have been two more killings while you've been gone; two more young peoples' lives cut short.' Adam explained about Jane and her village lover. 'It seems to me,' he went on, 'both must have been murdered by someone who'll go to any lengths to protect some secret. These poor innocents must have stumbled on it by chance and paid a heavy price. It's best if you leave off any more questioning for present. I don't want to put you in danger. Besides, if these people, whoever they are, think we've given up, they might come more into the open.'

'Is any of this linked to the murder of Betsy Wormald?' Charles asked.

'I wish I knew. I cannot easily bring myself to accept there are two, unconnected killers at large in the villages around here. Yet I can see no definite link either.'

'So how can we proceed? All the people killed have been from the artisan or labouring classes. Who can persuade them to tell what they know? I, for one, have rarely had any dealings with that sort. They're eager to avoid lawyers like me — and physicians like you, I shouldn't doubt.'

'That's simply explained in my case. They can't afford my usual fees. Since I treat some of the local poor without charge, I know they're no different from the rest of humanity. They fear lawyers because the law is so often used against them in ways they find confusing and harsh. Lawyers spout Latin at them and make them feel foolish. The rich who hire these lawyers have so much wealth, yet still seem intent on taking away what little the poor have left. As they see it, gentlemen like us too often ignore their problems in favour of enriching —'

Adam stopped, stared and then banged his good hand down hard on the arm of the chair.

'Good God, Scudamore! What an addle-pated idiot I've been. Of course! She said that was what the milk-girl's lover must be called, because she kept on about him. Not Pain, Paine with an e. That Paine.'

'What pain, Doctor? Where does it hurt you? Shall I call your maid and tell her to run for the apothecary?'

Adam ignored him. He was smiling and chuckling to himself

like the village idiot. Indeed, Charles was starting to think he must have suffered a brain-storm and was half out of his chair to go and call for help. Adam, seeing this, tried to move his left arm to restrain hold him back — and yelped aloud at the sharp spasm it brought.

'Damn this arm! Please, Scudamore, sit still and listen. I want you to do something for me as quickly as you can . . .' He trailed off into seemingly inconsequential muttering, while staring into a dim realm of conjecture hidden from anyone else. 'I said the other two got mixed up in something dangerous by mistake. That's wrong . . . is it? . . . Yes, at least . . . the girl, I suppose . . .'

'What is it you want me to do?' Charles had little patience for Adam's tendency to drift away into some world of his own.

'What?'

'You said you wanted me to undertake an errand, Doctor. Then you started muttering about something else. What is it you want me to do with such urgency?'

'Go back to Mosserton Hall via Holt. There you must seek out a friend of mine, an old seafarer called Captain Mimms. Ask anyone and they'll direct you to his house. Tell him to come and see me as soon as he can. If he's not there, leave that message — but stress it's urgent. More lives are at stake in this matter, of that I'm sure. Now go! Go fast as you can.'

It would be an understatement to say that Adam was cast down by Charles' news about his aunt. For almost two hours after Charles left, he did little but stare at the wall opposite where he sat. Partly his frustration was due to feeling trapped by his injuries and forced to rely on others. He had always relied on questioning people for himself and judging their responses at first hand. What might they have added, if only the person speaking to them had seen what he would have seen and probed what he would have probed? All he had to go on were second-hand accounts obtained by heaven knows what kind of questioning.

Of course, that wasn't the worst of it. When he should be

focussed on these murders, more than half his attention was claimed by uncertainty about what Lady Alice was doing. Just when he had found himself certain about his emotions and his wish to make her his wife, it seemed she was set on quite a different future. He wanted to believe she felt the same towards him. She had hinted as much — but could he be sure? Might she be expressing gratitude rather than any deeper affection? He loved and desired her, he had no doubt of that, but did she love him or want him as her husband? After many years of valuing his head over his heart, should he even be as certain of his own feelings as he thought he was? People talked about love enough, but he'd never heard anyone define it in a rigorous, scientific manner. Might he tire of her, once his desire had been satisfied?

Angry with himself for these doubts and fears, Adam tried to thrust the problem of Lady Alice from his mind and turn back to the other matters at hand. It was no use. He could not prevent his fears from tormenting him. The fact of Lady Alice leaving Mossterton and the uncertainty about her motives lay in his chest like a cold slab of ice.

Grinding his teeth together with misery and frustration, he forced himself onwards. Three people had been murdered. Remember that. Three young people with their lives still before them. Two of them, he was certain, had paid with their lives for nothing worse than misplaced curiosity and careless chatter. He was less sure of the precise reason for the death of the third, Betsy Wormald. It had to be linked somehow. It had to be. If only he could see how.

Three people dead. He repeated this over and over to himself, as if it alone could block out that other pain. Three murders brought about by the need to protect a secret. What was so important it was worth killing to keep safe? He could make a shrewd guess where to look for the answer. Had he been able to go himself, he wouldn't have hesitated an instant. To ask another person to go — and expose that person to considerable danger — was another matter. If anything went wrong, if another murder was the result, he would never be able to forgive himself. Yet to stand aside and risk the maiming or killing of more innocents was unforgivable.

'Damned if I do and damned if I don't!' he said aloud. 'Haven't I got enough wretchedness in my life without adding this too? Damn it all! God damn and blast it all!' That was when Mrs Munnings came into the room to see how her patient was doing. Fortunately, she seemed not to have heard his words.

'What is the matter with you, Doctor?' she said. 'You're staring at that clock on the mantelpiece as if you would like to smash it into pieces. Does its ticking annoy you? I can take it away if it does.'

It took Adam some moments to convince her the clock had not upset him in any way. Several more to persuade her that his lack-lustre spirits were not signs of a relapse. Even then, she must have harboured doubts, for she made no mention of helping him go downstairs. He should have pressed her, but his present mood made him loath to make the effort. In the end, he settled for bland reassurances and agreeing she might look in on him every hour or so for the rest of the day.

She was about to leave the room when she recalled what had brought her there. 'I almost forgot, Doctor. A servant came from your brother's house with a letter for you from your mother. Perhaps that will cheer you up.'

It didn't.

It was obvious her visit to Trundon Hall was not going well. Giles' attention was monopolised by his work as a magistrate, his mother wrote, made worse by the demands for local defence against an invasion by the French. He was obsessed by the idea the country-side was teeming with radical republican sympathisers. These, he kept telling her, were longing to start a revolution and deprive men like him of their property. The smugglers were also more active, so that the Revenue men besieged him with complaints about the complicity of the local people. Everyone who lived along the coast kept their eyes and their mouths shut — and their stables conveniently unlocked.

Amelia did her best to act as a proper hostess, but, with her husband so distracted, the whole burden of running the house and estate now fell on her. Even Sophia was no help. Instead of providing conversation or companionship, she had taken to staring out of the window with a silly smile on her face. Half the time, Mrs Bascom was convinced the young woman didn't notice anyone else's presence.

His mother's complaints about Adam himself were saved to the end of her letter. Why didn't he write or send a servant to let her know how he was? What was he doing with himself all day? Was Mrs Munnings looking after him properly? Since no one bothered to keep her informed, she would have to come and see for herself. Giles said he was too busy to escort her and Sophia to Aylsham, so she had told him he must provide servants in his place. They would leave Trundon Hall on Saturday and be at Adam's house soon after noon. They would stay in Aylsham for one day, then Mr Scudamore had kindly offered to escort them back to Norwich. She understood he had business in the city and would stay there for several days. As a mark of gratitude for his kindness and attention, she had agreed that he might accompany Sophia to the Vauxhall Pleasure Gardens to take the air on her own. It would do her good to be in the company of someone of her own age for a change. For herself, she was eager to pay the proper visits to her many friends in the city and catch up with news of any events of note that had occurred in her absence.

Adam folded the letter and sat in silence for a while, stroking his cheeks as he often did while puzzling over an issue. So, Giles was convinced there was some devilment abroad in the countryside. Some stirring of radicalism and dissent, even sedition. His brother was prone to exaggeration, it was true; never more so than when dealing with some threat to property and the stability of the existing social order. Yet though he might be the most conservative of men, he was far from being a fool. If his concerns were such that he was unwilling to leave his house for as little as a day, they had to be serious.

That left Adam with yet another decision. Should he write to Wicken in London and make him aware of what he thought was going on; or should he attempt to gain greater clarity about the matter first?

If only he could leave this accursed house!

13

THE SAME DAY

ADAM WAS NOT GIVEN THE TIME TO WORRY FURTHER. BY LATE THAT afternoon, Mrs Munnings was back, eager to help him go downstairs for the first time. She would settle him into a chair in the library, she told him, and give him the small bell so he could call a servant if he needed anything. As a further incentive, she pointed out he might take his dinner in the library or in the dining room. He had complained many times of the difficulty of eating in bed or from a tray on his lap. Now he could sit at the table as usual.

Although Adam was not quite so keen to start moving around the house again, he could see the sense of it. Mrs Munnings must want to return to her home and that wouldn't be possible until she was sure that he could manage with the help of the servants alone. Going downstairs for some or all of the day was the only way to establish that he had now reached that stage in his recovery. All meekness therefore, he let Mrs Munnings help him up and they began the slow journey down the stairs to his library.

It was a fortunate move. No sooner was he seated than there was a knocking at the front door. Hannah must have gone to answer it, for he heard her squeals of protest, followed by Captain Mimms' hearty laughter. It was a game they played whenever she opened the door to him. He would catch her around the waist and place a hearty kiss on her cheek. She would pretend to be angry and fight him off. Both kept to the rules of their game. He never attempted to take any greater liberties and she made sure to stand within easy reach as he came inside.

The captain was delighted to see Adam was able to leave his bedroom already and marvelled at his swift recovery.

'That's what comes of being young,' he said. 'When you get old like me, the slightest cut or knock takes an age to heal. Here I am, Doctor, as you requested. Rather late in the day I agree. I took dinner with old friends last evening and drank more than was good for me. Until a few hours ago, I was not really in a fit state to under-take the journey here.'

The old man's reddened eyes and tendency to flinch at any loud noise proved he had not yet completely rid himself of the after-effects of all that fine brandy.

'Then I am doubly grateful that you have made the effort to come,' Adam said. 'I would not have bothered you had it not been a matter of considerable importance.'

'No bother at all, my dear Doctor. Always delighted to talk with you. The only problem is I will not be able to stay long. The roads are far too dangerous these days for any man on his own, especially when the light is failing, let alone one as decrepit as I have become. The last six months have seen a notable increase in highway robberies. Times are hard and food is short. This cursed war is proving the ruin of honest working families, both on the land and in the weaving trade. Some have been driven to theft to survive. I have brought my groom with me for protection, but even that will be of little use after dark.'

'I would not for the world put you in any danger, sir. My groom, William, will go with you on your return journey, provided you can offer him a bed for the night in your servant's quarters. Two such young fellows should be enough to dissuade most ruffians from trying to stop you. No, I have a better idea. Let us celebrate together this first day when I will be able to eat at a table like a civilised human being. You can take dinner here with me and my housekeeper will prepare a room for you. Yes, stay here tonight and travel home in the daylight tomorrow. We can find a bed for your groom too, I'm sure.'

The captain was delighted with the idea and the arrangements were soon settled. To make more of a party of it, Adam sent Hannah to invite Peter Lassimer to join them. The apothecary and Captain Mimms enjoyed one another's company and the presence of a third person would allow Adam to take a back seat if he became weary — or if this attempt to distract his mind from gloomy thoughts about Lady Alice should fail.

'There's one thing I must beg of you,' Mimms said. 'For heaven's sake don't allow me to drink too heavily again. My poor head is only just recovering.'

'You have my word. I'm sure that Mr Lassimer would disapprove if too much alcohol passed my lips, so we will be abstemious together. As I told you, this is the first day I have been allowed downstairs, so I cannot vouch for how long I will be able to remain awake when the meal is over. We may all be able to have an early night.'

The two men exchanged the usual pleasantries until Hannah returned with the news that the apothecary would be delighted to join them. She then brought in coffee and they were able to turn at last to more serious matters.

'You will know of the murders that have taken place recently,' Adam began. 'For various reasons, I am convinced they are connected, both to one another and to some wider enterprise that is being planned. What that is I don't yet know. If it is of sufficient moment to warrant killing to keep it secret, it must have a most serious purpose. You have helped me before, Captain. I hope you will do so again.'

'With all my heart, Doctor. You should have known that.'

'I did and I thank you. However, I must point out that doing so on this occasion may put you into deadly danger. As I said, at least three people have already been killed because they came too close to the heart of this matter. I would not have that happen to you for all the world.'

'Pah! Remember that I am a naval man, Doctor, and have faced death many times. It did not frighten me then and it does not frighten me now. Tell me what you would have me do and forget about the danger.'

'If I am right, items to support an uprising to overthrow the government — most likely money and weapons — are being smuggled into the county and passed to radical and revolutionary groups. The route enters through the coast north of here, I judge, via the free traders who abound there. Those who are behind this business probably rely on their other smuggling activities to mask the comings and goings of this far deadlier contraband. My information suggests the centre of these activities is between the villages of Cley and Weybourne. I would dearly like to have that confirmed. I also need to know whether we're dealing with the regular gangs of smugglers or a group formed specially for this purpose. As you can see, I am still unable to leave this house and so must rely on others to bring me information. I know it is a great deal to ask, but can you use your contacts to help explain what is going on? Until that is done, I see no way forward. It would be useless without more specific information to alert the authorities to stop up this rat hole. They're already struggling to cope with preparations to deal with an invasion by the French and it isn't feasible to patrol the whole coast in the hope of coming upon these men. Besides, such an action would probably cause them to transfer their activities elsewhere. Then we would need to start again.'

'You have it right, Doctor. The only way to deal with this kind of plot is to catch the villains in the act. We won't be safe until such traitors are dangling at the end of a rope. I'll get you the information you need, I promise you. Not only is it my plain duty, it will be my pleasure to frustrate the plans of such evil wretches. God damn them to hell, I say! The Frenchies are at least honest enemies. These curs want to stab us in the back and so deserve no quarter. If I have my way, none will be given either, by God!'

The old sailor's eyes flashed with the joy of battle and his face grew so red Adam feared he might suffer an apoplexy. It was high time to turn the conversation aside into more peaceful channels.

Adam asked about the captain's sons and the state of his business. That could usually be relied upon to distract him. Mimms was supposed to have stepped back from involvement in trade matters to let his sons take over. Yet, like many in a similar position, he remained convinced they needed his advice far more often than they did. They probably humoured him, then went their own way. Thus, it was the two men passed the time until Peter arrived and the three of them could settle down to a convivial meal.

His two guests helped Adam into the dining room and sat him at the head of the table. It turned out to be one of the best evenings Adam had spent for a long time. The others regaled him with stories, each trying to outdo the other in finding outrageous anec-dotes to keep him amused. The captain seemed to have recovered fully from his hangover, though Adam noticed he drank little more than a glass or two of wine and the same of brandy. Eventually, the combination of laughing, talking and eating took its toll on Adam. His head began to nod and his eyelids started to droop. He tried to wake himself up, but it was no use. He had to admit defeat soon after seven o'clock. Insisting the others must stay as long as they wished, he called for Mrs Munnings to help him back upstairs to his bedroom.

He was asleep even before she had blown out the candle.

14

MAY 6TH, 1793

By Monday morning, Adam had decided what he would say when he wrote to Wicken. It was too early to share his suspicions; better to wait until he had enough evidence to make them convincing. At present, his most important deductions amounted to little more than guesswork and he had no wish to make a fool of himself. He decided to write that day, but only to explain that he had found no trace of the missing Swiss professor.

He woke first at seven o'clock. That was his normal time to think about rising, but today he'd promised another half an hour of relaxation. The day before, though it was a Sunday, had seen him rise rather early. Captain Mimms had stayed the night and was eager to get on the road to return to his home. It would have been impolite for Adam not to be ready to take breakfast with his guest and bid him a suitable farewell.

Naturally, once he had decided to delay rising for a little longer, he fell heavily asleep. When he next awoke, his clock told him it was now well past nine. Then it was all hustle and bustle. Mrs Munnings was called to bring a clean morning-gown and he had only just risen from his bed when the barber arrived. Shaved and dressed, he hurried as fast as he could to take breakfast. Mrs Munnings wanted to assist him down the stairs, but he said he was sure he could manage on his own. In fact, he was quite apprehensive about descending unaided. The stairs looked steeper than he remembered and he gripped the bannister tightly all the way. Fortunately, there were no mishaps.

'Well done, Doctor,' she said as he reached the bottom. 'If your progress continues like this, I shall be able to return to my own home in a day or so.'

'I expect you will be glad to do so, Mrs Munnings, but I'm most grateful for your kindness and care during the time you have been here. Do you have any further employment awaiting you?'

'Had you asked me before this morning, I would have said I had not. However, before he left yesterday, your guest pressed me to accept the position as his housekeeper. His current housekeeper is elderly and not in the best of health, it seems. She has lately told him she would like to retire to live on the small annuity he has provided for her. Captain Mimms has decided I would be the ideal person to take her place. I thought about his offer after he left and have decided to accept — subject to any advice you wish to give me, of course. You know the Captain well, I understand.'

Like most sailors, the captain has an eye for a handsome woman, Adam thought. Still, there's no harm in him. He's very different from Peter Lassimer. He might feast his eyes on his new housekeeper from time to time, but he's not the kind of man to attempt to take advantage of her. Besides, she's strong and in the prime of life, while he's far advanced into middle age. If it came to a wrestling match, Adam knew who would win.

'Believe me, Mrs Munnings,' he said, 'you could not do better. Throughout all the time I have known the captain he has always struck me as the kindest of men and the most honest too. I'm sure that you would be very happy in his household.'

Adam did not sit long over his breakfast, for he was eager to write to Sir Percival Wicken and see the letter on its way with all speed. As soon as he had finished his third cup of coffee, he therefore made his way through the hall to his library, still a little unsteady on his feet but safe enough if he took his time. Then, having written and sealed his letter, he called for William and instructed him to seek out the carrier with all speed.

'If you hurry, you might catch him before he leaves. Tell him to hand this in at the post office in Norwich the moment he arrives. Here, give him this shilling from me to ensure he does so. After that, I want to talk to you and your mother. I will be here in the library, so the two of you should come to me as soon as you return.'

Fifteen minutes later, a timid tapping on the door announced their arrival. Adam told them to find themselves chairs and sit down. Both were horrified at such a suggestion, for it was unheard of for servants to be seated in their master's presence. They swore they preferred to stand. Adam insisted they should not.

'What I have to say to you may take a little while,' he told them. 'I cannot have you looming over me all the time. The circumstances are unusual, so we will set aside formality this one time.'

If they had both been nervous when they came in, Adam's words made them yet more apprehensive. What on earth could the master want? What had they done wrong? While Adam collected his thoughts, mother and son sat in silence, trying to recall what grave misdemeanours they must have committed in the past few days.

Adam had spent much of the time he was eating breakfast debating with himself whether he should take the step he now planned. To put himself in danger would not have bothered him much; to risk harm to another, especially to a young servant, weighed greatly on his conscience. Again and again, he had tried to think of another way. Only when he had exhausted himself in what proved a fruitless effort did he steel himself to what had to be done. He began to explain.

'You both know about the murders that have taken place and that I am trying to discover who the killer might be. Since I am unable to leave this house, I must rely on others to find me the information I need. Now I find there is an urgent task for which none of those who have been helping me so far are suitable. The reason for that is simple. I need someone who can pass unnoticed amongst a crowd of ordinary working people. It must also be a man who is unknown to those I wish him to observe. They have seen Mr Lassimer and would recognise him at once. Mr Scudamore, however he tried to disguise his appearance, is every inch the gentleman. He would stand out like a thoroughbred amongst a herd of carthorses. They could not fail to notice him as soon as he entered the room and be on their guard. No lady could go on her own, so I cannot ask Mrs Munnings or you either, Mrs Brigstone. William, on the other hand, would fit the bill admirably — No, don't say anything yet. I haven't finished.'

Now came the most difficult part.

'I have asked you both to be present, because this decision is one which you must take together. I must tell you plainly that considerable danger may well be involved. If my reasoning is sound, two people – maybe three – have died because they stumbled on the secret this group is protecting. I am sure they will not hesitate to kill again if they feel threatened. That is why I cannot instruct you to do what I want, William. It must be your joint decision, you and your mother's, entered into with no pressure from me. Whatever you decide, I will not think the worse of either of you. Save in time of war, no man is justified in forcing another to go into mortal danger.

'I have planned this as carefully as I can. If William follows my instructions to the letter, I am as sure as I can be that he will return unharmed. Yet you must both be aware I cannot guarantee his safety. Much depends on him passing unnoticed amongst the crowd who will be present. I have no doubt the conspirators will watch everyone who enters the room, alert for spies or government informers. If he draws their attention to him, he will be in danger of a severe beating — or worse. Now, I have told you all that I can. If you wish to talk together in private, leave now and I will await your decision.'

For a moment, Mrs Brigstone and her son looked at one another. Then William nodded and his mother smiled. Their decision was made. Mrs Brigstone spoke for them both.

'My son will do it for you and gladly, Master. That is our firm decision. These are evil men and they must be stopped. The fact that they have killed should only strengthen the resolve of all honest people to bring them to justice. William is a brave lad, sir, well able to look after himself in most circumstances. If you tell him what to do, I promise you he will do it.'

It was what Adam had expected, but he was still relieved. If William had refused to go, he had no idea who could have gone in his place.

They got down to business at once. Adam had read in the news-paper that Professor Panacea was holding a fresh series of public lectures at the Assembly House in Norwich. The next one would be on the following day at noon. William was to take the chaise, drive to the city and leave horse and carriage at The Maid's Head Inn. From there he should go forward on foot.

'When you arrive, make sure you do what everyone else does. If possible, find yourself a seat in the middle of the hall. Sitting at the front would make you too conspicuous; to hide in the back could make them think you suspicious. All I want you to do is observe those who sit behind the professor. Not the man himself. Those who sit behind him at his lectures and go with him everywhere. The ones people call 'The Disciples'. These are the ones I am interested in. Don't stare at them, whatever you do. Try to keep your eyes on Professor Panacea, as if you are listening with great attention to every word he speaks. It would be natural for anyone to look around from time to time, so make these the opportunities to take note of the men I have told you about. By the time you return, I need you to be able to describe, in detail, as many of them as you can. For the rest of the time, take your lead from the other people present. Applaud when they applaud. Laugh when they laugh. Whatever you do, don't ask questions or give any sign you aren't completely taken in by the professor's words.

'I will give you enough money to pay the entrance fee and a small amount extra. Use it to purchase a bottle of the elixir that the professor sells at the end of his lectures, so that I can ask Mr Lassimer to work out what it contains. Don't rush forward to buy and don't hang back. Try to stay amongst a group of people, if you can. The same applies at the end. Don't be the first to leave and don't be the last. If anyone asks who you are and how you come to be there, you may tell them the truth – or at least part of it. You are groom to a doctor in the north of the county. He has sent you to the city, as he does from time to time, to collect various medical items he needs for his practice. Since you had to wait for these to be ready, you decided to take a walk. Then, seeing the notices announcing the lecture, you decided to go to listen to the man you'd heard others were making a fuss about.

'In case anyone decides to check up on your story, I have written to an apothecary I know in the city. He will have a package of drugs ready for you to collect when the lecture is over. Go to the address I will give you and don't hurry. Remember you're supposed to be a servant who has found himself with a few hours of leisure which he didn't expect. Look in the shop windows as you pass, admire the pretty girls you will doubtless see along the way. Do everything you can to convince any watchers that you are no more than you say you are. Once you have collected the package, return to The Maid's Head Inn and come back home. I hope, most sincerely, that these precautions will be unnecessary, but be sure not to omit them. They might save your life.'

William promised that he would do exactly as he was told. Since he was a steady lad, in no way given to acts of reckless bravado, Adam had to be content with that. All he could do was to wish him well, hand over the few shillings he had promised, give him the address of the city apothecary and settle down to wait for his return. The next day was going to try his patience to its limit.

At the time, even Adam could not know William's visit to Norwich would prove the turning point in the whole affair.

15

RUTH SIPPED AT THE TEA AND TRIED TO STOP HER EXPRESSION revealing how little she was enjoying it. She was used to the finest Bohea. The Reverend Oliver Marshall, Rector of Melton Constable, could clearly not afford such luxuries. This tea was third-rate — or even worse. Why didn't he buy his tea from the smugglers, as so many people did? Was he too principled or couldn't he afford even their prices? His twin daughters, Charlotte and Jessica, must be used to the loathsome stuff. They kept prattling on, interrupting each other and gulping at their tea. Talk, talk, talk and all about nothing.

Ruth had long since given up trying to introduce any remarks of her own. As long as she appeared to be listening, smiling and nodding her head from time to time, they were content. She longed — oh, how she longed — to take her leave, but as yet they had told her nothing of value. She had to keep reminding herself she was doing this for Dr Bascom, not for her own pleasure. She only hoped it would be worth it.

Now, instead of paying attention, she had let her mind wander. What on earth had possessed her aunt to decide to leave Mosserton Hall? It was such a beautiful house. How could she be so selfish? Had she considered the effect this would have on Ruth and her brother? She had said nothing about them going with her to her new address, wherever that was to be. Was she was trying to encourage them to return home or find their own accommodation? That's what Charles had suggested. Very well, they would find somewhere together. And yet — for some reason her brother was reluctant to accept this solution. He could not wish to live on his own surely?

A swift return to the present informed her Charlotte was describing a hat she'd seen on her last visit to Norwich. Ruth had little interest in hats or clothes. If Lady Alice hadn't taken charge of her wardrobe, she would wear the same things until they fell apart. There were so many more interesting things in the world to think about. Back to her present problems. Should she return to London? There she might interest some of the scientific societies in purchasing her botanical paintings, or at least attend their meetings from time to time. That kind of society attracted the finest scientific minds in the world. It would be a joy to talk with people who had something worthwhile to discuss.

Ruth was well aware why she was unmarried and likely to remain so. Most young men bored her. When they weren't mouthing empty compliments, they talked about horses, or the price of corn, or shooting, or – heaven help us! – the weather. Regrettably, the majority of women bored her just as much, since they were as empty headed as the men. Her father and mother wanted her to go out in Society to meet eligible bachelors, hoping they could get her off their hands. She could understand that. Few parents wanted their daughters to turn into old maids. She had tried, but Society meant all those tedious young men and feather-brained women. She'd rather knit socks!

What now was hurting her almost beyond endurance was the suspicion her brother Charles wanted to be rid of her too. The two of them used to be inseparable. Over the last two weeks he had been away on his own a good deal of the time. When he was present, he was often withdrawn and distracted, mooning about like a love-sick idiot. What a selfish brute he had turned into! He either didn't care that his sister was lonely and bored, or he hadn't even noticed.

She knew who was to blame. Since he first met Miss LaSalle, he had lost interest in everyone else. He'd had infatuations before, but they hadn't lasted long. He'd stare glassy-eyed at some young woman, then rush to tell his sister all about her. Praise her eyes, her hair or her skin. Those times he'd talked and talked, but without any action to follow. What if his present silence about 'Miss Perfect' LaSalle meant he'd decided on action rather than words?

What on earth could Charles even see in her? Her family barely qualified as gentry and she was as poor as the proverbial church mouse. She was pretty enough, Ruth supposed — at least in that superficial, predictable way most men preferred — but good looks never lasted. Ruth assumed the woman wasn't entirely stupid either. But what did any of this matter when she was so far beneath Charles in status? She had tried to explain that to him, but he'd flown into a rage and forbidden her to speak of the matter ever again. As for her aunt's attitude . . . Ruth was appalled by the rebuke she had received from Lady Alice for pointing out Miss LaSalle's obvious drawbacks as a bride.

Charles had been bewitched. It was the only answer. Not in the literal sense, of course. Ruth's rational mind had no time for superstitious nonsense of that kind. Bewitched in a figurative sense. Taken in by a pretty face, an attractive figure, pleasing manners and the other means by which temptresses lure foolish men into unsuitable marriages. Ruth herself had no interest in finding ways to please men. She prided herself on being quite without the ability to flirt. It never occurred to her that was why she spent most of the time sitting by herself whenever she was cajoled into attending a ball or assembly.

'Please forgive us, my dear Miss Scudamore. My sister and I have been somewhat monopolising the conversation. As I recall, wasn't there something you particularly wished to ask us?'

Ruth returned to the present with a visible start. The grasshopper minds of the Marshall twins had made a random jump and landed on the recollection there had been a purpose to Ruth's visit. She must seize the opportunity to ask questions, before another series of leaps carried their attention far away.

'I was hoping you could tell me a little more about Miss Wormald,' she said. 'My aunt has promised to do all in her power to bring her killer to justice. In pursuit of that goal, she has involved one of the most skilful investigators in the county. But none of us met Miss Wormald when she was alive. As you can imagine, many rumours about her are circulating in the area. Without a better knowledge of her character, it's impossible to sift the truth from the idle gossip and innuendo.'

'Betsy Wormald, you mean? The delightful Betsy? That's easy.' Jessica had decided to take the lead. 'A common girl with ideas above her station. Neither of us had any personal dealings with her, as I'm sure you can understand. Her father was only the village blacksmith. Not our class of person at all.'

'My sister has hit the nail on the head,' Charlotte chipped in. 'We saw her at church on Sundays, but it would never have done to speak to her. Her family are mere artisans.'

'What did she look like?' Ruth was determined to extract every piece of information she could. She had endured an hour of the twins' company already. She would not leave without obtaining something useful, however meagre.

'I suppose you would say she was pretty enough, in a vulgar way, naturally. It wouldn't have been so bad if she had dressed according to her station. Her father spoiled her, you see. She would come to church wearing clothes that were quite inappropriate.'

'Flaunting herself like a fine lady in the latest fashions. Ridiculous!' It was clear Jessica shared her sister's opinions in full measure.

The sisters could have been describing themselves, Ruth thought. Their true complaint was that Betsy Wormald had been far more attractive and better dressed than either of them.

Jessica leant forward and lowered her voice in the manner of someone about to impart a great secret. 'We heard . . . well, people said, Betsy's greatest wish was to leave this village and live in the city as a fine lady. We all know what that means, don't we? Aside from the Quality, there's only one type of woman who is able to live like that. If you ask me, she would have been perfect for the role of a trollop.'

Ruth braced herself. 'Did she have many male admirers?' she asked.

'Oh, my dear — hordes!' Charlotte had spent hours practising the merry tinkle of laughter that accompanied this remark.

'Like wasps round a jar of jam.' That was Jessica's contribution.

'And her father did not object?'

'Her father did not know. At least, we assume he did not. He is a staunch member of the Independent Chapel, you know. Not a proper Christian, but still very strict in his morals. That was why he was trying to persuade his daughter to marry that paltry fellow, Joseph Carse. Mr Carse did have expectations, I suppose. Some rich elderly relative near to death. He was also a member of the same group of dissenters. But Joseph Carse — really! A man of straw!'

'Do you know if she had agreed?'

Charlotte took this as an opportunity for a second performance of her irritating laugh. This was a mistake. It allowed her sister to answer in her place.

'We would be amazed if she had. She'd have gained a husband no one could be proud of. She would also have been forced to abandon her high-and-mighty ways and her dreams of moving to the city.'

The moment had come. Ruth knew exactly what she had to do, though her whole being revolted against it. Gathering all her willpower and telling herself it was in the best of causes, she leant forward and lowered her voice, exactly as Jessica had done.

'But I heard . . . people said . . . oh dear, this is so difficult. Miss Wormald was, I believe, found to be in a . . . certain condition . . . when her body was examined.'

'Oh yes, there can be no doubt she was with child. We weren't surprised, were we, Sister? The real question is, who was the father?'

'What do people in the village say?'

Charlotte wasn't going to be upstaged again. She jumped in with her response while Jessica was still collecting what passed for her wits.

'That it could be any one of half a dozen young men — and a good few older ones as well.'

'Was she so abandoned? Surely her father must have heard of her behaviour, if it was so blatant?'

Realising they had allowed themselves to be carried away, the twins tried to correct at least some of what they had said earlier. Now they claimed these were only rumours — and scurrilous ones at that. They did not believe them. To do so would be unchristian. They were only reporting what other people said.

After five more minutes of their wearisome conversation, Ruth was sure the Marshall daughters had no idea who had fathered Betsy Wormald's child. It was not due to the number of potential candidates either. The plain facts showed Betsy had behaved in a perfectly normal manner. Several young men had been attracted to her. Her father's reputation for strict morality and her own views on what made a man suitable husband material kept all at bay. On the face of it, Joseph Carse had been her only actual suitor.

Ruth decided she could take no more. If there was anything else to be gleaned from these two, Dr Bascom would have to go without it. She quickly made her farewells, relying on vague smiles and grunts to deflect the sisters' requests she should come to see them again. She also somehow forgot to invite the twins to visit her at Mossterton Hall. At last the housemaid — more likely the sole household servant and a maid-of-all-work — was instructed to tell Miss Scudamore's coachman she was ready to leave. The carriage clattered round to the front of the rectory and Ruth almost leapt aboard, calling out to the coachman to drive on as she did so.

Her ordeal was over.

16

THE SAME DAY

R<small>UTH HAD INTENDED TO RETURN TO HER AUNT'S HOUSE, THEN SHE</small> thought better of it. Why go back with half a story? If Betsy's younger sister, Fanny, proved to be at home, she would see what more she could discover from her. Attracting the coachman's attention with sharp raps of her knuckles on the side of the carriage, she instructed him to take her to the smithy.

The smithy at Melton Constable was in no way unusual. As they approached, Ruth saw a low, white-washed building of flint and brick standing by the side of the road with lofty wooden doors open at the front. Trees shaded the rear, while a cottage of typical Norfolk fashion lay on the left-hand side of the smithy itself. The cottage looked well-kept and had a neat garden already showing signs of the many flowers the summer would see there.

As Lady Alice's carriage drew up outside, Ruth could see through the tall doors open to the road that the forge was in use. Jets of scarlet, orange and blue flame erupted from the coals as the bellows were worked and the air rang with the noise of a hammer on metal.

Caught at his work, Matthew Wormald, the smith, didn't know whether to be delighted or horrified. He was in his working clothes;

the forge was roaring away and he had a bar of iron near ready for the anvil. If he left it now, he would have to start all over again. Ruth had to endure a stream of apologies for the clutter, noise and heat. He was sure they must offend any gentlewoman. Only when he paused for breath could she make her request to be allowed to speak to his daughter.

'Ah . . . yes . . . well, now . . . your ladyship . . . madam . . . she'll be inside, working in the kitchen. Begging your pardon, but this hot iron won't wait for any man. I must stay here and deal with it. If you would be so good as to ask your coachman to knock on the front door of the cottage next door, the maid will come and conduct you to my daughter.'

Pray God she's looking more respectable than I am, the smith thought to himself. If she's wearing her old dress with her hands covered in flour, she'll be right mortified.

Ruth thanked him and followed the coachman up the short path to the cottage door. As she had noted from the road, she could see someone was more interested than most working people in making good use of the plot between house and road. The path was edged by well-tended beds, all filled with the signs of the flowers to come. There were even a few already coming into bloom.

The coachman knocked on the door with the handle of his whip and they waited for a response. It came in the form of a young maid who opened the door, stared at the visitors in horror and promptly fled back inside, leaving no chance for the coachman or Ruth to say anything. Again, they waited, listening to a buzz of voices within. Finally, an astonished Fanny Wormald came to the door. Either she had not believed what the maid told her, or the poor servant was too frightened to return herself.

Fanny's hands were indeed coated with flour. Seeing a grand lady on her doorstep, she was too embarrassed by her appearance to be able to speak at first. It took a few moments for her to recover herself enough to show Ruth into the parlour. Then she hurried away to wash her hands and tidy herself as best she could, calling for the maid to make tea and be sure to use the best china cups.

Left to herself, Ruth looked about the room. She hadn't often entered the homes of ordinary people, so was curious to see what she might find. She didn't realise to have a parlour free from any other use was a luxury and proved the relative prosperity of the Wormalds. The furnishings might be sparse, the walls decorated with no more than two samplers and a single print, but it was more than their neighbours had.

The short journey to the smithy had given Ruth enough time to plan her approach. She needed Fanny to feel relaxed enough with her to talk frankly. That wasn't likely to happen at a first meeting. The girl would be far too nervous. Ruth was almost certain her father would also leave the smithy at the first opportunity and come to join them. The best she could do was establish some level of rapport, all the harder given their obvious difference in social status and wealth. That was why, after a polite offering of condolences and acceptance of tea, Ruth tried to find a subject on which they could converse more equally. As luck had it, she hit on the perfect answer at once.

'I was struck by how pretty your front garden is, Miss Wormald. The flowers will make a fine show in a few weeks. I even saw one or two butterflies, though it is early in the year for many to be about. I am surprised your father has time to keep the garden so neat.'

'You are quite correct, your ladyship . . . madam . . . err . . .'

'Miss Scudamore will do very nicely. It is my aunt who bears a title, not me.'

'Well . . . Miss Scudamore. The garden, such as it is, is my work. I have always loved plants and the creatures they bring with them.'

'I do so agree with you. The natural world is a source of endless delight. My greatest love is to observe its wonders and apply my poor efforts to capturing some of them in drawings and water-colours.'

'How wonderful it must be to have the skill and talent to do that, Miss Scudamore. I imagine a grand house like Mossterton Hall has splendid gardens. We do not have much ground here and some of it must be given over to growing herbs and vegetables for the kitchen. Then there are the chickens. They ruin the garden at the rear. I have put fences round the vegetable plot to keep them out. If I had not, their continual scratching and pecking would bring havoc there too. The garden to the front of the house is the only place where I am able to grow a few of the flowers that I love.'

'Would you like to see the gardens at Mossterton?'

'That would be wonderful indeed, Miss Scudamore, but we are humble people and quite unsuited to such elegant surroundings.'

'Nonsense! I can assure you, Miss Wormald, that many of the haughty people who think themselves more than worthy to visit my aunt's estate are quite mistaken. Most, I declare, are quite unable to tell the difference between a box tree and a holly bush. If you showed them a dandelion, they would not know its name. Amongst the ladies, to walk outdoors is something to suffer only if they can be the centre of attention while doing it. The gentlemen, of course, think of nothing but hunting whenever they are out-of-doors. It would be my pleasure to share the gardens for a change with someone who could appreciate what they contain. If you are willing, I will also show you some of my drawings and paintings. I am not an artist of the first rate, but I do strive to be accurate to the finest detail. Some of the leading experts in the field of natural history have praised my work. Do you think your father would allow you to come?'

'There is no doubt of that. He could not have any objection, save for the obvious one; that I have neither the fine clothes nor the manners appropriate to such a place.'

'You need not worry on either score. Only you and I will be present, I will make sure of that. Not that you would find my aunt, Lady Alice Fouchard, at all terrifying. Like me, she treats people as she finds them. There is nothing haughty or patronising about her. If you would like to come, I will send the coachman to collect you at a time when we can be on our own. Would tomorrow be convenient?'

The arrangements were made and Ruth took her leave shortly afterwards. It had been unforgivable to descend on the family in that way, unannounced. That the meeting had gone well was purely a matter of chance. She could not have known that Fanny Wormald would share her interest in nature. Still, fortune favours those with the wit and courage to seize an opportunity when it is offered. She was confident that, by walking an hour in the gardens at Mossterton and showing Fanny some of her better pictures, she could induce the girl to relax. She hoped it would be enough to get her talking freely about her sister. Time alone would tell.

17

THE SAME DAY

WHILE RUTH SCUDAMORE WAS ENDURING THE CHATTER OF THE
rector's daughters and visiting Fanny Wormald, William the groom
was in Norwich, bound for one of Professor Panacea's lectures.

William was not a frequent visitor to Norwich, save to drive his
master to his mother's home by the cathedral. Usually he would
return to Aylsham the same day. He wasn't often told to wait. When
he was, his usual practice was to stay in the servants' part of the
house. The city didn't appeal to him. Too busy, noisy and confusing.
For a lad born and brought up in a village, it was too easy to get lost.
They said Norwich was near as great a city as London itself and he
could believe it.

Today he had no choice. His master had told him to walk to his
destination, looking about him like a yokel on his first visit. As he
made his way up towards the Market Place, the great houses seemed
to overshadow him, blocking out the sky. People pushed past him on
all sides and the streets were choked with horses, carts and every
other kind of vehicle.

The huge Market Place should have given some relief. It did not.
If anything, the noise grew louder and the press of people denser.
Cheapjacks and street-vendors yelled their wares on all sides; shop-

pers threaded their way amongst the stalls loaded with every type of produce. Every so often someone yelled 'Stop, thief!' as a pickpocket found a victim. The smell was still worse. Meat, blood, fish, every sort of rotting rubbish mixed with human sweat and the dung from the dogs that hung about, hoping to snatch up scraps. The people who worked and shopped there must be used to it. He found it hateful.

William clutched his purse to him and made his way through the mob as best he could. Twice he had to jump aside as men carrying heavy loads thrust their way past him. Once it was a giant of a man, red-faced, bearded and wearing a long leather apron, with two sides of beef on his shoulders; once it was a poor fellow staggering under the weight of what smelled like a sack of cheeses. Then he was through, only to be brought to a halt by the immense mass of St. Peter Mancroft church, its tower seeming to reach into the clouds. The buildings here looked older, more jumbled together — a tangle of narrow alleys, edged with houses of wattle and daub, the remnants of an older city, now being swept aside by brick and tile.

Of a sudden, there it was; the great Assembly House, less than fifty years old, its wings stretching out like arms to engulf any who ventured to come close. That was where the lecture was to take place, so his master had told him. If Professor Panacea could afford to hire such a prestigious venue, it spoke volumes for the success he was having in the city. The doctor had said William was to join the others making their way inside, paying his entry fee of a shilling and taking a seat for the lecture.

At this critical point, his courage almost failed him. The place was too grand for the likes of him, too elegant, too sophisticated. A lordly facade of brick and stone, its many lofty windows edged in dazzling white. Servants entered the grandest houses only through meagre entrances to the rear, set aside for their use. He would never dream of using the front door, even of his master's more modest home. As for Mossterton Hall — that was too far-fetched even to imagine. How could he be expected to pass through a grand door-way, edged with what looked like fine stone and covered with a portal shaped like half a circle? It was too much.

Luckily for him, William had come to a halt in the middle of the pathway leading up to that door. Behind him, others arriving to attend had become impatient and were now pushing forward in a body and seeking to thrust him aside. Failing in that, they drove him ahead of them, so he was up to the door and handing over his shilling before he could escape — then through and inside, into the main hall facing row upon row of benches set ready for the audience. Bewildered and afraid, he automatically sought safety in the densest part of the throng already assembled there. All recollection of his master's instruction about where to sit had left him; it was mere chance that placed him in the middle of the hall and well towards the side. There William found himself amid the artisans and minor tradesmen, for the centre places had all been taken by wealthy shopkeepers and the wives of professional men. He would have stood out there like a dirty mark on a rich piece of cloth, despite wearing his best clothes for the occasion.

As it was, the man to his left must be a carpenter from the paper hat he wore and the sawdust still clinging to his clothes. On the right and behind him were a group of fellows whose talk revealed them to be weavers. In front sat a large lady, maybe a lodging house owner, with her skinny companion. All, like William, were staring about them. He wasn't the only one who had never ventured inside this building before.

When Thomas Ivory built the Assembly House, he and his backers wanted a venue fit for the most exclusive entertainments. A building where balls, routs and assemblies might be held in proper style and a credit to the place that still rated itself the second city of the realm. If the outside was grand and all in the latest style, Sir James Burroughs had designed the interior to impress still more. His design called for tall columns, fine plasterwork everywhere, a high vault to the ceiling and a forest of chandeliers and candle-sconces. All well calculated to convey both the city's wealth and the builders' exquisite taste. William felt like an insect, an ant maybe, on the floor of a mighty palace. To say he was in awe of what was around him was to be guilty of the grossest understatement.

'Pretty, ain't it?' the carpenter said to him. 'What would it look like filled with all them rich folk, dancing and prancing about, I wonder? The likes of us won't never see that, will we?'

William said he supposed they would not, then he fell silent again.

'This the first time you been inside? Me too. Probably the last as well. I only come because my wife badgered me. Says I'm getting fat and unhealthy. She should look in a mirror, I reckon. Why're you here?'

Tell as much of the truth as you can, his master had told him. 'Curiosity, I suppose,' he said. 'Don't like wandering around and can't go home before I collect a parcel for my master which ain't ready yet. He gave me a few shillings to enjoy myself.'

It must have been a sufficient response, for the man grunted and turned to speak to a woman sitting on his other side. Meanwhile, the pointing, staring and chattering gave William an opportunity to take a good look around. The stage had been set up at the far end of the room. In its centre, stood a wooden lectern like the one that held the Bible in William's parish church. That must be where the professor was going to stand. Behind it a dozen chairs were set in a semicircle. Already half of them were occupied by young men, all busily scanning the faces of the people filing into the hall. From time to time, one would turn to his neighbour, say a few words and nod or point towards someone in the audience. On one occasion, this brief conversation extended to three or four of the watchers. They must have seen someone of interest, for two rose, moved to the side of the stage and stepped down into the hall. A moment or two later, William caught sight of them escorting a man towards the door. He did not dare stare, so could not be certain their action was hostile, yet no other explanation seemed to fit.

William didn't have a watch. Only when some of those seated around began to consult theirs, did he realise the time for the lecture must have arrived. Sure enough, a tall, grey-haired man dressed in black came onto the stage, accompanied by more young men. He walked up to the lectern; they took their seats behind him.

At once, the audience fixed their eyes on the grey-haired man. William made sure his were directed too, so he could only sneak a quick, sideways view at the twelve men now occupying the semi-circle of chairs to the rear. They were still all watching the audience.

As the hubbub of voices stilled, the professor began to speak. He didn't shout. He didn't wave his arms or perform magic tricks. You people have come to hear the secret of how to enjoy long and healthy lives, he told his audience, and I will offer you nothing less. He urged them on, told stories, made them laugh. At times, they interrupted with applause or cries of wonder. For the rest, they sat in silence, seeming to hang on his every word. Even William found himself caught up in the general enthusiasm. It wasn't hard to obey his master's instruction to look as if he was paying attention, but far more difficult to keep watch on the men behind the speaker. The best he could do was snatch occasional glances in their direction. For the rest, he kept his eyes on the lectern and the man standing behind it like all the rest.

A man seated towards the centre of the semicircle of chairs seemed familiar. Had he seen him before somewhere? A casual acquaintance, perhaps? Someone he had known at some time in the past? William would have loved to take a longer look, but his master's words echoed in his mind. 'Whatever you do, don't stare at the men who will be sitting behind the professor. You mustn't let them think you have any interest in them at all. I cannot impress that upon you too much.'

The lecture ended with a rousing invocation to follow the professor's advice in all matters, followed by an earnest invitation to come forward and buy a bottle of his world-famous "Universal Elixir". It would, Panacea assured his audience, place the final crown on the lifetime of perfect health which now awaited them.

Many of the audience rose and pressed forward at once, waving coins towards the men on the stage. Two of the young men left their chairs and came forward with crates rattling with the distinctive sound of glass bottles. William went up as well, making sure that he stayed in the middle of the group. He took out his purse, selected the necessary coins and held them out in exchange for one of the bottles. All this time, he was careful to keep his eyes only on the two selling the professor's wares, exactly as he had been told. If anything else was happening, he couldn't know.

With the bottle in his hand, William followed the other purchasers through the doorway and back into the street. Only once did he allow himself to glance back before he left. The two men were still selling bottles of the elixir to late comers. All the others had disappeared, as had the professor.

Out in the street, William intended to go at once to the apothecary's shop and collect the parcel waiting for him there. He didn't see the group watching him, all men who had been seated behind the professor, until three of them stepped forward to block his way. The rest started to jostle him. All the time, the man William thought he had recognised stood a little apart, his eyes never leaving William's face. What if the recognition had been mutual? Despite all William's care, something must have alerted them.

'Stand a moment, friend,' this same man said. 'We want to talk to you. Why are you here? You aren't the normal kind who attends the professor's lectures. Look more like a servant, I'd say. Where did you get money enough to buy a bottle of the professor's magic drink, eh? Speak up! Who are you?'

So that was it. Buying the elixir, which was what his master had told him to do. He must have forgotten no servant could have afforded so much.

For a moment, William's mind went blank. Then he recalled how the doctor had urged him to tell as much of the truth as would serve to let him conceal the rest. Another thought came to him. On any other occasion, would he give a meek reply to such an abrupt demand? He would not.

'What are you up to?' he said. 'Get out of my way. I don't have to answer questions from the likes of you.' He tried to push forward. 'Stand aside, all of you.' Hollow enough words, he knew. Still, they fitted the part he'd decided to play in the hope it would get him out of this mess.

As William had expected, the men moved closer to him, forcing him to stay where he was. The one he'd identified as their leader, the one who had spoken to him before, now spoke again. 'Oh, but you do have to tell us, I assure you. That is, if you don't want us to get the information we want by rougher means.' His voice had taken on that purring quality bullies used the world over, whenever they had a victim at their mercy and were looking forward to what came next.

If only he could recall where and when he'd met this particular bully-boy before.

'Persuade him, Gort. Better still, let's all do it.' That was a second man.

As soon as he heard the name 'Gort', William remembered. A fellow calling himself Peter Gort had come years ago to the mansion where William was the lowliest underling in the stables. He'd asked Mr Chamberlain, the head groom, for work, but been turned away — roughly too, as William recalled. Mr Chamberlain told him he wouldn't employ anyone whose father was a criminal. Gort had gone then, but not before he'd told Chamberlain he'd live to regret what he'd said. Of course, no one took him seriously, least of all the head groom. Mr Chamberlain had been a pompous fellow, always demanding what he thought was the deference due to his position. A few days later though, he was leading a horse to the farrier in Aylsham, when he was set upon, robbed and very badly beaten. Someone had been lying in wait for him by the gates of the estate. Chamberlain swore it was the man who had come asking for work, though he admitted he'd not had much of a view of his attacker. Whoever it was had come at him from behind, struck him over the head and driven his senses from him for a time. By the time he came to himself again, he'd been stripped naked and struck or kicked enough times to break several ribs and leave his body a mass of bruises. The horse was never found. It was most likely taken into Norwich and sold.

William knew now he was trapped. All the others who had attended the lecture had gone on their way, leaving him alone with these men. It would be the work of a moment for them to drag him into one of the narrow streets that led off this part of the Market

Place. His only hope was to convince them he was harmless by playing the part of a country yokel who knew nothing and was none too bright either. There seemed to be no other option.

'All right,' he said, trying to sound as dull as he could. 'You wants to know who I am? I'm Dr Bascom's groom, I am. That's who. He's a good doctor too. Lives in Aylsham.'

As he spoke, he took a good look at Gort. The man was bulkier and darker than he remembered; a heavyset fellow now with a mass of pockmarks on one cheek. The kind of ruffian who made you think twice about getting involved with him. Thirtyish? Not more. William must have been sixteen or seventeen when he saw him last and Gort couldn't have been much older. That was ten or eleven years ago.

Gort smiled, but there was no humour in it. 'So why is this excellent doctor's groom wandering about in the city, far from home and with money to spend? Is it your money or his? Has he sent you to spy on the Professor? To try to find out something to discredit him?'

The second man, the pudgy, pasty-faced one, had scented blood. 'Pigface', William named him. The sort of pallid, pudgy fellow who's always ready to turn to physical violence — but only when he knows he faces no personal risk. 'He's a spy, Gort, that's what he is,' Pigface said. 'We know how to deal with spies, don't we?'

'Are you a spy?' Gort turned back to William, very calm, very relaxed. 'If I was a doctor, I wouldn't trust an ignorant groom with a mission of that kind. I'd come myself, or send someone who had medical training. No, my friend, you're not a spy — not of that kind anyway. So, what is your game? I know I've seen you somewhere before too. I'm right, aren't I? Speak up, Groom! I haven't got all day to waste on trash like you.'

Peter Gort. There'd been a second encounter; a mob of labourers and cottagers on the same estate coming to the Hall and demanding better wages and lower rents. Times were hard then, just as they were now, and the cost of grain had risen to heights unknown before. For a while things looked nasty, until the constables arrived and the crowd fled. To be taken up meant punishment, followed by dismissal, eviction or both. Even a poorly-paid job and a hovel was better than none at all. This man, Gort, had been one of the ringleaders. Yet the land agent said afterwards he was sure Gort neither worked nor lived on the estate.

'The doctor sent me here,' William said. 'I've got to collect some things he's ordered from an apothecary in the city, only they weren't ready and I had to wait. When I saw the poster advertising the professor's lecture, I thought I could at least sit down for a while. I didn't intend to buy anything, but I got carried away.'

'You spent your master's money? That's it, isn't it? He gave you enough to pay the apothecary and now you've spent it. I bet you'll lie and say a pickpocket took it from you. Yes, I remember you now, right enough. It was years ago, but you were some sort of groom then. No, not a groom, a horse boy — the lowest of the low. A grovelling underling in a rich man's household. Still the same then. I wonder. What if you're trying to earn a few pennies by working for someone else as well?'

'I don't work for nobody else. Only the doctor. I ain't no spy either!'

'No, you aren't bright enough for that. You could well be an informer though. That's more your level. A skulking, snivelling little informer.'

'I ain't either of those things I tell you. I'm a proper groom.'

'He's lying!' Pigface again. 'Come on, let's take him into the alleyway and beat the truth out of him.'

'Shut up, Huggins! I'm handling this and don't you forget it. So, doctor's boy, you say you're a proper groom. You've come up in the world. Done well for yourself. What does your master pay you, eh? Doctors are wealthy men. I'll bet he isn't making you rich.'

'He pays me well enough.'

'Can't see the truth, can you? I bet that rich doctor of yours pays you next to nothing while he wallows in luxury. We're going to turn the tables on his sort before very long. Wouldn't you like to help us do that?'

'What're you talking about? My doctor's a learned man, been to university and everything. I can't barely read. How could I ever be like him?'

'Very easily, if you had his advantages. His sort has held us down for far too long. The time has come to stand up and refuse to be exploited any more. Honest working folk, like my friends here, are ready to demand the elite hand over what they owe us. If they won't, we'll take it. That's what the ordinary people have done in France. Thrown out the aristocracy and the gentry. Aye, and all the rest of the scum who've been living off the fat of the land while they starve. It's our rights we want. You read what Tom Paine says.'

'I told you. I can't hardly read. I never heard of no Tom Paine neither. What you're saying sounds like sedition to me.'

'Gar, listen to 'im! Using long words like 'sedition', even though he's so stupid he can't read.' That was Pigface Huggins, trying to draw attention to himself again.

William began to feel a thread of hope. Maybe Gort and the others were finally beginning to believe he was too stupid to be a threat to them and whatever they were up to. What would a stupid man do next? Bluster? It was worth a try.

''Ere! Who're you calling stupid? I ain't stupid.' He turned towards Pigface. 'Not as stupid as you are anyway.'

Pigface was furious. His little eyes grew even smaller and his face turned a nasty mottled-red colour. He was desperate to see William get a beating.

'Didn't I tell you to shut up, Huggins?' Gort snapped. 'This fellow's only saying what's true as well. You are stupid — bloody stupid.' He turned back to William. 'Well, Groom? What if I said you could soon be employing a groom instead of being one?'

'I'd say you was off your head. I've got a good job and I'm happy as I am. I don't want to find myself in the lock-up or dangling at the end of a rope. Leave me alone. Let me go and do my job.'

'Send him on his way with something to remember us by!' Pigface said. 'I don't take insults from the likes of him.'

'Shut your ugly face, Huggins! I won't tell you again. You'll take insults from anyone I say. God knows you deserve them.' Gort was growing tired of the game now. 'Go on then, Groom. Be a lackey, if that's what pleases you. When the time comes and you see what you've missed, remember I gave you the chance to be on the right side. Yes, you're like Huggins here, thick as shit. Now turn around and piss off!'

For a moment, William was so far into his role he wanted to stand and argue. Then common sense and his master's instructions prevented such foolishness. He did as he was told; walked away, all too conscious of eyes watching him. Behind him, Huggins was protesting again. William heard Gort's voice rise in real anger, then a slap and the protests stopped at once. William knew he had a narrow escape. It was still possible some of the others would follow him to see where he went. Very well, best not to take any risks then.

Walking as calmly as he could, William made his way back across the marketplace to the apothecary's shop. There, as his master had told him, the owner had a package waiting. A simple package, wrapped round in blue paper. Yet to William, alert every moment to hidden danger, it was a magic talisman to get him home in safety. He left the shop, quite certain that somewhere Gort and his gang were watching his every move.

Were they acting for Professor Panacea? There hadn't been anything political in the lecture he'd given. Nothing about the downtrodden rising up, or changing the government, or even what was going on in France. He'd spoken only about taking charge of your health, eating the right diet and, of course, dosing yourself with his 'Universal Elixir'. Gort had been willing to stir up trouble before and that had been about claiming justice and the rights of the underdog too. What if he was taking advantage of Panacea's popularity to serve his own ends? Leave it, William told himself. That's the master's problem to work out, not yours. Your job is to get back home in one piece and report what's happened.

William headed down the hill towards the cathedral, his mind fixed on The Maid's Head Inn and safety. To his right, the huge bulk of the castle loomed over the rooftops. It was a prison now; the place fools like Gort, Pigface and the others would be sent to be hanged if they were caught stirring up treason. That's what they deserved too. Into Tombland next, while every sound he heard behind him, every footstep, made his nerves jangle and his legs tense ready to run for his life. Keep walking. Don't look round.

When he wasn't far from Mrs Bascom's house a wild thought came to him. Why not go there instead? Her servants knew him. They'd be sure to give him a pallet to sleep on overnight. It must be well into the afternoon. By the time he'd harnessed Fancy, got her hitched to the carriage and made his way out of Norwich to Hellesdon and the north, evening would be approaching. It was almost ten miles home and no one travelled in the dark if they could avoid it. Too many places to get into trouble or meet up with robbers.

It was a wonderful idea, but he knew at once it wasn't a sensible one. If he was being watched, what would they make of him going into a house like Mrs Bascom's? They wouldn't know she was his master's mother. All they would see was the fellow who'd sworn he was only a groom from a little town to the north going into a grand house in the city itself. Easy enough then to lie in wait in the morning and deal with him as the spy he'd just proved himself to be.

Then he was at the inn, asking that his horse be brought out of the stables; putting her harness on and fixing her into the shafts. Moments later, he urged Fancy out of the yard into the road and joined the traffic crossing the Fye Bridge into Magdalen Street, on the long road back to Aylsham. He'd done it, even if he wouldn't breathe easy until he was back in the stable yard behind the doctor's house. He'd managed to get descriptions of the men his master was interested in. He'd even got two of their names. His mother would be so proud of him! He hoped her pride translated itself into asking Cook to get him a larger than usual helping of dinner. He'd been too keyed up for food before the lecture and too anxious to get away from Norwich afterwards. In fact, he'd had nothing to eat since taking breakfast soon after dawn that morning. If he didn't get home soon, Gort's thugs wouldn't need to worry about trying to silence him. He was too close to starving to death.

18

STILL THAT SAME DAY

THE DAY WILLIAM WENT TO NORWICH DID NOT SEE ADAM AT HIS best. He slept little during the night and rose well before his accustomed time, determined to see William leave. The weather did nothing to cheer him either. A cloudy, misty dawn, with the dew thick on the hedges and walls, revealed a sky heavy with rain still to come. He had planned to lean from his window to call out a farewell, but the cold air which struck him the moment he lifted the sash put that idea out of his head in an instant. Instead, he had to content himself with looking down into the stable yard from behind a closed window.

William appeared and harnessed the horse. Adam hoped he would look up and see his master watching him, but he did not. Damn and blast this wretched arm! If only he could have gone to Panacea's meeting himself. It wouldn't serve, of course. He knew that. He'd stand out more than enough to put Panacea and his minions on their guard. Not that the man was likely to say anything suspicious in public. It was what he might make of Adam's presence that mattered. Would the fellow assume it was another local physician trying to gather evidence against him or something worse? Adam knew he couldn't afford the risk of frightening Panacea and sending him somewhere else to stir up trouble. Especially before he even knew what kind of trouble was being planned. When it came down to it, almost everything he was trying to do was based on nothing but guesswork.

Adam tapped on the glass to attract William's attention. Nothing. The lad hadn't even glanced up. He tapped again, harder, but it was too late. The noise must have been drowned out by the clatter of the chaise setting off, out of the yard and into the road that would take it to Norwich.

Adam sighed and turned back into the room. He felt too restless to go back to bed and it was too early to ring the bell and call Mrs Munnings to help him dress. He couldn't even do that by himself yet. He had trouble getting the sleeves of his day-gown over his broken arm and putting on his stockings by himself was beyond him. Too early to go downstairs. What would he do when he got there? Twice he sat in the chair by his bed and took up a book. Twice he put it back down after reading a few pages and went back to stand at the window. Twice, then three times he went to the bell pull and turned away. The fourth time he pulled it so hard the bell in the passage by the kitchen set those either side of it jangling as well.

Breakfast was a woeful affair. Adam usually ate a hearty breakfast. That day he drank little of his coffee and set his roll aside after a single bite, fearing it would stick in his throat. All the time his mind tormented him with fresh fears and imaginings. What would await William in Norwich? Should he have sent someone older, someone quicker to sense danger and stay clear? Who? Not Charles. Certainly not Peter after his last experience. Giles? The idea was ridiculous. There was no one available save William. No one better suited either.

All day Adam tormented himself in this way. Had he pushed William into accepting the task? Had it truly been open to William and his mother to say no? He was their master. Mightn't they have feared some punishment for refusing; some lessening of his estimation of their value? No, no, no. He hadn't demanded their agreement, he hadn't. He'd gone out of his way to give them every opportunity to refuse. None of this was any consolation. If anything happened to William, he knew he would never be able to forgive himself.

Round and round the house Adam went, while the look on his face was more than enough to warn the servants to keep as far out of his way as they could. Once he even went into the kitchen. There, his new cook, Mrs Driscoll, and Molly, the kitchen maid, were making bread. He'd peered at their hands busy in the dough and noticed their faces were smudged with flour, yet never noticed how much discomfort his presence caused them. He made matters worse by walking around staring at the pots, pans and other cooking implements. What was the purpose of that flat copper disk with the handle, he asked Mrs Driscoll? What did she cook in this huge pot? He could not have recalled what she told him two minutes later. Finally, warned by their looks at one another that he was causing great hindrance to their work, he left. It was a wonder people passing in the street outside didn't hear his servants' sighs of relief.

Back in his library, Adam's mind jumped to another topic. Why hadn't Lady Alice come to see him? It must be several days since she last visited. She hadn't written to him either. Something must be wrong. Had he offended her in some way? Then, since he couldn't recall anything he might have done, he started down another path. Why should she come to Aylsham? He was no more to her than a family friend and adviser to be consulted, or not as the whim took her. The rest was only in his mind. He should have seen any supposed change in the way she had treated him recently as just his imagination running riot. However warm his feelings for her had become, it was plain they were not reciprocated. How could they be? Why should any woman be interested in becoming his wife, let alone one as beautiful, intelligent and rich as Lady Alice? Nonsense, all nonsense! When had he turned into this lovelorn idiot, this ninny full of silly dreams and impossible desires?

As the full realisation of his foolishness gripped his mind, Adam sank into a chair and gave himself over to the deepest melancholy and despair.

It was in this state that Harrison Henshaw, his new assistant or pupil — Adam was still not sure which — found him. The young doctor was perturbed and not a little irritated. He had been allowed very little time with Dr Bascom since he arrived. He had been told to expect a mentor and instructor in advanced medical practice. Instead, he had been almost ignored, left to cope with the practice and patients as best he could. It was high time to rectify this lamentable state of affairs. He would beard the lion in his den and demand better treatment — or at least a chance to talk on a regular basis. He gathered his courage, tapped on the door and, when there was no answer, decided to step inside anyway.

Dr Bascom's posture and appearance filled him with alarm. The doctor was slumped in his chair, head lolling forward, apparently unconscious. Had he suffered a relapse? Had he risen from his bed or left his room too soon? Had he fainted or — heaven forfend! — suffered a seizure or some kind of paroxysm? Should he, Harrison Henshaw, barely six months qualified, try to cope with the situation on his own? Should he send at once for Mr Lassimer?

It took a few moments for Adam to realise who was in the room. All the while, Dr Henshaw was shaking him, calling out his name and demanding to know how he was feeling. Adam couldn't explain the true reason for his state, of course. Instead he did his best to make light of the whole episode, poking fun at himself for falling asleep during the day. Wasn't that something only old men did? He must be aging faster than he imagined. Maybe he was tired because he was rather concerned about one of his servants as well. Since he was confined to his house, he explained, he'd been forced to send his groom out on an important errand in his place. The roads were plagued with ruffians and robbers in these hard times, the lad was on his own and his route might prove hazardous. It was only natural to feel worried about him, wasn't it? He had been fretting about the dangers and somehow dropped off to sleep.

Adam babbled on and on, desperate to convince Henshaw that there was nothing wrong with him. At first, Dr Henshaw had been going to ask Dr Bascom to let him undertake an examination for any medical issues, but now that felt too presumptuous. Much easier to accept what he was told and turn instead to a general discussion of his role in the practice. Henshaw didn't have to mention how neglected he'd felt either. Adam felt so guilty about the way he had treated the young doctor since his arrival, that he raised the subject himself, poured out fulsome apologies and devoted more than two hours to the young man. This was exactly the distraction he needed. By the time Henshaw departed, Adam felt his capacity for rational thought had returned.

It didn't last long. Hardly had the library door closed behind Henshaw, when it opened again to admit Hannah into the room, bearing a letter from Lady Alice. Adam took it from her, snatched up the paper knife from his desk, freed the flap from the seal of wax holding it shut, and began to read.

'My dear Dr Bascom,' the letter began. 'I am conscious that you may be wondering why I have not written to you earlier. The only excuse I can make is both poor and obvious. I have been much occupied with certain business matters which have arisen sooner than I had anticipated. I hope my distraction will not have hindered your investigation too much.'

Damn! Damn and damn! Why this cool, business-like tone without the least sign of affection or regard? He read on, his heart sinking into even greater depths of misery.

'Charles has told me you need more information from Melton Constable. We can all see how difficult you must find it to get proper answers from the villagers, when you cannot go yourself. I might be able to help you with this at least. I asked amongst my servants and found that my coachman's family live in that village. His brother is a saddler there. Today I have given him a day free from his duties to visit his brother. I have told him he is not to ask too many questions, but simply encourage his family and anyone else he meets to talk about Miss Wormald's death, then keep his ears open. I hope this action will meet with your approval.'

Still nothing in the least intimate — or even personal.

'Now that my business is complete, I plan soon to pay you a visit to explain in full what has kept me here. Believe me, I wish most heartily that it had not. I long to speak with you again and see how far your recovery has progressed.

'I am ever your affectionate and devoted friend,

'Alice Fouchard.'

That was all.

His first impulse was to tear up the letter and throw it into the fireplace. At least he resisted that. Then he read it through again, found it no more comforting than before and gave himself over to an orgy of despair and self-pity. Indeed, for the rest of the after-noon, he sat at his desk staring at the wall, while his mind produced explanations that grew more bitter and hopeless as each hour passed. He refused to take any dinner and would have spent the whole evening in a similar state, had not Mrs Brigstone ventured to disturb him to say her son, William, had returned safe and sound and desired to speak to his master at once.

Adam realised it must be late, for he'd heard Mrs Brigstone touring the house a while ago, closing the shutters tight against the night air and barring them to keep out intruders. Heard, but taken no notice, so sunk was he in gloom and sour thoughts. His library was already dark. Stirring himself, he rang for Hannah to bring extra candles and told his housekeeper to bring her son to him at once. William was back, safe and unhurt. That at least was a little good news.

In reality, William had driven into the stable yard almost an hour before, when his mother was just finishing her nightly rounds. She rushed out to greet him at once, quite overjoyed to have him back home, so that he had to suffer a period of hugs and kisses before she would let him unharness Fancy and lead the horse into her stable. It was no use her rushing off to tell the master he was back yet, he told her, until the horse was rubbed down, watered and given her feed, his place was in the stable.

By the time Mrs Brigstone had tidied her son to make him fit for the master's presence, Hannah had set two candelabra on the library table and lighted the wall sconces. That made ten fresh candles, all lit. Even so, it made little impact on the darkness that had now fallen. When Mrs Brigstone and her son came to see the master at last, they were half-way across the room before Adam could make out their features clearly.

All the way back, William had been practising what he was going to say. He would set everything out in order, neat and concise, being sure to miss nothing out. Now, standing in the library before his master, with his mother at his side, all the fine words he'd rehearsed somehow left him, so that what tumbled from his mouth instead was barely coherent. He jumped from the topic of the professor's lecture to the surprising size of the audience. Digressed to marvel at the splendours of the building in which they had gathered. Described how the chairs and lectern had been set out. Suddenly mentioned that the leader of the group of bullies who had accosted him afterwards was none other than Peter Gort — he knew Peter Gort of old and considered him to be the very worst kind of character.

At first, Adam tried to excuse the lad's confusion and let him ramble on. It was clear he was exhausted. All that was keeping him on his feet was a mixture of excitement and relief. After a while though, Adam realised that if he let this farrago of a story continue, the poor lad would only become still more confused. Holding up his hand for quiet, he therefore made a rapid summary of what he had been told so far.

'Let me see if I have all correct. Nothing exceptional happened during the meeting itself. Afterwards, when you were leaving, this man Gort and his bully-boys detained you. Gort is the leader of the group known as The Disciples. You've encountered him before, when you first began working. At that time, he was already stirring up trouble, trying to persuade farm workers to riot for better wages. Am I right so far?'

William nodded. The excitement was wearing off and he was too tired to do more.

'Good. Gort, aided by a lout called Huggins, threatened you with a beating, because they thought you might be a spy. Gort must have remembered you, just as you had recognised him. When, at length, you convinced him you were no threat, he started preaching sedition and tried to get you to join him in some way. You managed to get away, collected the package I'd had prepared for you and then came home.'

William nodded again. He felt himself swaying, then his mother's hand gripped his arm and held him still again.

'That will be quite enough for now. You can tell me anything more tomorrow. You've done a fine job, William, and I'm proud of you. I'm sure your mother is too. The information you've brought me is of the very highest importance. I'm truly sorry I put you into danger. Sorrier still that you had to deal with Gort and the bullies he's drawn up around him. That's why I want you to understand that it's all been worthwhile. What you have told me makes sense of a major part of the problem I've been wrestling with.'

Mrs Brigstone couldn't remain silent any longer. 'I told you he was a good lad, Master,' she said, her hand on her son's shoulder and her eyes shining with pleasure. 'I said you could trust him.'

'You were right, Mrs Brigstone. Your son has done everything I could have asked of him and more. I won't forget this, believe me.'

'I remember that Peter Gort too,' Mrs Brigstone continued. 'What a nasty piece of work he was! His father too, if my remembrance is correct. The family used to live in Saxthorpe. Old Gort had a good job with the squire at one time, but threw it away by stealing from his master. Made it worse by taking the coward's way out.'

'How was that?'

'He cut his own throat and left his wife to go into the workhouse and his children to the mercies of the Poor Law Overseers. If that wasn't the work of the very worst kind of coward, I don't know what could be.'

'Indeed. It seems this Peter Gort had a bad start in life and hasn't made things better since then. Now, I'm sure William must be tired and hungry. Take him into the kitchen, get him a good meal and make sure he has an early night.'

'Don't you worry about that, Master. Cook's got his favourite food waiting for him. Plenty of it too and a whole jug of good ale. That'll put him back on his feet again.'

'You know, Mrs Brigstone, I'm think I'm hungry myself. I couldn't face my dinner earlier and now I can feel my stomach rumbling. Do you think Cook could find me something to eat as well?'

'I'm sure she can, Master, and right gladly too. She was fair cast down when you wouldn't eat the dinner she'd prepared for you. We'll go down to the kitchen right away and let her know your appetite has returned. That'll put the smile back on her face.'

'Thank you both. Tell Cook I'll eat in the dining room. Hannah can carry a few of these candles in there. No need to waste them. The rest will do for another day.' He had a sudden thought. 'She can also send in a bottle of the best claret — and a decanter of good port. Then I can raise a glass to your son's success.'

When Adam thought about what he had been told, he realised William had returned with much more that he had expected. Not just descriptions of the key individuals but two names as well, together with a strong clue about Panacea's real purpose. Even so, what mattered to him most was that William was safe. The lad had shown surprising coolness and flexibility in dealing with what could have been an extremely nasty situation. It would be worth a guinea as a reward, without any doubt.

William and his master both dined well that evening and slept well afterwards, both exhausted by the day's events. Never mind that the servant had encountered real danger, while his master had faced only imaginary terrors, all conjured up by his over-anxious mind.

19

ADAM AWOKE THE NEXT DAY TO fiND SPRING HAD DECIDED ONCE again to assume its finest garments and brightest colours. The sun shone from a cloudless sky. The birds sang as if taking part in a grand festival concert. Hundreds of bees and butterflies danced to their singing in air filled with the scent of flowers and the earth steamed gently as the sun dissolved the last of the previous day's mists.

Adam should have been as cheerful as the birds. Before he was out of bed, one of Lady Alice's servants had delivered a note promising that she would come to see him later the next day. Instead, he felt wretched. He had grown certain Lady Alice's coming must provide the final proof she was not only quitting Mosserton Hall, but leaving him behind too. During the night, he'd dreamed he was reading an account of her new life in London. She was, his dream had told him, soon to be married to one of the many well-born beaux who had flocked around her since her arrival. It had been so clear he'd been half convinced, when he first awoke, it was a memory.

In her note, Lady Alice hadn't indicated a precise time when she might arrive, beyond saying it would probably be well after noon.

That left Adam an ample interval in which to return to the state of dejected self-pity which had characterised almost the whole of the previous day.

By the time noon came, even that had begun to lose its attraction. It was the day on which Mrs Munnings was leaving to take up her new position as housekeeper to Captain Mimms. When, as his clocks were striking twelve, she came to bid him farewell, he struggled to put on an appropriate show of gratitude and good wishes. Maybe she would assume his low spirits were because he was sad to see her go. If so, she wasn't wholly mistaken, for he had come to like her as a person, as well as value her skills as a nurse.

After she left, Adam would have returned to pacing about and annoying the servants had Peter not arrived. Sadly, he was not in a cheerful mood either. The two men now glowered at one another, while Peter sought to justify his contention that his patient was almost fully recovered and should be returning to a normal life as soon as his injured arm might allow it. Adam, taking a sour delight in defying his friend even in this, questioned everything he said, especially the contention that, save for his arm, he was as fit as he had ever been.

This might, in time, have led to a serious quarrel. Trying to annoy his friend still further, Adam declared Mrs Munnings's departure to be a triple act of kindness. She needed to support herself in a suitable manner. The captain needed a reliable housekeeper — and he, Adam, had grown to like her too well to let her fall prey again to Lassimer's dubious attentions.

'Fie on Mrs Munnings and Captain Mimms both!' Peter said, his voice betraying disgust more than the anger Adam had expected. 'Far too many people of my acquaintance are falling prey to this malevolent plague of matrimony. They should both be old enough to know better.'

Adam stared. He was so surprised at this non-sequitur he found he'd lost track of his plan to provoke the apothecary. 'Who mentioned matrimony? She's left to be his housekeeper, not his wife. As far as I know, you're the only person who seems to feel the duties of the two positions are identical.'

'Much good it has done me! Take my present housekeeper. She's a good cook, an excellent manager, possessed of a fine figure and . . . since I know what a prude you are, Bascom, let's say she has a pleasing enthusiasm for amorous sports. Now, damn her eyes, she's also become infected with a desire for marriage. It's as bad as the tertian ague. Worse!'

'What nonsense you do talk, Lassimer! It's your own fault anyway. You should choose a steady, older woman as a housekeeper, as I do, and then keep your hands to yourself. I've warned you before about this obsession with young women and widows of marriageable age.'

'I should have listened. You were right, there's no doubt of it. Never be tempted to take a young widow into your household, Bascom. They enjoy their freedom for a time, then begin to hanker to drag you into marriage. I swear to you, in future I mean to avoid them altogether, whether as servants or bedfellows. Far better to fix my sights on the kind of women for whom being the mistress of a prosperous trader like me is the height of their ambition.'

'And who might they be?'

'I haven't worked that out yet. Probably the better kind of servant — or the daughters of skilled artisans.'

'Wouldn't such women also hope for marriage? Only the richest men can afford to sow their seed wherever their fancy takes them. Even mistresses have a habit of producing children who must be raised and educated. That's expensive.'

'Those fellows lack my advantages, Bascom. Thanks to my fine potions, I've never left any bastards behind. I'm too well aware of the financial disadvantages, let alone the tendency of such mistakes to afford a route into marriage. Of course, there may be a better solution. What if I make sure to stop paying attention to any woman after a set period — say a year — and transfer my affection elsewhere?'

'Take women out on loan, you mean, like books from a circulating library? Really, Lassimer. I must protest at such a cold-hearted attitude.'

Peter laughed, realising he'd won the struggle to prise Adam out

135

of his woeful mood. 'I wonder if you'll say the same once you've spent a few years safely gathered into Lady Alice's grasp, my friend? I know a good many married men who would give a king's ransom to be able to live the kind of life I do. As it is, they have to break their marriage vows to come even close — not that doing so deters them overmuch. I, on the other hand, can indulge myself with a clear conscience.'

There was no way Adam was going allow the conversation to stray onto the perilous ground of his dealings with Lady Alice Fouchard — or what he was now sure was her lack of any amorous feelings for him. Casting around for a way to bring this exchange to an end, he decided a cold drench of basic common sense might serve.

'All you need do is make it clear you're not ready for marriage and stop your philandering. Better still, find yourself a wife. Marriage is a sovereign remedy against the advances of unsuitable women, I believe.'

'You know, Bascom, that's an excellent idea. Why hadn't I thought of it? Not the wife part, of course. We're not all dull dogs like you. No, the bit about making it clear marriage to me isn't desirable — or even a possibility. Once my housekeeper realises it's not going to happen, she'll either take herself off or learn to be content with what she has. Either way, that will solve the problem. Thanks for the advice, old friend. I'll be sure to let you know how it turns out.'

Adam sighed and rolled his eyes. He knew well enough nothing would divert Peter from his distinctive attitude to womenfolk. But at least the awkward subject of Lady Alice had been avoided — at least for a while.

He was soon proved mistaken.

'The rumour is that Lady Alice is planning to leave Mossterton Hall,' Peter said. 'Is that correct? I don't know why she would want to give up such a fine mansion. Unless, of course, the alternative is a better one. Not many of those around here though, are there? So, with Mossterton gone, where are the two of you planning to live?'

'There's no 'two of you', Lassimer, and well you know it. I've told you before not to listen to gossip or let your imagination get the better of you.'

'But the news about Mossterton wasn't gossip, my good Doctor. I was told by an unimpeachable source — no less a person than the lovely lady's niece. I happened to be in Melton Constable, taking the benefit of my infallible healing balm to a lady who lives next door to the rectory, when who did I see there but Miss Ruth Scudamore. What's more, she hailed me with the greatest condescension imaginable and asked me if I could direct her coachman to the Wormald's smithy. Naturally I could. The two of us then spent a few moments in conversation. She expressed serious interest in the chemical composition of the balm I had in a jar in my hand. I enquired how she was enjoying her stay at Mossterton Hall. That was when she told me she and her brother must leave the place by Michaelmas, since their aunt had decided to live elsewhere. You see? Not gossip at all.'

'Very well, I concede that point. Yet why you persist in the belief that her ladyship and I are more than acquaintances I cannot understand.'

'Because my eyes and ears tell me so, Doctor. Who rushed to your house the moment news reached her that you had been so clumsy as to fall from your horse? Who came again, more than once, while you were at death's door — and saved only by my amazing skills from crossing the threshold of that dread dwelling? Who told your mother that she could not bear to lose such a dear friend?'

'Yes, Lassimer, friend. Mark the word well.'

'We all know what it means when a lady calls you "a dear friend", Bascom. She is but a step away from calling you her dear husband —'

'Go away, Lassimer! You forget I am a sick man. I am not to be troubled by having to listen to such nonsense.'

'A moment ago, you were telling me you are as fit now as you ever were.'

'That was before you started to weary me with your reprehensible views on women and your fantasies about Lady Fouchard and myself. Either is more than sufficient to sicken any sensible man. Together they have a more violent effect on the constitution than the strongest purgative. Go away, I say. Hannah! Hannah! Mr Lassimer is leaving. Show him to the door and see it is shut firmly behind him. I am not at home to visitors for the rest of the day.'

'What do I say when Lady Alice arrives, Master? You told me earlier to expect her this afternoon. Are you not at home to her either?'

'Ahah! You are caught out, Bascom —'

'Hannah, do as you have been told at once and don't ask foolish questions.'

'But Master —'

'Hannah! I'm warning you. Take this man out of my sight — and yourself too. Let Mrs Brigstone answer the door for the rest of the day. She at least will have the sense to know what I want without being told. Go! Now! Both of you!'

The two of them left, one trying not to cry and the other grinning from ear to ear. Only then did Adam realise he was a full day out in his reckoning. Lady Alice had not said she was coming that day, but the day after. He'd told Hannah to expect a visit on the wrong day.

20

THE SAME DAY

BARELY five minutes later, Mrs Brigstone knocked again at the library door and announced that Adam's mother and Miss LaSalle had arrived and wished to see him. She need not have bothered. Mrs Bascom swept into the room right behind her. She had obviously decided this was no time to wait on ceremony.

'Adam! I demand to know what has caused you to behave thus to your maid,' she said at once. 'I come in through the door and am greeted by the unmistakable sound of crying from the kitchen. What do I find? Your maidservant is sobbing her heart out because her master shouted at her for no reason at all. For shame! I didn't bring you up to be a bully and a tyrant. If you go on in that way, you'll have no servants whatsoever. Don't sit there with your mouth hanging open like some village idiot! On your feet when a lady enters the room!'

Before she had left Trundon Hall, it had been her duty to tell her elder son several home truths; now the younger one had also contrived to arouse her anger. It was high time she reminded him of the standards of behaviour she expected.

'Mother, please.' Adam knew it was little use trying to reason with her in this state, but he had to try.

'Don't "mother" me in that tone of voice! What have you to say for yourself?'

'If I might just —'

'No, you might not, whatever it is. I'm not going to allow you to fob me off with some feeble excuse. I'm ashamed of you, reducing the poor girl to tears. What you need, my boy—'

'If you would let me speak —'

'Where is Mrs Munnings? I want to hear exactly how you are progressing. None of your lame attempts to pretend you're better than you are.'

'Mrs Munnings is no longer here, Mother. She left this morning.'

'What? Have you driven her away too? You wretch! No sooner is my back turned than you turn on those who are trying to help you. What you need is a sound thrashing. If you weren't grown so big, I'd do it myself. Ah, I see it now. The fever must have affected your brain. Sophia? Send someone to fetch Mr Lassimer at once. Mrs Brigstone and I will get my son back into bed before he does any more harm.'

This was too much. To be declared insane in your own house and in front of a servant! By your own mother too! Adam's voice cracked with anger. 'Mother! Be quiet and listen! I did not turn on Mrs Munnings, nor on anyone else. She has gone, of her own will, to take up the position of housekeeper to Captain Mimms —'

Mothers are not easily scared by their own children.

'— who will, I am sure, treat her far more kindly that you seem to have done,' Mrs Bascom interrupted. 'Mrs Brigstone, you are a sensible woman. Pray tell me what my son has been doing. You need not fear for your place. I will make sure he does not take out his bad temper on you.'

'He has done nothing, Mrs Bascom, I assure you. From what I understand, Mr Lassimer was here and provoked him to anger in some way. Hannah found herself caught between them. The silly girl hadn't the sense to keep quiet and let them work out their irritation on each another.'

'But the crying —'

'Hannah is much given to tears, especially . . . as a woman I'm sure you can understand what I mean, Madam.'

'Ah, quite . . . quite. So, you assure me this reprobate son of mine has not been behaving as I assumed when I arrived?'

'Not at all, though he has been in somewhat low spirits this past day or so. Of course, his arm must still be very sore.'

Mrs Bascom wasn't in a sympathetic mood. 'Only fools and weaklings give way to low spirits because they have a few aches and pains. What you need, Adam, is a wife. A wife who will see that you are not allowed to indulge in this kind of maudlin self-pity —'

Really! His mother was impossible at times. Today, for some reason, she was determined to vent her anger on him. Maybe calmness and reason would rob the game of any pleasure.

'Did you enjoy your stay at Trundon Hall, Mother?' Adam asked, in as sweet a voice as he could muster.

'Don't try to change the subject. No, I did not. Your brother has an excellent wife — far better than he deserves — and what does he do? He neglects her and spends all his time on his so-called duties as a magistrate, or — worse! — playing soldiers with the militia. Sophia and I hardly saw him. He couldn't even spare the time to escort us here and visit his sick brother. When I look at the two of you, I ask myself where I failed. I was only saying to Sophia on the way that she should be grateful she remains unmarried. The responsibilities of a wife are many and grave, while the rewards are minimal. So, you have sent your nurse away. Why did you do that?'

'I do wish you'd listen, Mother.' Adam gave up on conciliation and opted for firmness instead. 'I did not send Mrs Munnings away. She agreed that I could now manage on my own, so she was no longer needed. By a fortunate accident, I happened to mention to Captain Mimms that she was going and he said he had need of a housekeeper. Might she be suitable? I assured him that he could make no better choice and he decided, there and then, to offer her the position. Since I knew she was in need of employment, I encouraged him. They already liked each other and the matter was soon agreed.'

'I will go to my room now,' Adam's mother declared, ignoring

Adam's response to her question. 'Such a poor welcome has wearied me and I am in sore need of the chance to recover my strength.'

Adam clenched his teeth. How typical of his mother! A good flounce was Mrs Bascom's usual way of avoiding having to admit she had been wrong.

'Sophia will stay and entertain you,' she continued. 'Mind you do not reduce her to tears as well. If you do, I swear I will box your ears as I used to do when you were little. When you marry, I must remember to advise your wife —'

'Go and lie down, Mother!' She might have been a dog, only dogs were more easily controlled. 'I'm sure it will do you good. Miss LaSalle too, if she wishes. I do not need to be entertained by anyone. Send Hannah to me, Mrs Brigstone, if you please. My mother is correct in saying the girl was not at fault. I should have shown more restraint and I am most ready to apologise.'

'I'm sure that will not be not necessary, Master. I will tell her what you have said and all will be well again. If she is somewhat . . . over-sensitive to your words, it is only because she holds you in such high regard. As do we all.'

Adam's mother subjected her son to a look that indicated she might be prepared to leave matters there for now, but was far from satisfied with him or his replies. Then she left and Mrs Brigstone slipped out too, relieved to be able to escape to the safety of the servants' quarters.

Sophia stayed. Adam thought she looked different somehow. Distracted? Absorbed? Intent? Lost in her own thoughts? It was quite possible she hadn't even heard his suggestion of taking a rest after the journey. She couldn't have missed hearing the exchanges between him and his mother, yet she seemed neither embarrassed nor concerned.

Still wrapped in her daze, she walked over to the window and stared out into the garden. 'Isn't it a wonderful day, Dr Bascom?' she said. 'The sun is shining, there is hardly a cloud in the sky and the whole earth seems full of happiness. Doesn't it make you glad to be alive?'

Adam agreed that the weather was indeed most clement for the time of year, though it was clear, even to him, that Sophia hadn't expected an answer. She certainly gave no sign that she had heard what he said.

'As we drove here, I could not help marvelling at the beauty of the landscape. The heathlands covered in golden gorse flowers. The sides of the road thick with — what do you call those tall plants with the yellowish flowers? Alexanders, that's it. The May trees will be in blossom soon. The blackthorn is over already and I could see fronds of bracken uncurling here and there. Now we are here and tomorrow . . . tomorrow Mr Scudamore is coming . . . to take us back to Norwich, I mean. Do you think the sun will shine?'

'I hope it will for your sake, Miss LaSalle, since you take such joy in the beauty of nature.'

'Do you not also, Doctor? I cannot imagine any person of sensibility could be immune to wonder at nature's infinite riches. I'm sure Mr Scudamore . . . but I should not waste your time with my fancies, Doctor. I am sure you have matters of far greater importance on your mind. Yes . . . of course. Will you indulge my curiosity a little? Have you solved the matter of who killed that poor young woman in Melton Constable?'

'Alas, I have not, Miss LaSalle. I remain blocked by ignorance of who was the father of the child she was bearing. Whether he was her killer or not, I am convinced he must have played some part in those events.'

'How burdened his conscience must be then, Doctor. To have taken two lives in a single act of violence, mother and unborn child, argues for a most depraved nature. Only Our Lord could have mercy enough to offer forgiveness for such an act. You say you cannot see what his identity might be. Did she not have a suitor whom many accused of the crime?'

'She did, but he will not do. Those best placed to know agree neither he nor Miss Betsy viewed the 'courtship' as more than a sham; one brought about by her father's desire to see her marry a person of his choosing. The fellow may well have run away to avoid any more of it and not because he bears the guilt for her death.'

'Did he not find her to his taste? I heard she was beautiful.'

'According to several reports, he may not feel much attracted to anyone of the female gender.'

Miss LaSalle blushed, but nodded her head to show she understood what the doctor meant.

'Forgive me, Miss LaSalle,' Adam said in haste. 'I should not have spoken in such plain terms. Such matters are unfit for a lady's ears. All I will add is that I have found no indication Miss Wormald behaved other than in the ways expected of an upright young woman.'

'There may lie your answer,' Miss LaSalle said after a moment. 'You told me her father is a strict Christian — something of a puritan in his morals and outlook — yet she proved a poor custodian of her virtue. Why would any girl brought up in such a household depart so far from their upbringing? She would be well aware of the importance of remaining inviolate before entering upon marriage. Do you not agree?'

'I suppose so. Yet there is no doubt Betsy had yielded to at least one man.'

'That is my point. If she did — as we know was the case — what was the reason? What if she had been led to believe marriage was imminent? What if — given she would be defying her father's wish to marry the other supposed suitor — she felt sure her new choice would prove just as acceptable? Why else would she have rebelled so much against her upbringing as to engage in intimate relations outside wedlock? Did you not tell me before that Betsy Wormald dreamed of rising above her present station? That would never be possible if she flouted the dictates of society to such a degree. No, I think she had found someone who promised to fulfil her dream, not abandon it. Someone fully acceptable to everyone. It is not so unusual for rural couples to, as it were, anticipate their marriage vows, is it?'

'No, but —'

'You must look for someone who seems entirely respectable; a man of some substance and standing. He might have nothing but seduction in mind, but she would not. She would desire what all would see as a good marriage; one that enhanced her standing.

Her father might worry about any prospective husband's religious inclinations, but I doubt if she would. Her mind would be set on a husband to make her the envy of her friends and neighbours. An older man, perhaps. If, after a time, she thought he might escape . . . what more obvious way of bringing him to the altar than carrying his child? Do you know of any such man in the locality?'

Adam's mind was running at such a speed through the implications of this idea that some moments elapsed before any words came out of his mouth.

'I do not, Miss LaSalle. No one at all. Yet . . . I mean . . . now I know the kind of person to look for, it may be that . . .'

'I fear I have taken up too much of your time, Doctor. Might I have your permission to walk a while in your garden? It is too lovely a day to waste by staying indoors.'

'What? . . . Yes, of course you may. Yes, indeed.'

As Sophia turned to leave, she hesitated long enough to ask another question. 'There was another matter about which I was curious, Doctor. Were you not seeking word of a Swiss gentleman who had disappeared?'

'I was. It was for Mr Wicken — I should rather say Sir Percival Wicken now. He asked me to see if I could find any trace of a learned Swiss professor believed to be in this area. I regret to say the fellow has proved elusive — if he was ever here. Indeed, I confess that I had almost forgotten about him until you asked.'

'You could ask Lady Alice when you see her tomorrow.'

'You know of her visit?'

'Mr Scudamore has been kind enough to write to me several times while we were at Trundon Hall. In his last letter, he told me he would be bringing his aunt and sister when he comes to escort your mother and I home to Norwich. They will all come in Lady Alice's carriage and a groom will lead his horse. According to his information, the carriage will wait here to take the ladies home, with the groom as escort, while Mr Scudamore will ride alongside us to Norwich. Once we have arrived, he intends to stay in the city for a day or so, I understand. That is if you had no pressing need of his help. He will stable his horse at a suitable inn until he is ready to return to Mosserton Hall.'

'I can think of no pressing duties for him at the moment.'

'Then I am most grateful to you, Doctor. You have made my day.'

'On the contrary, Miss LaSalle, you deserve my gratitude. I told you that my investigation into the murder of Betsy Wormald had become blocked. Thanks to you, I see a way forward. I will arrange at once for enquiries to be made for a respectable man who might have won her heart. My only regret — and it is profound — is that this fellow was lying to her all along.'

21

ONCE AGAIN, ADAM WOKE FAR TOO EARLY. THE WEATHER WAS TO blame, being all that anyone could wish from a day in May. It was too light and noisy to sleep for long after the dawn. Bright sunshine pushed its way through every tiny crack and hole in his shutters and the dust motes danced in the rays it made across the room. The birds sang as if they would burst. Their noise alone would never have allowed him to go back to sleep. The whole world seemed full of joy. Well, not quite the whole. All this exuberance in nature made Adam's mood darker and his sense of foreboding weigh heavier on his mind.

Since he was much too restless to lie awake in bed, he rang the bell for Hannah to bring him water and towels. After that, his toilet completed, he dressed himself in a clean day-gown and sat down to wait for the barber. That damned arm still prevented him from shaving himself.

By eight, Adam was downstairs and ready for his breakfast — still far too early, of course. To take his breakfast alone would be seen as impolite, yet neither his mother nor Miss LaSalle would put in an appearance before nine. He scowled at the clock and wondered how should he spend the time while he waited.

In the end, he decided to withdraw into his library and write to Wicken. Thanks to Miss LaSalle's remark of the day before, he realised that he had failed to report finding no trace of the Swiss professor. The quack doctor had been his one, frail hope, until Lassimer's experience in Holt proved the so-called Professor Panacea had no medical knowledge and didn't fit the description either. There wasn't anyone else who could make a likely candidate. Wherever Wicken's quarry was hiding, it didn't appear to be in Adam's neighbourhood.

As he was about to write the closing words to his letter, Adam hesitated. Should he mention his other suspicions? So far, he'd shared them with no one. Was that sensible? If he turned out to be right, there might well be a need for swift and decisive action. Wicken could provide that — and would do so without asking unnecessary questions.

He put his pen down and tried to think the problem through. What he had to say must cause a many people profound disquiet, yet he still had no firm proof of any of it. William's experience in Norwich was of little use, for it might easily be put down to bullying by an old enemy. The suggestion of radical leanings in Gort's words weren't proof either. Plenty could be found in Norwich and the countryside roundabout who might say the same. They had formed themselves into groups to discuss Tom Paine's writings and their dreams of a British Revolution — and Wicken would know far more about them than he did. Even if one group was planning to go further than dreaming, he couldn't point them out or offer any evidence to substantiate his fears. If he was proved wrong — if all his suspicions came to nothing — he would have proved himself a credulous fool.

With a sigh, Adam took up his pen again, added an appropriate farewell to his letter and signed his name. Then, before he could change his mind, he arranged wax and seal, folded the paper carefully and sealed the edges together. He would send William to take it to the Norwich carrier right away. That done, he could return to fretting about what the day — and Lady Alice's visit — might bring.

Her ladyship, accompanied by Charles and Ruth Scudamore, arrived soon after ten o'clock. Adam went to greet them and found his hallway somewhat crowded. It now contained not only Lady Alice, Miss Ruth Scudamore and Charles, but also his mother and Miss LaSalle. Both these had preceded him, eager to greet one of the new arrivals, albeit a different one and for different reasons. Mrs Brigstone and Hannah were also there, trying, in the crush, to collect the arrivals' travelling clothes.

Despite his anxiety, Adam could not help his spirits rising at the sight of Lady Alice. She had seemed aware of him the moment he entered the hall, yet the look she gave him was more expressive of concern and timidity than warmth. The next moment it had changed to alarm. Did he look so forbidding? Never before had she shown the slightest apprehension at meeting him.

At this point, Adam knew he must face a difficult problem. His mother would want to engage Lady Alice in extended conversation. Whatever her thoughts about the deficiencies of her younger son's character, she was delighted with the company he was keeping. Talking with Lady Alice and taking note of what she was wearing would provide his mother with a fine topic of conversation amongst her many friends in the city. She'd once arranged for him to join them for afternoon tea, so he knew their habits. These ladies represented the cream of Norwich society. They always wore their best clothes to these meetings, took care to behave impeccably and practised the arts of politeness — especially those of tearing other peoples' reputations to shreds and putting one another down by recounting anything which proved them to have a superior acquaintance.

Happily, while Adam was still wondering how to divert his mother so he might speak to Lady Alice on her own, matters were taken out of his hands. Charles had been staring at Miss LaSalle as if he had never seen a woman before. Now he stepped forward. Might he suggest she accompanied him to walk in the doctor's garden? It was a beautiful day and it would be a shame not to take advantage of the opportunity for some exercise. The journey into Norwich would be quite long enough to be seated. Sophia, looking at Charles like a faithful dog whose master has returned after a long absence, accepted at once. Never mind that she had come inside from the garden only moments before. At once the two of them, oblivious to anyone else, made their way towards the French windows which opened from the dining room to the terrace beyond.

Ruth took a hand next. She had not met Adam's mother before and Adam, of course, had neglected to introduce them now. Ruth at once pointed this out, so that Adam hastened to make good his omission. Then she managed to monopolise Mrs Bascom's attention with a series of questions. She had been driven past Trundon Hall on more than one occasion, Ruth told her, but had never been beyond the gates to the park. Indeed, she was quite ignorant of its history or of what treasures might be found within its walls. Would Mrs Bascom be so kind as to tell her a little about the place? After all, at one time it had been her own house, so none would know it better. Mrs Bascom could hardly refuse such a request and was forced to allow Ruth to steer her into the parlour.

The moment had arrived. Adam and Lady Alice were left alone in the hallway. The trouble was that Adam could think of nothing to say. He stared, but kept silent. Lady Alice, if anything, looked even more apprehensive then he did. Thus, the time passed, each second at least three times its normal length.

The two might have remained, had not Lady Alice proved the more courageous. In a thin voice which sounded strange, even to her, she suggested they should retire to the library, where they could speak in private.

Once inside that room, with the door shut behind them, Adam again left Lady Alice to take the lead.

'I hardly know where to begin, my dear Doctor,' she said, 'despite asking Ruth and Charles to assist in allowing us an opportunity to talk in private like this'. Her voice trembled and she kept her eyes directed away from Adam's face. 'I would have written to explain, but there are too many actions for which I must seek your pardon and I did not know where to begin. Now I am here, it is no better. You have every right to be angry with me — even to break off our former friendship. All I can do is plead with you to hear me out and allow me to make what amends I can.'

Adam had been steeling himself to cope gracefully with the blow he knew must fall upon him; expecting rejection, not this plea for forgiveness. He was dumbfounded, his mind unable to grasp what was happening. Her ladyship must have seen this continued silence as confirmation of her own worst fears, for she fell silent too. Only the tears slipping down her cheeks revealed her misery. It was those tears which at last jolted Adam into a response.

'You cannot believe I am angry with you, your ladyship. You cannot! What have you done that could provoke such unkindness on my part? As for breaking off our friendship, I would rather cut off my own leg. Lady Alice . . . your ladyship . . . my dear friend, it is I who must throw myself on your mercy, not you on mine. Whatever I have done to offend you, please accept my assurance it was never my intention —'

'You have not offended me, Doctor. How could you? I am the one who has rushed into precipitate action. I knew I should have sought your opinion in advance. Afterwards, I was too ashamed of my behaviour even to tell you of it. Instead, I relied on my nephew to bear the news, while I hid my head and waited for the storm to break. No! Do not speak. Please, I implore you, allow me to explain how I came to be in such a state of foolishness.

'After my husband's death . . . once the sharpest pain of bereavement had passed, I wondered how I should spend my life. I have little taste for the empty round of visits and social occasions with which many ladies fill their time. I am not as accomplished as my niece. She has the talent to make fine botanical drawings and paintings. I have little talent for anything of an artistic kind. I therefore grew bored, for I could find nothing to satisfy my need to occupy myself with something worthwhile. Then, at length, I found the answer. I have long wished to busy myself making a home of my own — choosing decorations and furnishings and setting all out in a way of which I could be proud. Mossterton Hall could never provide this, for, as you know, I hold but a life tenancy. It would be inexcusable for me to take it upon myself to make changes. That is for Sir Daniel's heir to undertake, should he wish to do so.

'What I had overlooked was the other mansion and estate Sir Daniel owned; the one he had bought soon after we married to be my Dower House, had I managed to produce an heir for him. After his death, our son would inherit Mossterton and I would live at Irmingland Abbey. It is only six miles distant, yet was never part of the Mossterton Estate and so is not covered by the entail. To be honest, I do not recall that I had even visited the property before. Now I had myself driven there to see what I owned in my own right. The house is empty, as it has been since Sir Daniel bought it. The only people living there are the couple he employed to keep the place clean and in good order.

'The estate is not as large as Mossterton, yet extensive enough. I ascertained from my agent it brings in a significant amount in rents from half a dozen tenants. I am no farmer, yet even I could see that, with proper improvement, the land could yield more than it does at present. The house itself is old. As its name implies, there was once a house of religion there. That was seized for the crown by the last King Henry, then sold to a favoured courtier, who demolished the abbey itself and used the monks' dormitory and refectory to form a new house. The land closest to them became his park and the abbey fishponds a series of ornamental lakes.

'The more I looked, the more idyllic the site seemed and the more suitable for what I had in mind. I could enclose the oldest parts within a larger, more convenient mansion designed in the latest fashion. The architect might do as he wished outside. Within, I would have all decorated in the best Italian manner. Marble pillars for the hall and fine plasterwork everywhere. The present house has small windows with stone mullions and meagre panes of glass. Mine would have openings large enough to admit far more light. Instead of dark, low-ceilinged rooms, I would have finely-proportioned apartments. Within them, I would place elegant furnishings, fine paintings and the treasures I hope to accumulate. I have ample means for such an endeavour and it would give me great joy to plan it out and bring it to fruition.

'That was how I fell in love with what I planned to create at Irmingland. I became so besotted I ignored such whispers of prudence as tried to make themselves heard. All, I told myself, could be accomplished long before any move away from Mossterton became necessary.

'I should have left it at that. Instead, I rushed to acquaint Sir Daniel's heir with my decision. I told him I would renounce my life tenancy of the Mossterton estate and allow him to enter into his inheritance. My late husband always described him as a dull man of infinite caution, so I expected a series of protracted negotiations over the terms.

'We were both wrong. I wrote outlining my willingness to hand over his estate and suggesting a settlement I thought much to my advantage. He must return my dowry in full and pay me an annuity large enough for me to live on in comfort. That way, my other funds would be free for use at Irmingland Abbey. To my amazement, he wrote back at once, agreeing to everything. My immediate thought was that I should have asked for more. Yet what more did I need? Why endanger my dream by giving in to base greed?

'He made one proviso which did cause me much thought. He wanted me to leave Mossterton by this Michaelmas. Six months away, Doctor. Can you imagine the arrangements I must make in so short a period? I will barely have been able to appoint an architect to undertake the renewal of Irmingland Abbey, let alone see the work underway.

'Now I wanted your advice and counsel, believe me, but fate had intervened. Instead of being there to save me from the anxieties I had brought upon myself, you were struck down with fever and close to death. I knew I should abandon my dreams at once, but I could not. They had become dear friends and I needed all the friends I could muster to help me face what threatened to be another tragedy. I therefore shook myself free of the business of legal agreements and arrangements by the simple expedient of agreeing at once to his stipulation. I would leave Mossterton Hall by the date he set and live either in Norwich or in London. From time to time, I would visit Irmingland to supervise the work and add any final touches. Should the very worst happen and I was alone again, I would stand in even greater need of some project to occupy my days. Only when you began to recover did the full magnitude of what I had done become clear to me. While I had set in train changes that must alter my whole life, you — the man my husband had charged to look after me and help me cope in this world — remained ignorant of all I had done.

'Now you know why I have come here to plead for your forgiveness, Doctor. You are the last person in this world I would ever wish to offend, yet I have done so most grievously. Can you ever excuse me? May we be friends again, as we were before I undertook such rash and thoughtless actions? I would go upon my knees, if I thought it would help convince you of my penitence.'

'You have not offended me in any way. How could you?' Adam said. 'There is nothing I need to forgive. It is I who must ask for your pardon. I have let myself become so bound up in solving these murders that I have neglected all my duties — aye, and my feelings — towards you. Please, I beg of you, give me your hand in token of accepting this my most abject contrition.'

'I will give you more than that,' she said. Leaning forward, she pressed her lips on his and he experienced a moment of euphoria enough to take away his breath.

'Now,' she said, straightening again too soon for him to gather his wits and respond as he wished. 'We have been alone together for much longer than strict propriety would allow. Let us find the others. Your mother will be eager to set out for her home and Ruth will have exhausted her questions.'

'You are wrong about my mother. She will be burning with curiosity. Indeed, I suspect I will have to send her on her way by brute force. Poor Charles will have had time to walk around my small garden near a dozen times.'

'Poor Charles would be willing to walk around it a thousand times, as long as Miss LaSalle was by his side. If your mother will be curious about how we have been spending this time together, I admit to being almost apprehensive about those two. Have you ever seen two people more smitten? If my nephew does not ask Miss

LaSalle to marry him very soon, he will drive me mad with frustration. My only concern is how your mother will react. Do you think it would help if I told her that both I and Charles' parents will not hesitate to give the union our blessing?'

'Do that and she will agree at once. You do know Miss LaSalle has no fortune?'

'Of course. In many situations that would be a barrier. Here it is not. The young lady's lack of a dowry is a stroke of luck. You must have noticed my nephew's character might best be described as cheerfully indolent. He is like my pet cat; able to spring into action should the need arise, but otherwise content to remain idle. A rich wife would ruin him. He would live on his capital and never bestir himself to seek any accomplishment. He is not without means, Doctor. My brother has seen to that. Yet he has also taken care to arrange matters so that Charles must either work or live in relative poverty — poverty for a Scudamore, that is.'

'Can he support a wife?'

'If he puts his mind to it. While you were so ill, I talked at some length with Miss LaSalle. It was a way to stay alert in the depths of the night. I found her to be a clever and determined young woman. She will be well able to manage Charles and do it without any outward appearance of doing so. Charles will surprise himself with how well he prospers. He will never guess who is the true director of his fate. Am I right?'

Adam nodded. 'I would say that you are. In the time she has been with my mother, Miss LaSalle has made herself more a trusted friend than a companion. In my view, Charles will be the one to gain the most from a union.'

'Miss LaSalle will not be the loser, I assure you. Charles may lack ambition, but he has a warm heart and a loving nature. Once his heart is pledged, it will be for life. I know he prizes honesty and loyalty above almost all other virtues.'

'You do realise their marriage will cause my mother to submit me to endless questions about why I remain single?'

'You will need to find a way to set her mind at rest then, won't you? Now, let us go into the parlour before either of us commit further indiscretions.'

'But I have so many questions about your plans for Irmingland Abbey. And . . . and . . . there is something else I must ask you' The last thing Adam wanted was anyone to be present at that point.

'Both must wait for another day. Before we return to Mossterton Hall, Ruth and I have a good deal to tell you. We have made discoveries and I, for one, am eager to tell you what I have found out. I know Ruth is too.' She smiled and patted his hand. 'Patience, my dear Doctor. It will not be so very long before my period of mourning will end and I will be free of the obligations imposed by Society. Till then, let us be content to remain, as I hope we are, the very best of friends.'

22

THAT SAME DAY

IT WAS NOON BEFORE THE PARTY SET OFF FOR NORWICH. STOPPING at Adam's house had not required the servants to unload any of their baggage. Had that been necessary, Adam was sure they could not have departed before two o'clock. His mother deemed a mountain of luggage necessary even for the briefest stay.

In the meantime, Adam suggested Lady Alice and her niece might like some refreshment. He was glad he'd asked his cook to have something ready, since both accepted with visible eagerness. It was some time since breakfast and he'd noticed his mother had arranged for a hamper in the carriage. Charles, riding alongside, would have to starve, unless they stopped somewhere to let him eat too.

Their hunger and thirst dealt with, the three returned to the library. Ruth wanted her aunt to begin. Lady Alice insisted the information she had would be better understood in the light of Ruth's discoveries. Losing the battle, Ruth spoke first.

Adam listened to her tale with a growing sense of unease. Had he been wrong not to link Betsy Wormald's murder to the other two killings? He'd imagined some jealous village Lothario as her killer. A man ridding himself of an unwanted marriage and a bastard child by a single act of violence. Nothing to do with events elsewhere. The picture Ruth was presenting argued against that theory and agreed with all Miss LaSalle had said. Betsy was far from being the kind of young village girl for whom men's admiration took precedence over all else. The Marshall twins' assertion that Betsy's attractiveness had been matched by looseness of morals was mere jealousy and spite. Betsy had been more beautiful than either of them and that was sin enough to damn her in their eyes. They would never accept young men might prefer her for sensible reasons. She had to be a wanton and a temptress, whether she was or not.

Betsy Wormald may well have imagined herself a romantic heroine from the pages of the novels she read. She might have dreamed of handsome men on thoroughbred horses coming to whisk her away to a life of bliss. None of that mattered. Ruth's findings showed she was very much her father's daughter in terms of attitude and calculation. This was a young woman who wished to rise in the world. Thoughtless at times, even gullible and romantic, yet with an ambitious nature. She knew what she wanted — to leave Melton Constable for the city, where she would live the life of a lady of means. She also knew she wouldn't do that by going with the first lusty farm lad or journeyman who came knocking.

So, there was no evidence to suggest Betsy was promiscuous. Quite the reverse. Whoever persuaded her to yield her maidenhead to him must have taken a different route to winning her over; one that wasn't based on romantic dreams or wanton thoughts. Had it been a promise of early matrimony and enough means after to set up the kind of household she craved? One that fitted a prosperous family of the middling sort? The identity of this man was still unclear. That he had never intended to keep whatever promises he made was plain. If he had, finding she was carrying his child would have hastened his marriage plans, not been a stimulus to murder.

Why did he kill her? Why not abandon her, as he had most likely abandoned others before? There had to be a stronger motive. Jealousy? It was not unknown for a seducer to assume his victim's morals were as frail as his own. Yet, if all he wanted was to take his pleasure and go, why should he care whether the child in her belly was his or not?

One of Adam's more irritating habits was a tendency to pursue his own thoughts to the exclusion of everything else. Now it caused him to miss Ruth's explanation of how Fanny Wormald had come to Mossterton Hall. She had already reached the point where the two of them had settled into private conversation before it registered in his mind. Then, of course, he was all attention.

'What was that, Miss Scudamore? You talked with Betsy's sister in private and at length? Did she say anything of importance?'

'That is what I was telling you, Doctor. Were you not listening? I thought that expression on your face betokened abstraction and not —' She caught her aunt's warning look. 'Miss Fanny Wormald came to Mossterton Hall yesterday, as we had agreed. I will leave aside our time in the gardens and discussions on the natural world, since it is clear your capacity for attention is limited. Now, are you paying attention? I do not wish to be made to start again.'

'I am all ears, Miss Scudamore, I assure you. No more wool-gathering.'

'For shame, Ruth!' Lady Alice said. 'Dr Bascom is not some child you may scold in such a manner. Apologise at once.'

'No apology is needed, your ladyship. Miss Scudamore was quite justified. I was the one at fault. Now, Miss Scudamore, please proceed. I will do my best to make amends by paying closer attention this time.'

Ruth blushed. She knew she had a sharp tongue — many people had told her so — and she had not intended to rebuke the doctor in such a forthright manner. As so often, her words were spoken before she had taken time to consider them. Now the doctor's graceful acceptance of blame made her feel ashamed to have spoken in such a way. She sensed her aunt's irritation though and thought it best to press on.

'Fanny told me she was sure Mr Carse and her sister would never have married. They pretended to a courtship only to content Miss Betsy's father. Neither wanted it to go further. I asked her whether there was anyone else in the village Betsy might have considered as a husband. At first, Fanny said there was not — then she added, "not of late".'

'Not of late. So, there had been. Did she say how long ago?'

'She was picking her words with care. I don't think she wanted to tell me anything about it, so I didn't press her too much for fear she would stop altogether. Instead, I asked if the man had left for some reason. She said that he had and Betsy had been beside herself as a result. What sort of fellow was he? Betsy admitted she had assumed him to be the gentleman who appeared in the village without warning, then stayed for no more than a few weeks. You note she said "gentleman"? She had not used this word of Mr Carse.'

'That is most perceptive of you, Miss Scudamore. This person was of a different stamp, it seems.'

'So I thought also. Fanny told me he had rented a small house on the edge of the village. When I asked for a description of him, she said he was unremarkable, save that he looked like a gentleman. Well dressed. Fine manners. Spoke well. An older man, around forty or so — too old for Betsy, in her opinion. No one knew where he came from or what his background was, for he said little about himself when questioned. Only that he was seeking refuge from the chaos in France. His mother had been English and that was enough to place him under suspicion. Betsy told her he spoke English very well, Fanny said.'

'Was this man seeking solitude?' Adam asked. 'It seems odd for a gentleman to take a house in a small village like Melton Constable. I would have expected him to settle in Norwich or London.'

'My thoughts exactly,' Ruth replied. 'I also wondered if he'd been trying to hide. Yet, according to Miss Fanny, he delighted in walking about the village, talking with everyone he met, rich or poor, high or low. That was how he came to meet her sister. Betsy had been talking with Reverend Marshall's curate when this Mr Dewmark — that was his name: Mr Morris Dewmark — came along and bade the curate good-day. Naturally, Mr Burgess, the curate, introduced him to Betsy. After that, she encountered him several times. Fanny said her sister thought he was wonderful. There was something mysterious about him, like the heroes in the novels she read.'

Adam was intrigued by Mr Dewmark. What if Wicken's Swiss professor had shown himself at last?

'Did Miss Fanny tell you whether this Mr Dewmark is still in the village?' he asked. 'He sounds an engaging character.'

'He left after around six weeks. I had to work hard at this point. Miss Fanny was reluctant to go further. She wanted to tell me more — that was plain — but something held her back. I asked questions. She answered with sighs or said she barely knew what to tell me. In the end, I remained silent and let her struggle with her conscience.'

The turning point had come when Fanny asked whether it was true that Lady Alice had engaged 'some grave physician' to enquire into her sister's death. Was Miss Ruth acquainted with him?

'I told her I was, Doctor. I knew him to be a most dignified and solemn gentleman. An elderly man, greatly experienced in under-standing the human condition.'

'Ruth!' Lady Alice said. 'That was wicked of you.'

Her niece was unrepentant. 'It was necessary, Aunt. Had I said he was a gay young dog who galloped around the countryside falling off his horse, our conversation would have ended there.'

Lady Alice seemed about to protest, but Adam raised a hand. 'Go on, Miss Scudamore. I care not how you described me, so long as it served to draw out more information.'

'It did, I assure you. She said her sister's behaviour after this Mr Dewmark disappeared convinced her they had been more than casual acquaintances. Betsy was too cast down, too morose. Despite her denial of any interest in his comings and goings, Fanny felt convinced her sister had been sorely hurt by his departure. No, more than hurt. Stunned.'

'You said he disappeared.'

'That was the word Fanny used. According to her, one day all was normal. The next day there was no sign of him. He left as mysteriously as he had arrived.'

'Did anyone else in the village know where he went?'

'Here is the oddest thing of all, Doctor. Fanny told me her sister accompanied their father to Norwich one day, weeks later. When she came back, she seemed in a daze. Eventually she told her sister she'd seen Mr Dewmark walking down the street. When their father stepped aside to look in the window of a shop, she seized her opportunity. She went up to Mr Dewmark and asked him why he had left Melton Constable in such a precipitate manner. To her amazement, he denied any knowledge of the place or of her, saying she must have mistaken him for someone else. He had never been to the place she mentioned or met her before. Then, before she could recover herself, he walked on.'

'Could she have been mistaken?' Adam asked. 'There may have been a resemblance only. Her sadness at the man's departure might have served to turn it into an identity.'

'I asked the same, Doctor. Fanny said her sister had tried to convince herself she'd been wrong, though it was plain she'd never believed it. Then she grew more and more determined to uncover the truth. She told Fanny that amongst the men Mr Dewmark had walking with him that day was someone she recognised. His name was Peter Gort, he had lived in the village of Corpusty, but had walked each day to the Dame School the sisters both attended. He was older than Betsy, so must have left before Fanny was of an age to go to the school herself. That was why Betsy knew him and Fanny did not. Betsy had determined to send Gort a message and a letter for him to give to Mr Dewmark. The reply would then serve to clear up the mystery.'

'Did she do that, Miss Scudamore?'

'Fanny said she didn't know. She thought it likely, because her sister seemed so determined, but she was not sure. If the message had to go to Norwich, it would have taken several days to get a reply. By then, Betsy had been murdered. No message had come back by post or carrier afterwards, or she would have known.'

Adam's expression grew more sombre. 'Poor child,' he said, his voice heavy with bitterness. 'That message would have brought about her death. Even that chance meeting . . .' He lapsed into a silence so disconsolate that neither of the ladies dared break it for several minutes.

Ruth set the conversation in motion again. 'There's more.'

Adam raised his head. 'More?'

'Fanny found a diary Betsy kept. Their father asked her to go through Betsy's clothes and her few possessions. He couldn't bear to do it, even though, like the good Christian he is, he wanted to see anything they couldn't use given to the poor. Not things of sentimental value, of course, but all the rest. While she was doing this, Fanny found a small book hidden at the back of a drawer. It was obvious what it was. She told me she was reluctant to read any at first. She felt it would be intruding into areas her sister had wanted kept private. She even considered destroying it unread. If her sister had died a natural death, that's what she would have done.'

'She kept it?'

'Yes, Doctor, she did. Kept it and read it, hoping to find some clue that might unmask the murderer.'

'Did she?'

'She didn't know. What was plain, she told me, was her father would be deeply hurt by some of what Betsy had written. She had to keep it from him, whatever the cost.'

'What has she done with it?'

'She gave it to me to give to you — or rather, to this grave, elderly physician I'd told her about. I had to swear not to open it or look at any of what her sister had written. I also had to promise that you would destroy it after reading it. That was a binding condition to be agreed by you before I could hand over the book. I was to obtain your most solemn promise to that effect.'

'You have that promise, Miss Scudamore. No one else will read even a single page but me and I will burn it afterwards. If it becomes clear before I have finished that the diary contains nothing relevant to the murder of its writer, I will destroy it at once.'

'Thank you, Doctor. I was not in any doubt of your reaction, but now I can tell Miss Fanny what you said. I'm sure it will put her mind at rest.'

After that, Lady Alice's news seemed something of an anticlimax. The servant she'd sent to Melton Constable to pick up what he could had merely confirmed what Fanny told Ruth about the mysterious Mr Dewmark. When Dewmark arrived, the villagers had been suspicious. Later, the sympathy his tale of fleeing the murderous sans culottes in Paris evoked, together with his easy manner, won most of them over. They were surprised when he began to attend the Independent Chapel on Sunday, but no one associated it with any interest in Betsy Wormald. They'd assumed he was doing his best to make a new life in England. Some suggested his English mother must have been able to keep him out of the clutches of the Catholic priests. Others claimed he was turning to a purer form of worship, once he was free of the influence of Rome.

The villagers found his disappearance shocking. There seemed no reason for him to leave, let alone so secretly. The house he had been renting was owned by the local squire and his agent confirmed the rent had been paid in full and there had been no dispute of any kind. True, the rental period had only been six months, but the lease allowed for that to be extended without limit. There had never been any reason to expect he would go before even the initial period of the lease was finished. When the agent had entered the house to confirm nothing was amiss, he found all in good order. There were even some clothes belonging to Mr Dewmark in the clothes-press in the bedroom.

This evidence served to strengthen the general village view that Dewmark's disappearance was due to some disaster. Perhaps some dire news had come from France; the death of a close relative or something of that kind. Perhaps he had been set upon by highway robbers or suffered an accident. For days, people expected to hear his body had been found somewhere.

Only one man expressed a different view of what had taken place. That was Lucas Varley, an old man much worn by the years and none too clean either. He spent most of the day outside the village inn, hoping to persuade some unwary stranger to buy him a mug of beer. A wastrel and a drunkard, most called him. So he was, but the passing years had not dulled his mind. He'd play the local idiot if it won him more beer, but that was an act. The real locals knew he was as cunning as any fox.

Lucas Varley swore Mr Dewmark had come up to him, shortly

before he disappeared, and asked him if he knew of a man called Jack Bretherton.

Of course, Varley knew of him. Everyone did. "Black Jack" Bretherton was feared up and down the coast and far inland — as feared as the gang of smugglers he led. Only a fool mentioned anything about him to a stranger and Lucas Varley was no fool. He denied all knowledge of Bretherton until Dewmark went away, presumably to ask someone else. Varley had been hoping to cadge the cost of a mug of good ale, but he was willing to forgo even that to make sure Bretherton couldn't trace any information Dewmark obtained back to him.

Varley's answer to the mystery of Dewmark's disappearance was simple. Black Jack would have heard about the curious Mr Dewmark soon enough and he didn't like folk who asked questions. He was always on the lookout for spies from the Preventives or the Revenue. By this time, Varley told everyone, Dewmark's body would be rotting somewhere off the shore, weighted down with old chains.

'Even I've heard of Black Jack,' Adam said. 'What this old fellow said is correct. Only a halfwit would go about openly asking for information about him. An imbecile — or a man who has good reason to expect Black Jack to come calling, yet has no fear of what might happen after that.'

23

STILL THE SAME DAY

Adam was a different person after Lady Alice and Ruth left this time. He sat in his library, humming a little tune to himself and watching the sky through the window. Why should he waste the day indoors, he thought to himself? He might also take a stroll around the garden. He was sure it could do him no harm. He went out as Charles and Sophia LaSalle had done, looked at the flowers and enjoyed one of the magnificent skies for which Norfolk was famous with those who painted the landscape.

At least, that was what it looked as if he had done. The reality was that he scarcely saw or appreciated anything. Lady Alice was not intending to marry anyone else and she had kissed him too! That must mean something, surely. Her period of mourning had five or six more months to run, but then . . . he felt euphoric at the mere thought and gave himself up to the most delightful fantasies.

Eventually, after half an hour or so, more rational thoughts slowly penetrated his consciousness and he realised it was time to leave off day-dreaming. Going back inside, he shut the library door fast, settled himself at his desk and took up Betsy Wormald's diary. She had written it in the kind of pocket-sized book of blank sheets you might buy in any stationer's shop; a cheap binding filled with poor-quality paper. The ink had blotted and showed through from the front of each page to the reverse in many places. Reading it was remarkably trying. The girl's handwriting was childish and her spelling atrocious. She'd also tried to save space by writing as small as she could, filling every morsel of each page. It was likely she had little money of her own to spend and hoped to put off buying another book for as long as she could.

Adam began to read, skimming each page in search of what might be relevant to his needs. He had toiled his way through more than half the pages before he found anything of interest. Most of the entries consisted of the minor doings and childlike secrets any girl of her age might be expected to confide to a diary. Romantic outbursts, criticisms of village people, painful adolescent poetry. If he hadn't known it already, he would have soon realised how devoted she was to popular novels. Some of the events mentioned had to be imaginary or taken from fiction. If not, the villagers of Melton Constable were a far livelier group than he would have imagined.

Adam was close to giving up his reading when a sentence caught his eye. Betsy must have written it sometime after the rest of the entry for that date, since she'd squeezed it into the space between what she had already written and the next entry. 'The first time I met M!' it read.

He took greater care after that, finding references to "M" cropped up more and more often. He had encountered her "by chance" when she was walking back from taking a gift of vegetables to "poor Goody Jowett". She had come upon him when searching for primroses to put in a vase on their dining table. He happened to be in the small circulating library she patronised on her regular trips into Holt. Adam's smile was grim. None of these encounters had been accidental on M's part. He was tracking the girl, ensuring their meetings grew more frequent, finding excuses to talk with her — impressing her with his city polish and his calculated flattery.

Soon she was caught fast and the diary contained almost nothing save mentions of M, their secret meetings and, finally, his professions of love. There were no more chance encounters in the

lanes and pathways about the village. Now they met by arrangement. Sometimes it was in the church at times when no others
would be present. Sometimes, when the weather grew warmer, they
walked outside or slipped into an empty barn. Finally, she was going
to his house by a route which shielded her from view. That was
when he began to promise marriage, telling her enough funds were
about to reach him from France to set them up in style.

The man was a practised seducer, yet not all went his way. Betsy
resisted longer than he expected. Instead of yielding quickly, she
asked for more information about him and the time before he fled
France. Did he have a wife? He did once, he told her, but his wife
had died some years ago. Children? No, he had no children. Why
had the sans culottes sought him out? He had been a famous actor,
a member of the Comédie-Française no less. She had never heard
of it, so he explained it was the royal theatre, patronised by the
nobility. What happened when the revolution started? He had to flee
for his life. Not only were his sympathies with the king and queen,
his own family were minor aristocracy. He was a marked man from
the beginning. Adam allowed himself a cynical laugh. Only a girl as
innocent as Betsy would have taken any of this for the truth.

M then started pressing her to "seal their love". It could be no
sin when he had pledged to marry her at the first possible opportunity. When she still held out, he had a tantrum, saying it was clear
she didn't love him. In time, she gave in, of course. According to the
diary, they lay together as often as they could. She wrote of her
"delicious surrender", complaining that M had been "a little too
rough" on several occasions. She'd even noted down some of the
ways he'd required her to enhance his pleasure. She'd started planning their wedding as well. Then he disappeared.

The very last entry suggested M had got in touch very soon after
their fateful meeting in Norwich and before she had been able to
send her message to him. Peter Gort, the man she'd seen by M's
side, had come up to her in the village just two days later and given
her a note from M. She was ecstatic. M specified a time and place to
meet, saying he would explain all. Nothing had changed, he wrote.

They would soon be married as he had promised. She should set her mind at rest.

She kept the rendezvous and the promised rest turned out to be eternal. Adam snapped the diary shut and swore heartily. The thought of that innocent young woman's fate almost ruined what had been a perfect day until then.

24

13TH MAY, 1793

Adam spent the weekend going over and over all he knew, trying to put it into some sort of order. The weather had remained fair, so he could divide his time between making notes in the library and walking in his garden. Peter came once, examined him and agreed he was now free to walk as far as the apothecary's shop whenever he wished. That had been their regular meeting place. Adam would join Peter in his compounding room and sit there, sniffing the odours of herbs and spices and telling his friend about whatever mystery he was trying to solve. Peter would bustle about, throwing out suggestions and ideas while continuing to mix up various potions and powders.

Despite all his efforts, Saturday and Sunday came and went without Adam feeling he had advanced further. Whichever way he fitted the pieces together, no firm pattern emerged. As the time passed, he grew moody, swinging from elation, as he recalled how Lady Alice had pressed her lips on his, to black fury when he thought of Dewmark's lies. How could any man be as depraved as Dewmark was? How could he bring himself to exploit her inno-cence in such a heartless manner, only to take her life when she threatened to get in his way? By God, if anyone on this earth deserved to hang . . .

When Monday came, Adam rose early. It looked as if the spell of sunshine had passed, though the air was still warm. The wind had changed direction overnight. It had been blowing from the east. Now the clouds showed it had swung around to a westerly flow and that usually promised rain before too long. He hoped it would hold off long enough for him to walk to Peter's shop as he had planned. But first, he had things to do at home.

He began by writing a lengthy letter to Wicken, starting with a summary of everything he had discovered so far. To this he added a series of requests. Could Wicken ask his sources for any information they had about Mr Morris Dewmark? That might not be his real name, of course. He had lied about so much else there was no reason to believe anything he said. Not that he was an actor, nor that he had ever been in France. Many French refugees had fled to England and most met with a kindly reception. Lady Alice's servant said the inhabitants of Melton Constable had received Mr Dewmark kindly. That might have been the purpose of yet another of his lies.

Next Peter Gort. Adam knew Wicken had spies and informers in Norwich. Could they find out more about Gort and the group who clustered around Professor Panacea? Did Wicken know anything about Panacea himself?

Lastly, he turned to the hardest part to explain with any clarity — his growing suspicion that events were about to take a perilous course. What worried him most was what the old man, Lucas Varley, had said about Dewmark asking where he could find Black Jack Bretherton. If he didn't know Bretherton's history and reputation, why seek him out? If he did, what did he want with that evil gang? There could be no innocent reason for ensuring Black Jack knew you were asking about him. You had either chosen a particularly strange and painful way to commit suicide, or you had a paying proposition. If the latter, it had better pay well. Bretherton wouldn't sell his services to anyone for less than a substantial amount in gold or silver.

Adam sealed his letter and called for William, telling the lad to take it to the carter and see he delivered it to the post office in Norwich the moment he reached the city. It was bound to take at least three days or more for Adam to get a reply, but there was no quicker way. All he could do was wait and hope his message would arrive in time.

Adam felt sure Morris Dewmark had killed Betsy Wormald. He might also have murdered the milk-seller's daughter and her hapless beau, but that was less likely. Another's name came to mind for that ruthless act. The trouble was, unless Adam could work out what else these ruthless men were planning, neither would ever face the hangman — and Adam wanted so very much to bring that about.

Despite all his good intentions, Adam never managed to go to Peter's shop. After breakfast, Hannah told him Captain Mimms had arrived and was asking to see him. Peter would have to wait. Mimms must have risen at dawn to reach Adam's house at this hour, so something important must be happening. At the very least, his news might offer a diversion from Adam's growing anxiety.

Luck was not on his side. What the captain told him served to increase it by an appreciable amount.

'Sorry to descend on you like this so early in the day, Doctor,' Captain Mimms began. 'Yes, some coffee would be most welcome. Roads are getting dusty, you know, and I drove hard to get here as soon as I could.'

'I'm most grateful, Captain. Please, sit for a moment and recover your breath. Once Hannah has brought us coffee, you can tell me whatever it is that has caused you to come here in such a hurry.'

'No time for niceties, Doctor. After you've heard what I have to say, you'll be wanting to send a message to that friend of yours in London. If I'm quick, your lad might even catch today's carrier before he leaves.'

'Very well. Ah, here's Hannah with the coffee. At least let her set it down so that I may pour you a cup before you begin.'

'Thank you kindly. Now, this tale I have was brought to me by an old sailor who used to serve under me. I did as you asked and put the word out among the fisher folk and mariners. They know I'm not going to let on who's told me anything, so a few of them will say things to me they'd never tell anyone else and Old Sam is one of those. He was a brave, strong fellow in his youth. Now he ekes out a bare living as a lobster fisherman off the coast at Salthouse.

'As he tells it, a few days ago some men came around the village telling everyone to stay indoors the next night. They weren't even to look out through their windows. No, not on pain of terrible punishment.'

'Smugglers?'

'Couldn't be. The smugglers round there and the village folk know each other well. Half the village turns out to help them when they're making a run and they'd never need to make threats like that. No, Doctor, Sam says this wasn't the usual smuggling gang. He reckons they weren't even seamen. Landsmen, more like, and a nasty-looking bunch too. They'd a Norfolk way of speaking though, so they weren't strangers. Just men who didn't know anything about how things stand between the smugglers and the locals. Of course, no one argued. The ruffians made it clear anyone who disobeyed them would face the consequences.'

'It sounds as if they weren't making the run. More likely waiting for what was to arrive and nervous about anyone seeing or guessing what it was.'

'My thoughts exactly, Doctor. Whatever they were waiting for wasn't going to be tobacco or Geneva spirit. Something much chancier than that.'

'Did this Sam tell you anything else?'

'Aye, he did. Like us, he felt something much more significant was going on than the usual smuggling. He was so curious about what this might be he made himself a kind of mask with eye-holes. Amazing how much your face shows up in the dark, you know. You can wear dark clothes, gloves and a hat, but the slightest light reflects from your face like a beacon. Got to be some light for a run too. If it's pitch black, no one will be able to see to bring the stuff ashore. As Sam tells it, this was two nights ago, when the moon was near the full and the sky clear. Sam understood he would have to be extra careful, so he got himself ready and hid behind a hedge where he could get a good view of the lane of the village through a gap.

'What he saw wasn't anything like the usual smuggling run. It was only two carts with no more than six or eight men around them. They weren't smugglers at all. Sam was sure of that. The fools hadn't even known to muffle the horses' hooves with sacking. Either they knew there wouldn't be any Revenue men about or the rest of the gang — there'd been at least twice as many going through the village earlier — were lying in wait somewhere, ready to ambush anyone trying to interfere.'

'What was in the carts? Could Sam see?'

'Plain enough, he said. The first one was carrying a good number of small barrels, each about the size to hold a half-anker of Geneva spirit. According to him though, whatever was in them wasn't liquid. He says you can hear spirits sloshing about as the horse pulls the cart along. When this cart passed, he didn't catch any sounds like that and he wasn't more than four or five yards distant. Still night too. No noise of wind or waves to mask the sound.'

'And in the second cart?'

'At first he could only see long bundles wrapped in old sacking or cloth. Looked like bunches of sticks. He wouldn't have seen any more, only the cart went over a bump in the road and one bundle fell over the edge. The men dashed to pick it up, but not before Sam saw a musket fall out into the road.'

'Muskets!'

'Aye, Doctor. Sam reckons there were eight or ten bundles in that cart. Say six muskets to each bundle . . .'

'You're right, Captain. I have to get this news off to London right away.'

'You'll be careful with it, won't you? Sam's risking his life by passing it on. He told me he stayed in his place for hours after the men had passed to make sure no one was watching. Wasn't until almost dawn he slipped back into his cottage. Today's market day in Holt and he had a few lobsters to sell to a stall holder on Fish Hill, who often buys his catch. After he'd made his bargain, he slipped over to my house to tell me his tale. It isn't unusual for him to spend a few moments with me, so no one would have seen anything suspicious in it. Still, if word got back somehow that he'd been watching, he reckons his life wouldn't be worth a rotten herring.'

'I don't need to mention his name or yours, old friend. I only wish there was some quicker and safer way of getting the news where it needs to go than using the post.'

'Aye, right enough. Even if the carrier takes your letter to Norwich today and hands it in at once, it's bound to take two more days at least to get to London and be delivered. That's plenty of time for whatever was landed to be miles away and safely hidden.'

Adam felt close to defeat. He'd set out to find who had murdered a village girl, then been faced with two more murders and a quack doctor who definitely wasn't what he claimed to be. He'd seen his closest friend assaulted for asking the quack too pointed a question. Now he had learned of a vicious gang bringing weapons into the country for some devilish purpose he could only guess at. It was too much for a country doctor to cope with on his own — especially when he wasn't allowed to travel.

Maybe Mimms sensed something of Adam's discouragement. The old sailor leant over and put a hand on Adam's shoulder.

'When wind and tide are against you and there's an enemy vessel to be fought, Doctor, there's only one way forward for a man of spirit. Load the guns, cram on all the sail you can and cry damnation to the rest. If you falter now, you'll regret it for the rest of your life. I'll leave you to write your letter.'

Adam managed no more than a weak grin as a farewell. His mind was made up, but he couldn't help wishing he didn't feel so close to bringing up his breakfast.

As things turned out, Adam never had to write anything. As he took up a pen, the sound of voices at the front door filtered through to him. In a moment, Hannah was in the room bearing a letter for him. She hadn't even knocked!

'It's one of those King's Messengers again, Master. The ones with the enormous horses and the fancy saddlecloths. He says he's been told this letter is most urgent, so I thought I should bring it to you right away. Would you mind if I took him into the kitchen and gave him something to eat and drink? He's all covered with dust, he is. Told me he and a colleague had come all the way from London. They only stopped once for a few minutes rest — besides changing horses, that is, and seeing to . . . what's necessary. Well, the other man started from London and they met at Ipswich or somewhere, so this one rode half the way. The poor man's exhausted. A handsome fellow too.'

'Of course, Hannah. Make sure he has a good meal and give him this guinea from me. Tell Mrs Brigstone to find him somewhere suitable to sleep for a while, if he wants to. Now, on your way and leave me to read my letter. And next time, even if it's urgent, remember to knock first.'

Adam recognised Wicken's handwriting right away, though this example was so untidy that he must have written in great haste. The ink had spattered in numerous places and several words were crossed out and corrected. Still, as with all Wicken's correspondence, the message itself was clear and concise.

My Dear Bascom,

I am glad you are so much recovered. On another occasion, I will express my satisfaction at this outcome more fully, but time presses and I wish to see this letter on its way to you within the hour.

I understand you have been much engaged in seeking the person who committed three murders in your neighbourhood. That is a most worthy endeavour, but I fear I must ask, nay beg you to set murder aside for the moment. You may also abandon any further attempts to find the Swiss I told you about. Much greater matters are afoot and I need your help with them, as you have helped me in the past.

Word has reached me that some outrage is being planned in Norfolk. We have long known that county to be a hotbed of radicalism and republican views. Indeed, it is second only to London itself in the number of groups and societies which meet to share their treasonous ideas and plan sedition. Hitherto all the talk has remained that — just talk. I have men keeping watch on the largest and most active of these societies, as you can imagine. The dogs profess patriotism and loyalty, even while they conspire to overturn the constitution and end the monarchy. One or two of the rasher sort try to spur them into action, but their plans are usually easy to frustrate.

What is afoot now is different. In what way, I cannot tell you. We have been unable so far to fix on the ringleaders or discover in any detail what they are planning. There is a cunning mind behind it — of that there is no doubt — but whose mind that may be is unknown. I have lost several good men when they have come too close to discovering the truth. Whoever these people are, they do not shrink from murder to protect their conspiracy.

I am not asking you to get involved in seeking what my own men have failed to uncover. That would be far too dangerous. I am also aware that you are, at present, still confined to your house as a result of your recent accident. What I need is someone in the area whom I can trust. Someone who can give orders for swift and decisive action, should that become necessary. If that sounds to be something others could do, I assure you I would have spared you this request if I could. You have proved a most able lieutenant on previous occasions for the same reason that rules out the rest. You think and reason in ways that step well outside normal boundaries. If I knew precisely what needs to be done, there are a hundred men I could ask to see it carried out. You are the only person I can trust to see what others cannot, then turn your understanding into the necessary action.

This is not a task for one man. One man — you, I hope — can divine the nature and direction of this conspiracy, but it will need many more to prevent it achieving its goal. I have therefore communicated with Maj. Gen. George Gorras, Deputy Military Commander of the Eastern District. We have a long acquaintance and I know him to be someone who will do what is needed without wasting time in needless questioning. I have given him your name and told him of my trust in you. In this matter, he will carry out your instructions at once and to the letter. He has ample forces at his disposal and is also in contact with the naval commander in Great Yarmouth and the civilian authorities. For a time, Bascom,

I am giving you plenipotentiary powers to act in my place, for I cannot leave London at present. Use them well.

I am, Sir, as always, your most humble servant,
Percival Wicken, K.B.
Deputy Permanent Secretary, Southern Department

What could Wicken mean? "Plenipotentiary powers"? "Act in his place"? Why him, why Adam Bascom, local physician? It was true he had once given orders to a few of Wicken's men, when there seemed no one else capable of doing so. He had also known Wicken to act on what he said without stopping to question its soundness. Now he was to have a Major General standing ready to do whatever he told him. He was a doctor, for heaven's sake, not a politician or a military man. Was there no one else? No one better fitted to such a role?

If he had judged himself unequal to the task before, that was doubly and trebly the case now. The letter read as if Wicken, with all his resources, was placing the frustrating of some seditious plot into his, Adam Bascom's, hands. All he had to go on were fragments of facts, a few promising ideas and a mass of guesses. Were they enough for him to load the guns, cram on all the sail he could and cry damnation to the rest? Hardly.

Adam was still sitting at his desk, too stunned to move or speak, when Hannah tapped at the door.

'Excuse me, Master. One of Lady Alice's men has brought a letter from her. I thought you would want to see it at once.'

Another letter. Had it been from anyone else, Adam would have set it aside until a more opportune time. Now he opened it, cheered even by the sight of her familiar, neat writing.

My Dear Doctor,

I did not intend to bother you at a time when I know you are much occupied with matters of a most serious nature. But last night I had a dream so strange

178

and vivid that it is burned into my mind. It will not let me rest until I send word to you.

The details of the dream are unimportant. The impression it left with me is not. I awoke convinced you stand in dire and pressing need of my support. Not in any material way, but in the form of sufficient assurance to enable you to undertake the task which lies before you, be it never so fearful. If I fail you now, the dream seemed to say, we will both face a future blighted by regrets and missed opportunities. I am not such a brave person, Doctor, but I can be determined when I know so much is at stake.

The purpose of this short letter is to tell you that my trust and belief in you are complete and unqualified. Whatever you decide, I place myself, and such resources as I possess, at your command. I do this without question and without regard to the outcome. Please believe me when I say that nothing can ever shake my faith in you. Nothing.

I am, Doctor, ever your most loving and affectionate friend,
Alice Fouchard

Adam wept. Then he wiped his face dry, took up his pen and wrote a note for Charles, whom he expected must still be in Norwich. Unless he was greatly mistaken, Miss LaSalle would know how to find him. He would send William at once to his mother's house to ask Charles to return, so that he could act as his emissary to General Gorras. A servant would not do. To write down the necessary explanation of what he believed was being planned, as well as how and where it might be prevented, would demand a small book. He still lacked one piece of the information necessary for the general to take action. Even so, he could explain, via Charles, all that should be made ready in advance.

He could not guess that Charles, when he came, would supply that final piece of the puzzle.

25

14TH MAY, 1793

WHEN THE NEXT DAY CAME, ADAM KNEW HE MUST ACT AT ONCE. No time to go over all he knew again, only to think his conclusions through and make his plans with proper care. Once he used the powers Wicken had lent him and set events in motion, it would be too late to draw back. Timing was all. Act too soon and it would leave an opportunity for those involved to call everything off and go to ground. Leave it too late and half the county would be flung into chaos. Yet, though he thought he knew what was going to happen, he still had no idea of where or when, save that it must be soon and somewhere close at hand.

Once again, the weather matched his mood. When he woke, he could hear the sound of rain dripping from the eaves and the swish of standing water every time a cart or carriage passed. Going downstairs, he sat almost in the dark to pick at his breakfast. When he returned to his library, he was strongly tempted to tell Hannah to set out candles.

Shrugging his shoulders, he got to work. What should he do next? Send out the alarm? Put everyone on alert, but hold back from more? Wait until news reached him that their enemies had declared themselves?

A sharp rapping on the library door told him Hannah was paying him back for reproving her omission yesterday.

'Mr Jempson is asking if you will see him on an urgent matter, Master.'

'Bring him in, Hannah, and warn Cook to start making a pot of coffee.'

She was back with Mr Jempson in an instant. 'I am relieved to find thee so much recovered, Doctor,' Jempson said, seeing Adam standing to receive him. He didn't look relieved. He looked tense and worried.

'Good morning, Mr Jempson.' It was really very early for the elderly Quaker to be paying calls. 'Save for my arm, I am quite myself again. Broken bones are slow to heal. These will take some weeks yet to be as they were. Please take a seat, sir. What brings you here to see me? Hannah, bring us coffee right away.'

'No coffee, Doctor. I must not stay more than a few moments. I am on my way to Norwich to my daughter's house and wish to reach it as soon as I can. I am come because, last evening, I received a letter from her which has worried me a good deal.'

'I pray your daughter is not ill.'

'No, she is well. The problem lies with the young servant girl I sent to stay with her.'

'The one who was threatened by a man with pockmarks on his cheek?'

'That is the one.' Jempson finally took a seat, though he looked ready to jump to his feet at any moment. 'I sent her to Norwich for refuge, as thou wilt recall. Now, my daughter writes, the danger I hoped to avoid by doing so has followed her there. Two days ago, the girl left their house on some errand or other and returned in abject terror. She had seen that same man who threatened her in Aylsham. He is in Norwich.'

'Was she certain of it?' Adam had little doubt the maidservant was correct, but it did no harm to seek verification.

'Quite certain. She said he had seen him talking to the owner of a livery stable as she was passing. As soon as she caught sight of him, she turned and fled. She didn't think he'd even noticed her. My daughter asked if she heard anything of what the men were saying. The girl claimed the only words she had caught were ". . . at the old ruin near Hempstead".'

'The old ruin near Hempstead. That village is close to Holt, is it not?' It made sense.

'I do not know it, I fear. I have not lived long in this area and rarely travel anywhere save to the principal towns. Hast thou any inkling of what these words may mean?'

Adam ignored the question. 'She heard nothing else?'

'Nothing. She made off as quickly as she could. Now, my daughter writes, the girl refuses to leave the house at all. That is why I must go. I sent her to Norwich and feel responsible for her safety.'

'Quite so.' Here was confirmation of at least one part of his version of events. Not a revelation, but still useful. He would tell Jempson enough to calm his fears, but no more.

'I know not whether to leave her there or take some other course of action.' Jempson was on his feet again.

'My counsel would be to bring the girl back to Aylsham. The danger here has passed. Indeed, there may well be more danger in the city. These are turbulent times, Mr Jempson. Events in France have thrown us back into war and brought the danger of invasion. Sadly, not all our enemies are on the far side of the English Channel.'

'Dost thou fear a rebellion?'

'The majority of the English people have more sense than that. Even so, there are those who dream of such an event and will do all they can to bring it about. They will fail — of that I am sure — though some are ready to die in the attempt. Bring your maid home, Mr Jempson. Tell your daughter and her husband to come here too, if they can. Evil is stirring in this county, great evil, which must soon come to Norwich too, if those who plan to carry it out are not complete fools. Many have told me there is rising discontent amongst rural folk. It must be far worse — and will be far more easily brought to a head — amongst the poor of a great city like Norwich.'

'Thou knowest what this evil may be?'

'Whatever it may be, I sense it is close upon us.'

'Here? In Norfolk?'

'In most grave events affecting this realm, this county is too remote to be much involved. This may be different.'

'An invasion? There are many places along our coast where a landing might be made.'

'Not yet, if I am any judge. Our navy is too strong and the French forces at sea are no match for ours. They cannot be confident of landing without heavy loss, nor of overcoming our defences. Not, that is, unless they create enough of a diversion to draw them away. There lies the danger.'

'As the Good Book saith, a people divided against itself must surely fall.'

'Indeed so, sir.' Adam had had enough of talk. There was much to be done and he longed to make a start. 'You wish to be on your way to Norwich, so I will delay you no further. My thanks for bringing me your news, grave though it seemed to be at first. It has rendered the pattern of this puzzle a little clearer and shown me what should be the next step.'

'May the good Lord bring thee success, Doctor. I pray with all my heart that He will.'

They clasped hands and parted. The moment Hannah had seen Mr Jempson to the door and on his way, Adam called her to him. She was to seek out the apothecary and tell him to come with all speed.

'Tell him to leave off whatever he is doing and come at once. I have urgent need of his help. Let there be no delay.'

'What ails you? Tell me!'

'I am quite well, I assure you.' Adam was standing, staring out of the window into the street beyond when the apothecary rushed in, his medical bag in his hand.

'Then why such haste?' He had been happy mixing compounds

when Hannah arrived, out of breath, to say her master was asking for him to come at once.

'I need someone to go to Holt for me.'

'And I am that person? Could you not have sent William?'

'He is already driving to Norwich with all the speed he can muster. You will not allow me to go myself.'

'Certainly not with this mood upon you. If you did not dislodge the bones in your arm again, you would probably break your fool neck. I admit you have progressed well. It was in my mind to come to see you today in the normal manner of Christian gentlemen. I was even planning to tell you that you may resume a good part of your normal life.' He held up his hand to stop Adam interrupting. 'With the express exception of driving anywhere, save at a walk and with someone else, such as your groom, handling the reins.'

'I am most grateful, but this will not wait upon your caution. You will not let me go in the manner necessary, so you must do it in my place.'

'What if I have other business to attend to? Is earning my living to wait upon your whims? Are my patients of no importance?'

'If I am right, you face nothing in the world presently that is more vital than this.'

'If you are right . . .'

'As I believe I am. Stop arguing and get upon your way. I know you love to torment me, but this is not the time. Sedition is abroad in our land. If we delay, innocent folk will be harmed or die before we can root out the infection that threatens our country.'

'Very well. Tell me what you want of me. I can be in Holt within the hour, if I drive fast.'

'Seek out Captain Mimms. Something is about to take place in that area. The only clue I have to the location are the words, "the old ruin near Hempstead". Mimms has lived in Holt ever since he retired from the sea. If he does not know to what those words refer, no one will. Find out and return as fast as you can. Tell him to be ready to do more at my word, only not yet. No prior warning must reach these rogues that we are aware of what they are planning. I mean to catch them unawares, if I can. Tell the captain to await my message first, then rouse the constables and every other loyal man he can reach and send them where I will tell him. I am about to write to my brother to be ready to use his people to patrol the coast and prevent any help coming to these treacherous vermin from there — if I can find someone to carry my letter to Trundon Hall.'

'What about Dr Henshaw? Would it not be sensible for him to make your brother's acquaintance? If there were any sickness at Trundon, he would be likely to be called under present circumstances.'

'Of course! I fear poor Harrison Henshaw is very far from my attention at present. I must try to make it up to him very soon. Matters are coming to a head, Lassimer. The next week or so should see all resolved.'

'Then you can turn your attention back to the murders.'

'It has never been anywhere else.'

26

THAT SAME DAY

ADAM KNEW HE WOULD HAVE HOURS TO WAIT BEFORE PETER returned, even if his friend found Mimms right away. While he yearned for movement and action, he was forced to remain where he was. That was the unkindest blow of fate in this whole sorry business.

Adam sat once more at his desk and composed a note to his brother that he sent swiftly on its way as soon as Dr Henshaw arrived. Poor Henshaw was expecting to collect medicines from the house, then go to see a patient living two streets away. Instead, he was sent to saddle Fancy for himself and ride like the wind to a house he had never visited before.

'Follow the road past The Black Boys Inn and Blickling House,' Adam told him. 'When you come to the road from Norwich, turn right and keep going until you reach Holt. Then straight through the town, down the steep hill into Letheringsett, second turn on the right and Trundon is about a mile ahead. If you get lost, ask. If my brother isn't there, talk to his wife. To be honest, I hope he is out. You'll get more sense and less argument from her.'

Next, he wrote another long letter to Wicken. He had no notion when he might be able to see it sent to London. Still, setting out his thoughts and evidence in order helped calm some of the fear that all he was doing would end in ridicule.

In his letter, he began with Wicken's request to look for the lost Swiss professor. That had arrived almost at the same time as the first murder — Betsy Wormald. It was also then that Lassimer had first complained about the activities of Professor Panacea. Adam wrote that he had first assumed Panacea and the Swiss were the same man, until Peter's painful experiences at Panacea's meeting proved that idea wrong.

What of the second and third murders? It was clear they had to be linked together. Were they connected with the first? It looked so at the time. Next, he summarised William's report on Panacea's meeting in Norwich and the aggressiveness of Peter Gort and the men named The Disciples. After that came the peculiar behaviour of Mr Morris Dewmark and his secret wooing of Betsy, the black-smith's daughter. On next to the information from Mimms about smuggled muskets and the link to Black Jack Bretherton. None of it was conclusive in itself, but, taken together, the interpretation was inevitable, at least to Adam's mind. All that remained was to discover time and place — which was what he was seeking to do.

Wicken's last letter showed his alarm at what little news had reached him until then. Maybe alarm was too mild a word. It was one thing to suggest Adam might need help to counter whatever was going on. Quite another to give him the authority to call upon the military resources of the Deputy Commander, Eastern District. Wicken must already know a good deal more than the little Adam had been able to tell him up till now. Enough for him also to fear at least a major riot, if not some kind of uprising.

The time dragged past. Peter had been gone three hours, then four. Five hours. Surely, he should be back by now. If his horse was tired, Mimms would have loaned him another. Could they not grasp the urgency of it all?

Adam jumped as if struck by an electrical discharge. Mossterton Hall! It lay right in the path of these men and was one of the grandest houses in the area.

Good God, why had he not warned Lady Alice, or made time to

urge her to move to a place of safety? What if they burned it to the ground with her inside? Damn and blast this wretched arm! He could not saddle a horse unaided or ready the chaise and put Fancy between the shafts. No, Henshaw had taken the horse. He'd sent Henshaw to Trundon himself. No horse then. William had taken the chaise to Norwich. He was trapped in Aylsham with Lady Alice in the greatest danger barely eight miles distant. Jempson was gone to Norwich, so none of his horses could be borrowed. Besides, who would bring it back and saddle it? Not Hannah or Mrs Brigstone, for sure.

In his frustration and fear, Adam raised his arms above his head and slammed both fists down on the desk before him. The scream of agony that produced brought his whole household running.

That was the moment Peter knocked at the front door.

'Even a physician should know better than to do such a foolish thing.' Peter finished making sure the splints were back in place. 'Are you sure you won't take a little laudanum for the pain?'

'Quite sure, Lassimer. I need all my wits about me. Have I managed to do any damage?'

'That I cannot tell yet. At the very least, you must have set the healing back some weeks, maybe more. We can make a better judgment when the pain and swelling has subsided. The bones seem still to be in place, so I judge you cannot have disturbed them that much. I suspect much of the force of the blow fell on the splint, not on your arm.'

'Very well. Now forget my silliness and tell me at once what Mimms said.'

'The good Captain did not seem much surprised by my tale of a moon-touched physician demanding his neighbour and friend leave everything to run off at his bidding. It seems he has seen you goaded into action before —'

'Leave off your foolery, Lassimer, damn you! What did he say?'

'There is a ruin not far from Holt. It lies near Hempstead and is known as Baconsthorpe Castle. It was a castle many years ago, but the Heydon family converted it into a mansion, since they owned many sheep upon the heaths around there and grew fat from the profits of their wool. What happened to bring them down, Mimms does not know. Much of their house is now uninhabited and in a state of dilapidation, with the walls breached and the roofs fallen in. Only the grand outer gatehouse remains intact. The inner gate-house is without its roof. The whole mansion occupies an extensive site, with a moat, a lake and other ditches around it.'

'That will be the place, I am sure of it. Are there any barns nearby, did he say?' Adam had almost forgotten the pain in his arm.

'There is a large barn which is part of the property.'

'Does anyone live in the parts that remain?'

'One tenant. However, the outer gatehouse is at present unoccu-pied. The last tenant and the landlord came into dispute and a new tenant has yet to be found. The farmland is yet unimproved. That was a good part of the dispute. The landlord wanted a better rent and the tenant refused to pay. Yet neither owner nor tenant is willing to do more than fold sheep on it for fear of the costs involved.

'The nature of their quarrel doesn't concern us. That it has left the place empty was the greatest stroke of good fortune for these conspirators. It must be the place! Not too far from the coast, easy to find — that gatehouse must be plain from miles away — yet remote enough for those gathering to escape detection. What else?'

'Mimms says he will speak at once to the leaders of the town. When I left, he was calling for his coat and hat. The old fellow seems to be a man of consequence there. He's sure he can persuade the leading citizens to call out sufficient men to make a sizeable band. Since the smugglers have been active thereabouts in recent times, there is also a company of a dozen or so dragoons quartered in Holt. If they join with the constables, the loyal townspeople and their servants, the muster should reach fifty or more. I have the feeling he will be amongst them too, even though he must be more than sixty years of age.'

'He misses a good fight, I expect, though he would prefer it to be upon the water. Now, I need someone —'

'Not this time, Bascom. I am sore and weary enough.'

Adam opened his mouth to protest when Hannah burst into the room, once again without knocking.

'Hannah! What did I tell you —?' Adam began. She took no notice.

'Mr Scudamore, Master, is come in great haste.'

Charles Scudamore's entry into the room stopped Adam in his tracks. Charles looked weary and furious. He had always treated Adam with deference. Now he gave free rein to his anger, even dispensing with any greeting.

'Damnation take you, Bascom! It had been my intention to walk in the Vauxhall Gardens with Miss LaSalle today. Your man would not allow me time to do more than leave a curt message for her with your mother's housemaid, saying you had called me away. I don't doubt she will want an explanation of your behaviour. I most definitely do. You seem to think everyone around you is at your beck and call. Is that not so, Mr Lassimer?'

'It is, Mr Scudamore. I myself have only this moment returned from going to Holt at his most peremptory insistence.'

This was too much for Adam in his present state of agitation. 'Be silent, both of you! I have no time for explanations or niceties. What is it to be, Lassimer? Either do as I ask or leave me in peace. There is no call for you to wait with your ears flapping for gossip.'

'Send this young fellow. He will be eager for action,' Peter said. 'First you spoil my morning, then you deny me my simple pleasures. It's too bad of you, Bascom. Watch that arm now! No more damage or I cannot answer for what may happen. Good day to you, Mr Scudamore. I wish you better luck with this surly fellow than I have found.'

'Eager for action?' Charles said. 'By no means. I want a chance to return home and rest before setting out on another wild-goose chase for our friend here. Good day to you, Mr Lassimer. It seems my arrival has saved you from further annoyance. Now it's my turn.'

The pain in Adam's arm returned twofold. His temper, never too secure under great pressure, escaped from his control entirely.

'For God's sake! Hell and damnation take you, I say! Why must both of you idiots behave like spoiled children? This is an emergency. Unless I can prevent it, there's going to be a bloody rebellion — right here!'

They stared at him. Surely, he could not be serious? You didn't have rebellions in Norfolk — at least, not since Kett's time and that must be two hundred years ago. The sight of their shocked faces and glazed looks drove Adam to still greater fury.

'Don't gawk at me like blasted sheep!' He swore fit to make a sailor blush. 'I mean what I say. I haven't the time to explain any further. Do as I tell you, or face the chance that a good many around here will die — including you. If I could be everywhere myself, I wouldn't have to rely on people who question and quibble like old women buying their groceries. Listen, damn your eyes! Mossterton Hall is in danger, as is Aylsham itself. Lassimer, rouse the town to its defence. Constables, sturdy townsmen, anyone who can hold a weapon of some kind. Tell the rector to fire the church bells to sound the alarm. Go, man! Now! Scudamore, where's William?'

'Gone to the stables to feed, water and rub down his horse and the one I was riding. They've been ridden a long journey at some speed. Neither's going be in a fit state for much else. But . . . What's this about Mossterton being in danger? My sister and my aunt are there. I must go to them at once.'

'Indeed you must, but not yet. You can hire a fresh horse from The Black Boys Inn, I hope. Will there be another horse you can ride at Mossterton?'

'Of course, but —'

'What news do you bring from Norwich?'

'Little enough. The place is all agog because Professor Panacea has disappeared. Two lectures were advertised yesterday, both in the Assembly House. Large crowds assembled, as they have for all his lectures of late, I am told, but no one arrived. Neither the professor nor those fellows who surround him. The ones who call themselves The Disciples, as if that quack were Jesus Christ himself.'

191

Adam grew still more frantic, if that were possible. 'Anything else?'

'The Duke of York is coming to the city in two days' time. He will hear speeches from the mayor and members of the common council. Then he will go to the Market Place to review several troops of Loyal Volunteers who will parade for that purpose. It promises to be a grand occasion.'

'A bloody occasion more like! Tomorrow night, then. Tomorrow! So little time . . . Listen and don't interrupt. This is what I need you to do. Go first to Mossterton Hall. Lady Alice and your sister are in peril. Gather all the most able-bodied of the male household servants. Do the same with all who work in the gardens, grounds and Home Farm. See they are ready with whatever weapons can be mustered. Tell her ladyship and your sister to remain indoors for the moment, but be ready to flee at once if danger threatens. I assume one or other of them can drive?'

'My aunt drives better than I do. She's a superb horsewoman. My sister, I fear, will be of very limited use in that respect. Her talent is for paints, pencils and books.'

'No matter. If one can handle horse and carriage, that is enough. Tell her ladyship to have all ready, including her carriage and horses, before nightfall tomorrow. Matters will come to a head by then, I am certain of it.'

'I can drive and ride. I will take care of them.'

'You will not be there. After you have done as I ask, take what rest you may. Then rise at dawn and go back to Norwich with all speed. You are to seek out Major General Gorras, the Deputy Military Commander for the Eastern District. Give him this message from me.'

'Gorras? His son, or one of them, must have attended the same school as I did. "Gormless Gorras" we called him. As I recall, his father was a military man.'

'Spare me your memories until a more fitting time. Here is what you are to tell the general.'

'He'll never see me. You do know that, don't you? You can't ride up to the military headquarters and ask to speak with the general.'

'He will see you, if you say you have come from me. He will also listen most carefully to what I am about to bid you to ask him. Then, unless my information is very far in error, he will act on it at once. Unlike certain people I can think of, he will not waste such little time as we have left on questions and idle reminiscences about his school days.'

'This is thanks to your friend in high places in London, doubtless.'

Adam ignored that comment. 'Tell the general there will be a muster of dissidents, malcontents and would-be rebels tomorrow evening at Baconsthorpe Castle, near Holt. The plan is to mount a rebellion, starting there and stirring up all those who wish for a revolution. They have muskets, thanks to the smugglers and the French. Their plan will be to march at once towards Norwich, collecting more followers along the way. Tell him I have roused the townsfolk in Holt and Aylsham. I have also sent word to my brother at Trundon Hall to guard the coast in case French troops land to help them.

'Mimms will send whatever forces he has managed to get together to Baconsthorpe. There is a small troop of dragoons in Holt, so they will add some military muscle to whatever townsfolk are willing to turn out. General Gorras, if he will be guided by me, should gather his forces and head at once to Baconsthorpe Castle. Do you know where it is? If you don't, ask someone at Mossterton Hall to tell you before you set out. It is near a village called Hempstead, some two or three miles to the south-east of Holt. If he moves quickly, he may catch the rebels between the two forces, like a crab closing its pincers on its prey.'

'I will leave at once.'

'Wait! There is one more thing. Your news about the Duke of York causes me great alarm. Ask General Gorras to send men into Norwich as fast as he can and alert the city authorities there. Wherever His Royal Highness is expected to go during his visit should be searched — and searched thoroughly. What better start to a revolution could there be than to encompass the death of the king's son? Oh yes, here's a letter for Wicken. Please ask General Gorras to see it is sent to him when convenient. I'm sure they'll be in touch soon. Now go!'

Adam had done all he could. Now he must wait in his house, far from events and powerless to intervene. He could only worry and pace up and down, helpless until someone should be able to spare the time to bring him news.

He kept going over things in his mind, again and again. What had he missed? What still remained to be set in motion? William could return to Holt at the same time that Charles was setting out for Norwich. Captain Mimms must not move too quickly — and not too slowly either. Tomorrow night! Would there be time for the general to muster his forces and get them close enough to Bacon-sthorpe before the men from Holt arrived. Could he spring the trap?

Adam had never had anything to do with military matters. Now his mind filled with unanswerable questions. How quickly could soldiers be turned out of their barracks and got on the march? How fast would they go? What if the general relied on cavalry? Would they take longer to be ready? It was close to twenty miles or so from Norwich to Holt. No horse could go all that way at high speed. How slowly would they need to ride for the horses to be able to cover such a distance? Would the rebels hear them coming in time to make their defence? Was the ground about the castle suitable for horses to cover? It was close to the heathlands and they were a dense tangle of gorse and heather, with plenty of rabbit holes. Would the general tell his men to dismount and approach on foot? Would he even be there? Senior officers might attend a battle between opposing armies, but he must surely delegate such a minor matter as this — at least in military terms — to a far more junior officer. How experienced would such a young man be? Would he rush in too rashly or hang back too far?

Round and round went Adam's mind, until he felt as tired as if he had ridden to Norwich and back himself. He couldn't eat, he couldn't sleep. His servants had taken one look at their master and decided to stay as far away as possible. Nothing could now ease his mind save news of success — which could not possibly come for another thirty-six hours or more. Was this what it would be like to be a general? To send your forces to carry out a complicated manoeuvre in the face of the enemy, then wait, alone, to hear if it had succeeded or failed? Thank God, he had never been tempted by an army commission — or a naval one either.

27

PETER GORT URGED HIS HORSE FORWARD. HE'D BEEN SO OCCUPIED with his thoughts the animal had started to amble along, stopping from time to time to nibble grass from the side of the road. Panacea would be expecting him back in Norwich. Let him expect! Greater things were in prospect than Panacea's petty concerns. No longer would he let Panacea order him about, sending him back and forth along the wretched road between Norwich and Weybourne. The hour had almost come. Tomorrow he, Peter Gort, would be leader. If Panacea wanted to survive, the so-called professor would have to learn to take orders instead of giving them.

This damned horse was as lazy as the rest of them. Still, there was no rush. He'd told the rest of The Disciples to meet him at Baconsthorpe tomorrow afternoon. Before they arrived, he needed time to go over his final preparations and make sure all was in place. He would bed down in the empty gatehouse for tonight. In the morning, he would open the barn and check the muskets and the rest. He'd made sure the two he'd left in Norwich had all they needed before he left. They were good men, committed to the cause. They wouldn't let him down.

He'd never liked the professor. Admired his skill and cunning, but no more than that. For a start, the man was much too arrogant and acted as if everything was his own idea. Without his, Gort's, prompting, Panacea would have accomplished little. True, he'd established the contact with Black Jack Bretherton, but even that was only a continuation of his predecessor's arrangement. Who was it who went to and from the coast to deliver messages and collect what Black Jack's men had brought from France? Not Panacea. Who recruited The Disciples, watched out for government spies and ran Panacea's meeting for him? Who told the professor how to contact the right people in Norwich and round about to stir up dissent amongst the working people?

Gort's horse stopped again. This time Gort gave it a sharp blow across the rump with the whip he was carrying and it broke into a shambling trot. Not for long though. The beast must have sensed its rider was too wrapped up in his thoughts to keep it moving at a steady pace.

The Disciples were a stroke of genius and that were his idea, not the professor's. Without them, Panacea would never have been able to keep in touch with all the groups of radicals; nor provide them with the pamphlets and money they needed to grow in numbers. Norfolk was riddled with spies and government agents. Did the professor ever consider what it took to keep his activities secret? Without Gort's men, every move Panacea made would have been reported to London, then somehow frustrated. The man was too squeamish. This was war. There were bound to be casualties. A few spies less should have been welcome news, not a reason to lecture them on the need to avoid anything that drew attention.

That was Panacea's worst failing, of course. The man was weak. He had no ambition. All he wanted to do was send messages to France and stir up discontent. Lurk in the background causing such trouble as he could. If that had been all the French revolutionaries had done, they'd still be bowing and scraping to a king. They had found men of vision and courage, who mobilised the mass of people to overthrow the monarchy and the nobility and take charge of their own destiny. Why shouldn't the British do the same? All it needed was a strong leader to set things in motion.

Gort had no doubt he was that person. Look at what he had accomplished so far, despite having to do it all without alerting Panacea to what was going on. If all went as he planned, there would be enough people armed tomorrow night to overwhelm any local resistance. Resistance? Gort laughed. Fat country squires and feeble aristocrats. Weaklings who spent their time eating, drinking and fumbling their mistresses. When was the last time any of them had handled a weapon or led soldiers into battle? By the time they woke up to what was happening, half of them would be hanging from their own gateposts.

He had the men, he had the muskets and he had the powder. Not much longer to wait either. The day after tomorrow, he'd be leading his forces into Norwich, then on his way to London. No more suffering at the hands of fools whose only claim to power and privilege came from being born in some grand house. No more being told by snivelling clergymen that to be poor and exploited was God's will and had to be accepted. It was time for the British people to rise up and overturn centuries of rule by self-appointed members of the so-called elite. The people would do it and men like him, Peter Gort, would be their leaders.

Fifteen years before, a pompous member of that same elite had thrown his steward — Gort's father — out of job and house. Done it without a second thought too. Made his father so ashamed he'd cut his own throat and left the rest of them to cope with nowhere to live and nothing to eat. His mother had died within six months — died in the workhouse. They sent his sister to be a servant to a baker in North Walsham. When she ran away, they found her and branded her a thief. What if she had taken a few things to sell? She had to eat, didn't she? The judge sentenced her to be transported and he hadn't seen her since. Didn't even know if she was still alive. Then they bundled him into the army and sent him to fight the rebels in North America. That was where his eyes had been opened to what ordinary people could do if they stood up to their oppressors. He'd soon had enough of wearing a red coat and suffering humiliation from the sergeants and officers. One night, he'd deserted to fight with the rebel colonists. When the war ended, he planned to make a new life for himself in a free country.

It hadn't taken him long to realise all he had done was swap one set of oppressors for another. Those Americans were full of fine words about freedom and their republic, but that was all they were — words. When it came to actions, they were no different to the British. Obsessed with making money and claiming rights over the land. They might not have titles or pretend to be gentlemen, but the rich still lived in fine houses and made the poor scratch a living as best they could. They even had slaves. When he tried to point out where they were going wrong, they soon turned against him and made him run again.

That was why he came back to England, determined to fulfil his destiny at last. To make everyone see that Peter Gort wasn't a man to be pushed around when he could fight back. It had been a hard struggle at first. No one would so much as listen to him. They were too ground down by ignorance and poverty; too afraid of losing what little they had to rise up and demand more. Even when he'd found the professor and realised this was his chance, his plans had nearly been ruined. By God, these Norfolk fellows were stupid! He'd told them what he'd do to traitors, but some of the fools still couldn't keep their mouths shut. He'd had to be ruthless in dealing with them after that. You couldn't be squeamish with the fate of the country at stake. Not when it was your own future in the balance as well.

Gort's horse had stopped again, cropping the long grass as before. This time, Gort hadn't even noticed. In his mind's eye, he was riding a magnificent charger at the head of his troops and all around people were cheering and shouting, the women throwing flowers. The shining path to glory lay open ahead of him. This was his hour! Nothing could stop him now. Nothing.

28

CHARLES SHIFTED IN THE SADDLE AND TRIED NOT TO THINK HOW FAR below him the ground was. He was used to horses of a reasonable size. Ones with placid temperaments. Not like this huge beast, which seemed to be waiting its moment to throw him off its back. Why in heaven's name had he offered to join the troop of dragoons sent out from Norwich? General Gorras didn't argue. He'd nodded and told one of his men to find Mr Scudamore a fresh horse. It hadn't occurred to Charles at the time how different a cavalry horse and a normal riding horse could be. Not only was this one far too lively for him, it was the largest horse he had ever ridden. He wished they could have provided him with a fresh backside as well. He must have ridden further in the past week or so than in the whole of the rest of the year. Backwards and forwards between Mossterton Hall and Aylsham. To and fro from Aylsham to Norwich. To Trundon Hall to escort Mrs Bascom and Sophia and alongside them back to Mrs Bascom's house in Norwich. Now he'd faced another twenty miles in the saddle. Twenty miles going as fast as they could without ruining their mounts.

It had been a beautiful evening when they set out. Charles had come to expect that in this part of Norfolk. You often started your day with a bright dawn, then the cloud rolled in and made everything look miserable. You might even have rain during the main part of the day, though that wasn't all bad. On the sandy soils, water ran away almost as soon as it fell. The farmers were more likely to worry about droughts than floods. Having had winter and spring in the same day, the evening once again brought summer. The sky cleared, the clouds retreated to the horizon and all grew calm. He'd never seen such spectacular sunsets as Norfolk could produce. On the right day, the western sky would blaze with colour. Yellow, orange and scarlet through to the darkest reds, streaked with the deep purples and blues of distant clouds. If only he could capture it in paint.

Now the sun was almost down. Long shadows everywhere and the blackbirds clucking and grumbling in the thickets and tangles. The captain told him there would be a full moon later. He stretched in the saddle, looking at as much of the sky as he could. No moon yet. As he settled back down, he groaned at the pain his backside was giving him.

'Saddle sore?' The captain was riding alongside him. Probably thought he should stay close in case Charles' horse grew too frustrated with its rider's limitations. 'I tell the new recruits it'll take about six months before they can feel comfortable. A year or so later, their backsides will be like leather.'

'I wish mine was!'

'Not far now. I'll slow the men down a bit soon. One of the troopers knows this area well. He says we'll come out of the heath into better land about a mile short of the castle. The only drawback is the area's damp for this part of the world. The castle itself has a moat and some kind of mere close by. Then there are various other ditches and hollows with water in them. Springs too. We'll need to pick our way carefully.'

Charles nodded. The captain was a likeable fellow who hadn't complained at a civilian tagging along. Most military men regarded civilians as an inferior species. He wondered if he was married.

The thought made him grin. A few weeks ago, it wouldn't have entered his head. Now . . . he let his mind wander, remembering Sophia's excitement when he had arrived to collect them. What would she be doing now? He'd been furious when Bascom's groom arrived and dragged him away from Norwich. Did Sophia know where he had gone? William said he'd gone to Mrs Bascom's house first and they'd told him where to find his quarry. She must know something at least. She'd told him once that she'd grown to trust Dr Bascom's odd ways. He supposed he did too, or he wouldn't be here now.

What about Ruth and Lady Alice? Last evening, after delivering Adam's dire warnings to his aunt, they'd sat for a while together in the withdrawing room. Then Ruth said she had a headache — fear most likely — and retired to her bed early. His aunt seemed excited by Bascom's warning. Before dinner, she'd summoned her butler, housekeeper and estate steward to give them their orders. It could have been the Duke of Marlborough speaking to his officers before the Battle of Blenheim. Once that was done, she ignored the danger. Dinner was served at the usual time, with tea in the withdrawing room after that.

Perhaps it was her resolution in the face of danger that had stirred up his own courage. That or Ruth's sly probing over dinner. Either way, he'd asked his aunt what she thought his father would say if he told him he'd asked Miss LaSalle to marry him and she'd accepted. Not that he knew if she would, of course.

'Thank God,' his aunt had replied. 'That's what he will say. He thinks it's high time you got married and applied yourself to your career in the law, not idle here at his and my expense. I could see this coming, so I've made some enquiries about the young woman in question. From Society's viewpoint, she's an unusual choice, it's true. She has no dowry, save what her brothers might scrape together to avoid shaming their family name. She also holds an ambivalent position as companion to a widow of gentle blood and modest fortune. That would be odd in other circumstances, because Miss LaSalle's family background is as good as Mrs Bascom's. However, I'm assured she's not a normal kind of companion, who would be a woman of lower status, hired to be an acceptable person to take when calling on acquaintances. Someone to make up a fourth at whist or to provide entertainment at the pianoforte in the evening. Things like that, with a great deal of fetching and carrying as well in most cases.'

'Sophia's an angel.'

'That's what all men say when their passions are aroused — and not always about their wives. I have written on the matter to your father and he agrees with me — as he is usually well-advised to do. Our conclusion is that she will do very well. She is clever, sensible and more than capable of running both your household and its master. The fact that she is good-looking, has a fine, slim figure and lovely hair may seem of great consequence to you now, but aren't nearly as important. Very well. You may make your proposal to the young lady with his blessing and mine. If she does not accept, I will be dumbstruck.'

As simple as that. He could ask Sophia to marry him without fear of the consequences. Now, when he longed more than anything to do so, he was stuck on a horse, somewhere to the south-east of Holt, emerging from what seemed an endless waste of heath.

'I'm going to halt the men,' the captain beside him said softly. He held up his hand and everyone halted on the instant. Charles was glad he'd been warned. He'd been miles away and wouldn't have seen the signal, let alone acted on it in time. 'We need to listen. We must be close to the place. If anyone's there, we should hear them.'

Charles strained his ears, but heard nothing. Just the soft noises from the horses, the occasional rattle of harnesses, and the noise of the wind blowing.

There! What was that?

'Parsons, you've got the youngest ears of all of us. Hear anything?' The captain had whispered to one of the troopers drawn up close beside him.

'Men, sir. Quite a few, I'd say. I can hear them talking to one another. At least one cart or wagon. There's also some dull noises like lumps of wood being knocked together. No horses, though — save for whatever is pulling the wagon.'

'Good man. I wonder how close we can get before they start to hear us?'

'We're downwind of them, sir. That should let us hear them before they hear us. It's hard to keep the horses quiet though.'

Another trooper rode up. 'I can see some lights, sir. Torches, I'd say. It's not that dark yet, so they must be doing something that needs a good light. Helpful to us, sir. A man with a torch in his hand makes a fine target.'

'We're here to round up these rebellious fools and hand them over to the law to be dealt with, not kill them. Listen, all of you. Try to avoid violence if you can. Defend yourselves, if you have to, but no more. Head for those you think are the ringleaders. If some of the rank-and-file get in your way, that's too bad. Show your carbines and swords, but try not to use them.

'I'm going to get us as close as I can before you men must dismount. This kind of ground won't allow us to use the horses. I'm told the castle has two gatehouses, one about fifty yards from the other. It's also got a moat and a mere to one side. I expect the mob will be collected inside the moated part. That's good. Only one way in and out, unless they jump in the moat. Once they've heard us, most will try to get away. You six, block the exit. The rest of you, round up everyone you can and take their weapons away.

'Now, Mr Scudamore. I suggest you stay back while all this happens. No sense in you getting hurt — nor having you get in the way of my men.'

'To be frank with you, Captain, I'm not keen to be hurt and I won't be much use to you. I've never been in this kind of fight. More likely to make a fool of myself than be any help. I'll just —'

Everyone heard that. Shouting, followed by several gunshots and more shouting. Close by too.

'That must be the men from Holt,' the captain said. 'Dismount and draw your weapons men.' He was shouting now. 'Bugler, sound the attack.' Moments later, Charles was alone.

He waited a few moments, then edged his horse forwards. He'd had the greatest difficulty in holding it back. The beast must be well aware what that bugle call meant. It had no intention of being left out of the action if it could avoid it. The more he held it back, the more it pranced and strained against him.

He was rescued by one of the troopers left behind to hold the other horses. 'I should dismount, sir. Dancer here knows what's going on. If you won't let him go where he wants, he'll have you off his back. Whoa, Dancer! Whoa. There, I've got his bridle now. He knows what that means. Slip off him as quick as you can.'

'Did you call him Dancer?'

'That's right. Light on his feet, ain't he?'

Charles felt much safer on the ground. He'd brought a brace of pistols from Mossterton Hall and he drew one of them — then prayed he'd not have to make use of it. Would he even be able to shoot a fellow human being? Most likely miss anyway.

Dusk had come on quickly once the sun went down. It was hard to see and Charles had to pick his way over very uneven ground. Ah, this must be the outer gatehouse — it was so difficult to make out much ahead — and those must be the ruins of the old castle, those broken walls showing against the lighter colour of the sky.

More shots and yells — the noise had risen to a crescendo — then still more shots, followed by the unmistakable scream of someone hurt. A man rushed past him and another came up out of the shadows. This second one stopped for a moment and brandished a knife, probably something used in his trade. It took Charles a second to realise the fellow was going to attack him. He raised his pistol and fired, but couldn't tell whether he had hit his attacker. One minute he was there, brandishing that knife and coming towards him. The next moment there was no sign of him. Another man burst out of the gatehouse as if all the hounds from hell were on his trail. He saw Charles' pistol and threw himself on the ground, howling for mercy. As Charles stood there, pistol in his hand, completely at a loss on what to do next, the shouting died down. It was all over.

A few moments later, one of the troopers stood before him. 'Captain's compliments, sir. He sent me to find you and lead you to where he is. Ah, well done, sir! You got one of them. On your feet, you treacherous bugger! Come on, get up or I'll fucking shoot you where you lie. That's better. You can walk in front of us. If you try to run off, this gentleman will kill you for sure, even if I don't.'

The captain was complimentary. 'Well done, Mr Scudamore! Very well done. This wretch must have got past us in the confusion, but you stopped his nonsense, right enough. Johnson, take this snivelling piece of dirt out of my sight and put him with the others.'

He turned back to Charles. 'All over now. We've got almost all of them, I'd say. They didn't put up much of a fight. We've had one man wounded by a gunshot and another stabbed in the thigh with a pitchfork. The men from Holt have one killed and two quite badly injured. Looks like they were hit with the stocks of muskets the rebels used like clubs. At least six or seven of the rebels are dead and a good few more injured. I hope we got all the ringleaders. I saw at least one man jump into the mere. If he can swim, he may well have got away. If he can't, he'll have cheated the hangman out of his pay by now.

'A good night's work, that's what I call it. Caught them fair and square, with no chance to do more than put up a few isolated fights. There are always some hotheads who want to make martyrs of themselves. It's bad to lose even one man, but I'd have expected more casualties in tangled ground like this. They lost seven at least to our one. I don't know who they are yet, save one. There's a brave old fellow here from Holt says he recognises one of the dead men. Knows you too, he says. A fellow called Captain Mimms. Naval man, so that rank means someone a long way above me. You'll hardly believe this, but he drove here in his dog-cart alongside the troopers and the local men on foot. Can't keep an old soldier — or sailor in this case — away from a good fight. As I said, he's recognised one of the dead as a local man, a nasty piece of work called Henry Huggins.

'Now, if you'll excuse me, I'll leave you to see to gathering up my men. The lieutenant here will take his troop back to Holt and the civilians say they'll look after the wounded. They'll also see the civilian dead dealt with in a proper Christian manner, for all that they were traitors. We look after our own dead and wounded, of course. Oh, I almost forgot. Captain Mimms says you're most welcome to stay with him for what's left of the night. It's a bit dark to go back to Aylsham or wherever on your own. Better to leave it until tomorrow. I'd guess midnight isn't more than two hours away by now.'

29

ADAM'S HOUSE WAS NEVER SO BUSY AGAIN AS IT WAS OVER THE NEXT two days. Charles arrived on the first morning just before noon. After the fighting was over the night before, he'd given up his temporary cavalry mount with considerable relief. Then he'd ridden to Holt with Captain Mimms in the dog-cart.

'I managed to hire a horse from the White Lion in Holt to take me to Mosserton Hall,' he told Adam. 'I wanted to give Lady Alice the news, so that she could send her people back to their usual duties. I've come now on a beast from the Mosserton stables. One of our grooms will return the hired horse.'

'You're becoming quite the rider,' Adam said. 'So, what news do you have?'

'The most important news is that my backside is never going to be the same. I hope you realise that, Bascom.'

Adam made a noise something like "Pfaff!"

'Get to the point, Scudamore,' he said. 'I am quite unconcerned about the state of your posterior, now or in the future. What happened last night? That's all that matters to me.'

Charles was going to continue teasing the doctor, but he noticed the gleam in his eye that indicated rising anger. Time to get down to serious business.

Over the next thirty minutes or so, Charles related all he had done the day before. How he had ridden to Norwich, sought out General Gorras's headquarters and been amazed to be taken at once to the general himself.

'Impressive man. Didn't want me to waste time on explanations or excuses. Told me he'd been expecting a message from you and I should deliver it at once. He listened carefully, asked no questions and called his aide de camp at once to carry his orders to the relevant officer.'

Adam permitted himself a small smile. Charles had obviously been sceptical about even seeing the general, let alone finding him ready to take immediate action. Perhaps next time he'd have more faith.

A troop of dragoons must have been standing by, because they were on their way northwards within thirty minutes.

'I don't know what got into my head,' Charles said, 'but I insisted on going with them. My own horse wasn't up to going further, of course, so they lent me a huge animal called Dancer. By God, Bascom, I hope I never have such a ride again. I spent the whole time trying to stay on the animal's back and not look down. I've never been at the top of a ship's mast in a storm, but I swear it must feel much the same.'

The Battle of Baconsthorpe Castle. That's what he and Mimms had christened the five minutes of fighting. It took longer for Charles to tell Adam what had happened than the actual affair had lasted. The outcome was the total collapse of the planned rising. They'd rounded up all the ringleaders — at least, all they could find who were still alive — and arrested about forty others who had been stupid enough to join in this supposed revolution. Around a dozen of the rioters had been injured and seven or eight were dead. He wasn't sure exactly how many.

'One came for me with a knife,' Charles said, 'so I shot at him with my pistol.' He was concocting a good story to tell Miss LaSalle.

'Did you kill him?'

'I don't know. He just disappeared.'

'You almost certainly did then. A pistol ball at close range would throw a man flat on his back, as well as making a fine mess of wherever it hit.'

Charles wasn't sure he liked that conclusion. Maybe he'd wait and see how Sophia reacted. She might not relish the thought that he'd been responsible for someone's death. On the other hand, if he wanted to appear to be a hero . . .

'Did you hear anything of Professor Panacea or that fellow Gort?'

'No, Panacea wasn't amongst them, nor any man of around thirty with dark hair and a pockmarked face. They must either have escaped in the confusion or not been there in the first place.'

'Hmm. I can believe that of Panacea, but I was almost certain Gort would be there. He's the driving force behind this business, you see.'

'Not Panacea?'

'No. If I'm right, Panacea thought he was using Gort and his band of thugs for his own purposes. In fact, it was the other way around.' Adam shook his head as if to clear that thought away. 'No matter. Go on with your tale. At least I was right in my estimation of what these rebels planned to do once they had armed themselves.'

'Armed was hardly the word,' Charles said. 'The dragoon captain reckoned very few, if any, had ever seen a musket up close and none knew how to load or fire one. A few had pistols or old blunderbusses. One of those killed a trooper. Such damage as they did with their fine, French muskets was limited to using them as clubs. Most of the rabble only had knives or pitchforks.'

'How many had gathered at Baconsthorpe? I couldn't decide if this was to be the sole focus of this revolution. Maybe Gort wanted it to be more of a fuse to start things off. That's most likely the answer. They'd march to Norwich, picking up others along the way, then join with a contingent from the city.'

'It was getting too dark for me to have any idea of numbers,' Charles said. 'The ground was so uncertain you had to keep your eyes on where you were going. There were dips and ditches everywhere, lots filled with water. That old castle had a moat as well. Several fugitives jumped in to escape capture, I believe, and rather fewer got out again. The captain of the dragoons told me he thought around a hundred to a hundred and fifty men had assembled. It wasn't much more than a mob. Most ran away as soon as they saw us coming.'

'Even a mob can start something serious. Have you heard ought of what has been going on in Norwich?'

'Nothing. I'm going to return there as soon as I leave Aylsham.'

Peter was the next arrival, soon after two. As ever, he was eager for news and gossip. Word of the events of the night had already spread about the immediate area. No one knew what to make of such a happening and so it caused more confusion than concern. Some dismissed it as little more than another riot against the high price of grain. Others nodded their heads and claimed innovations in farming were forcing poor labouring families out of work. Few gave any credence to the notion of an attempt to overthrow king and constitution.

That much Peter knew and relayed to Adam. What he didn't know was what had really taken place. Like all the others whom Adam had sent here and there at his bidding, he had seen only a part of the picture. What he wanted was to understand it all.

'What were these men doing at Baconsthorpe?' he asked. 'Come on, Bascom, out with it. You must have known what was going to happen or you wouldn't have been issuing orders like some tin-pot general.'

'So far as I understand, they were there to get weapons and powder. According to Scudamore, the dragoons captured two farm carts loaded with muskets and shot.'

'Where did those come from, in heaven's name? The French? But how . . . of course, the smugglers. That's why it had to be here they assembled. Too risky to take the weapons into Norwich and get everyone together there.'

'According to one of the prisoners, they did plan to march on Norwich. If all had gone as they wished, they would have numbered more than a hundred before then. Along the way they would collect more malcontents and arm them too. By the time they reached Norwich, their numbers should have grown large enough to overwhelm any opposition.'

'Fools! Did they imagine they could be like travelling players? Marching along, full of pomp and swagger, and expecting to draw a crowd to follow them?'

'I don't think so. Someone planned this with care. There are a good many groups of radicals and dissidents about here. Most would have known this was going to happen. They'd be ready to join in as soon as the group reached them. There would also be men waiting in Norwich for the sign that their revolution had begun. That's what is making me anxious now. If I'm right about what that sign was to be, it may have been prevented. If not, those in the city may still cause an uprising, even though the rural groups have been prevented from joining them.'

'Who was behind it? Was it this quack fellow? Panacea?'

'Peter Gort, I think. I still don't know who Panacea is or what he was doing behind the mask of his role as a so-called medical expert. He may have had a hand in what happened, but something tells me he's probably as surprised today as the rest of us.'

30

ADAM HAD TO WAIT UNTIL THE NEXT DAY FOR DEFINITE NEWS FROM Norwich. It came in the form of a smart young lieutenant with a message from General Gorras.

'General's compliments, sir.' The lieutenant stood to attention, almost as if he were speaking to the general himself. 'I am to tell you that all is now calm in the city. Thanks to your timely warning, he says, he was able to send a message to the mayor, who mobilised the constables to search everywhere the Duke of York was expected to go. They soon found what they were seeking. Someone had hidden six barrels of powder under the wooden stand built for His Royal Highness to review the Loyal Volunteers. When they found it, it was ready with fuses laid. Best of all, the general says, they seized two men who were waiting to put matches to those fuses. It won't be long before they tell everything they know so that all the other conspirators can be rounded up.

'General Gorras also says you will understand he has many duties that must keep him in Norwich today. The Duke of York's visit is to go ahead as planned. No sense in alarming the population. The conspirators wanted to cause disruption through an attack on the King's second son and the general says it's best to deny them both. I am to tell you he plans to give himself the pleasure of calling on you tomorrow, sir, if that will be convenient. He wants to tell you the rest of the details himself. He'll also be bringing another gentleman with him, but he didn't tell me that gentleman's name.'

Adam agreed it would be quite convenient for the general to call the next day and sent the lieutenant back to Norwich. What he wanted most was to send a message to Mossterton to ask Lady Alice to come as soon as possible — and preferably alone. That was going to have to wait, it seemed. In the meantime, there were other problems to be dealt with.

Where was Panacea? If he was trying to make his escape, where was he heading? London? It would be easy to hide in such a huge city. Overseas? Adam had included one possible destination in his warning to General Gorras. What if it turned out to be wrong?

Then there was Gort. Charles said they were sure he wasn't amongst the dead, the wounded or the prisoners taken at Baconsthorpe. Where was he then? He must have been at the muster since the whole thing was his idea. He'd not give up the chance to supervise this final stage, nor allow someone else to lead the "troops" in triumph into Norwich. He therefore must have escaped, unlike that lout Huggins. Where would he go? There were still the three murders to be solved. One of them anyway. Adam was sure he knew who was responsible for the other two.

Adam gave up trying to solve these niggling puzzles and turned to more immediate matters. Who was this other gentleman who was coming with the general? Wicken? Could he have reached Norwich so quickly? Hadn't his letter said he was unable to leave London for the present? Whoever it was, there was the question of how best to tell his servants about tomorrow's visitors without throwing them into a panic? Hannah had been reduced to a quivering mass of excitement by the arrival of the handsome young lieutenant in his red uniform jacket. What she would make of a general and his escort Adam could not imagine.

Adam remembered the rest of that day as a whirlwind of cleaning, scrubbing and polishing. For most of it, he hid in his library, trying to turn a deaf ear to the noises from the other side of the door. He couldn't see anything wrong with his house as it was, but when he'd said as much to Mrs Brigstone, she'd regarded him with something close to pity.

'If visitors think a house looks ill cared for, it isn't the owner they blame, is it? It's the servants. You go into your library, Master, and leave all else to us. That way everyone will be happy.'

The trouble was that Adam didn't feel all that happy — or not as happy as he thought he should. He had been proved right about what had been brewing in the area, the revolt had been stopped and most of the ringleaders taken. Shouldn't that make him satisfied, if not overjoyed? It didn't though. He couldn't be content until both Gort and Panacea had been captured. That brought his thoughts full circle, back to those irritating loose ends.

Panacea, Adam felt sure, hadn't been involved with the events at Baconsthorpe and had almost certainly never left Norwich — at least until he made good his escape. That was what was so maddening. Why had the man run away? It made little sense. There was no proof Panacea was involved in either the rebellion or the attempt on the life of the Duke of York. He could claim he was what he had always been — a travelling quack doctor peddling a dietary regime and a patented nostrum to go with it. Yet he had disappeared even before the gathering at Baconsthorpe. Did he get wind of what was about to happen? Did he fear he would be dragged into it somehow? His links to the smugglers had been used, that was certain, but what else might link him to sedition?

Peter Gort was a different matter. William's experience with him and his bullies had proved his link with the radicals. One, at least, of The Disciples, Henry Huggins — 'Pigface' in William's account — had died in the Baconsthorpe fight. There was little doubt Gort was a traitor and had left Norwich to take the lead of this ragtag rebellion. He had to run, but where?

Adam sighed. So much for trying to work it out for himself. Wouldn't it be much better to wait until General Gorras came? He might be able to shed some light on Gort's involvement that would explain both his disappearance and where he might have gone.

~

General Gorras arrived the next day shortly before noon. To the great disappointment of Adam's servants, he wasn't wearing military dress, nor had he come with an escort of cavalrymen. Only two men came with him. The young lieutenant whom he had sent to Adam the previous day and Sir Percival Wicken, fresh from London the evening before and beaming from ear to ear.

After the servants had collected coats and hats, the general told the lieutenant to wait for him in the servants' quarters, much to Hannah's delight. The other two joined Adam in his library, first to take coffee and then to be free to talk openly.

'You've done it again, Bascom,' Wicken said, putting down his cup. 'I ask you to undertake a small task related to a missing Swiss professor. You uncover a plot to kill a member of the Royal Family and an attempt to overthrow the government.'

'Whatever did happen to that Swiss, Sir Percival?' Adam asked. 'Did you ever find him?'

'Plain 'Wicken' will do very well, Doctor. I am most grateful for the honour bestowed upon me by His Majesty, but it makes for such a mouthful. The Swiss? Long dead, I'm afraid. In many ways, he was the beginning of it. I see you are both waiting for me to explain, so I'd better begin at the beginning.'

Wicken's tale proved to be both lengthy and complex. Added to that, Adam interrupted many times with questions and explanations from his point of view, while General Gorras added comments and details of his own. After a time, it all became somewhat muddled. This, however, was the gist of it.

About six months before, a British spy in Switzerland had reported that a professor at the university in Geneva had gone missing. The man was notorious for his denunciations of the revolution in France. A while later, the rumour went around that the professor was being held by the French authorities, but whether he had been kidnapped or had somehow strayed across the border was unclear. It's wasn't evident what the French wanted him for either, other than to silence his criticisms. The authorities in Geneva began demanding his return with some vigour, for they feared the worst. In reply, the French authorities denied all knowledge of the man.

Things that happen without any obvious reason cause spies to become alert. Why risk the anger of the Geneva Syndics to silence a single critic? There were plenty of others throughout Europe, many of them far more influential. Several British agents in Switzerland and France now set out to discover what was going on and quickly confirmed that the professor had been arrested. He was being held in the house of the mayor of the little town of Evian-les-Bains, on the south shore of Lake Geneva. This also seemed odd. Why was he not taken to Paris or some much larger place where the French could question him? Everyone went on the alert, waiting to see what happened next.

They did not have long to wait. The professor appeared again, leaving the mayor's custody after only two or three weeks, but did not return to Geneva. Another oddity then. He claimed to be on his way to seek asylum in England. At least, that was what he told anyone who asked. Asylum from whom? The man was Swiss and had been living in Geneva for many years. Why didn't he return home on his release? He would have been safe enough there. The Syndics would make sure of that.

British agents tracked him across southern Germany to the Low Countries. There they lost him. One moment he was in plain view on his way to the Channel coast; the next he had gone and no one knew where. They had a single clue, which they found when they searched the room he had hired at an inn in Rotterdam. In a drawer of the pot-cupboard beside the bed was a torn piece of paper bearing what looked to have been an address ending in "Norwich". The innkeeper swore no one else had occupied that room for many weeks. Trade was awful, he said, and all due to the war. The paper seemed fresh so everyone assumed the Swiss, whatever his reason for going to England, was heading not for London but for Norwich.

'That was when I contacted you, Bascom,' Wicken said. 'The messages sent from our spies had made me more than suspicious of this man. If he were now in England, which seemed most likely, he would become the business of those working for me. I alerted my men in Norwich, but they found no trace. Thanks to your two letters, I was able at last to discover the answer. Gorras here would have sent the second letter on to me, only he knew by then I was on my way north. I read it last night.

'The name gave it away. The "Mr Morris Dewmark" you wrote of was our man. His true name is Maurice Duparc and he's a notorious and cunning French spy. It's typical of him to enjoy making fun of us by using a pseudonym so close to his real name, merely pronouncing it somewhat in an English way. When you wrote that Mr Dewmark had transformed himself into Professor Panacea his plan grew plain at last. This morning, soon after dawn, my men went to the rooms where he had been living, but our bird had flown. What else they found there I will tell you later.'

Much of what Duparc had told poor Betsy Wormald and the people of Melton Constable was true then. He did have a French father and an English mother, both dead now. He was an actor by profession. Not in the exalted company he claimed, but in a series of provincial, travelling groups in the north of France. He was also well known to be a notorious womaniser. Duparc had come close to being executed himself barely a year ago when he abducted and seduced — raped would be a better word — the fifteen-year-old daughter of a nobleman. Her parents were destined for the guillotine and she was destined for the bed of one of the revolutionary leaders. That villain was not at all amused to discover Duparc had denied him the pleasure of taking the girl's maidenhead by taking it himself.

'Whether the Swiss died in prison or was killed there we do not know.' Wicken was into his stride now. He liked being the centre of attention. 'Either way, Duparc took his identity and used it to travel through Europe without hindrance. Once he reached the Channel coast, he evaded those following him and slipped into England. We don't know whether he used the same alias, or dropped it and became someone else. Whatever he did, he entered this realm and made his way not to Norwich, but to the village of Melton Constable. Why there, I have no idea. Perhaps because it was not far from the city, yet still remote.'

'I think I may be able to explain.' Adam said. 'The main reason, I'm sure, was to bring his fluency in speaking English back to the level needed. I was told he walked around the village on most days talking to anyone and everyone. Actors learn to imitate by listening to others. He must have already chosen his long-term disguise as Professor Panacea, a travelling quack, so he needed to conceal his French accent. Many quacks claim to be foreign, even if they aren't, but the last thing this fellow wanted was to be recognised as French. There was a stronger reason too. He had to establish a secure route by which information and people could pass to and from France. Someone — a predecessor perhaps? — had given him the name of the leader of the most powerful gang of smugglers on the north coast. Dewmark therefore went around asking how to find the man. "Black Jack" Bretherton will do anything for enough money, so he would be ideal and would have links with France anyway. Bretherton's gang could carry messages themselves, or take them out to sea and hand them over to a passing French privateer.'

'By George, you have the truth of it!' Wicken clapped his hands in pleasure.

'That will be Panacea's — I mean Duparc's — route back to France too, I'm sure,' Adam added. 'I've already written to ask my brother Giles to seal off his part of the coast. He's a local magistrate covering several coastal villages north of here, General. While a small boat could put off from many places, my guess is that Duparc is heading for a rendezvous with a privateer. If so, there aren't that many places with water deep enough close inshore to allow a ship with such a deep draught to come in close enough to meet a rowing boat. The best bet is Weybourne.'

Wicken and General Gorras exchanged glances and the general asked Adam to call a servant to send the lieutenant in at once. Then, too impatient to stay in his chair, he rose and met him at the door. Moments later, they heard the sound of hoofs outside. Hannah would be so annoyed.

'I have sent him to Great Yarmouth, Doctor,' Gorras explained, 'to carry a message to the senior naval officer there. Pray continue, Wicken.'

'Where was I? Duparc is at Melton Constable. His job done there, he turns to the next phase. He's an actor, so it must have been second nature for him to leave off one role — Mr Morris Dewmark — and take up that of Professor Panacea. In many ways that alias was a stroke of genius. It gave him the freedom to wander without suspicion, as well as a suitable disguise for the visits paid to him by those supplying information. They could pay for a bottle of his preparation and hand over a note or whisper a few words at the same time. If they had more to tell, they could request a personal consultation with the great man.'

'His performance was excellent,' Adam said. 'Mr Lassimer told me he would have convinced anyone who lacked a thorough medical training. That was why my poor friend was treated so roughly. He asked a question which exposed the emptiness behind the mask. Panacea — Duparc — couldn't risk losing such a convincing disguise.'

'Interesting,' Wicken said. 'I wonder if they forced the Swiss professor to write his script in hope of earning his release? That would account for it being so good. He might also have been the one who concocted the potions the quack sold.'

'Lassimer analysed the contents of a bottle that I told my servant to buy,' Adam said. 'It held cheap gin, heavily laced with opium, extract of coca leaf, some sugar and a whole range of herbs and spices to add an exotic flavour. That mixture wouldn't have aided anyone's health. The original one must have been far less potent. I imagine Duparc tried it, liked its effect and gradually grew unable to live without it. It is well known that those who become dependent on opium, for example, need larger and larger amounts to produce the effect they long for — until it kills them. What Duparc was selling recently must have been more or less what he now needed. It would have produced a startling effect on adults. I dread to imagine what it would do to any child to whom it was given.'

'More deaths to set down to his account?'

'Quite probably.'

Wicken had little more to add after that. Duparc, he said, had always intended to stay in and around Norwich. It was well known the French were planning an invasion. If the Norfolk coast was not the first choice for that, as some claimed, it would still be an ideal place to mount a diversionary attack, so the French wanted people collecting information about suitable landing places. Wicken's men had confirmed that Panacea also kept in close touch with radical groups in the area, in case they might prove useful when the invasion came. Quite why he had turned to organising a feeble attempt at an uprising was still unclear.

'He didn't,' Adam said. 'That wasn't his idea and I doubt he even knew of it until it was too late to prevent it happening. He was used by one of his followers, a fellow called Peter Gort. He was the hothead trying to set our country on the path to revolution.'

'Was he also the one who planned the assassination of the Duke of York?' That was General Gorras.

'I expect so. He had a deep hatred of everyone he classed as being amongst the elite, because of what happened to his father. Whether Gort senior was a thief or a wronged man, we'll never know. It's enough that Gort believed his father's noble employer had treated him unjustly. After he was dismissed as a thief, the father killed himself. That threw his family into the workhouse. This was to be Gort's revenge. What better signal for a city-wide riot and uprising could there be than killing the King's son?'

Wicken smiled, not at the thought of a royal assassination, but what he was about to share. 'He'll not have another chance, Bascom. That was the piece of news I left aside a moment ago. When my men broke into Duparc's rooms they found the body of a man, dark haired, bad pockmarks on one cheek —'

'Gort!'

'We didn't know who it was, but now you have been able to tell us. He'd been stabbed more than a dozen times. His body hadn't yet started to smell, so they reckoned he must have been killed not long before — probably as soon as he reached Norwich in his flight.'

Adam shook his head. 'So Duparc finally discovered how he had been betrayed. Gort must have escaped from the confusion at Baconsthorpe and ridden like the wind for Norwich, hoping he might still supervise the attempt on His Royal Highness's life. He probably went to Duparc — Panacea — for help and refuge, thinking Duparc would be pleased by what he had done. Naturally, Duparc was furious, since, thanks to Gort, all his patient work was ruined. Duparc was a spy and what the French call an agent provocateur, I believe. He had no wish to provoke open rebellion so far in advance of the planned landing. No wonder he stabbed Gort with such violence. Starting riots and uprisings now would allow time for them to be put down. He wanted them to happen only when there were French troops on hand to take advantage of the chaos. Thanks to Gort, the authorities had been warned in advance. That accounts for Duparc dropping everything and trying to take his escape route back to France.' He sighed heavily. 'So many deaths for nothing.'

'Without your help, there would have been many more, Doctor. These are violent times. Come, we will leave this poor man to get some rest, Gorras. He has been ill recently and you can see his arm is still in a splint. Farewell for the moment, Doctor. Both I and your country owe you a profound debt. You have many friends at court who will make sure His Majesty hears of the part you have played in snuffing out this treachery. His Royal Highness, the Duke of York, already knows of it, of course. It is not every day a country physician prevents a rebellion and saves the life of the King's son. Few generals could claim as much, could they, Gorras?'

'By no means. Nor admirals either. Good-day to you, Doctor. It has been a brief meeting, but a most pleasant one. Perhaps we may be able to renew our acquaintance at some happier time in the future?'

'One thing more, Bascom,' Wicken said, as he rose to leave. 'We cannot prevent news of the fight at Baconsthorpe being reported everywhere, since too many people were involved. What we will do is make sure the loyal newspapers report it in the right way — as an attempt by hotheads and traitors to cause trouble. An endeavour frustrated by prompt action by the military and local loyalists. We will also keep your name from being mentioned. How could you be involved? You are confined to your home and have been for many days past. Believe me, you are too useful to us behind the scenes to risk anyone else becoming aware of your activities.'

'What about the attempt on the Duke of York's life?'

'It never happened. Two local men were found to be in possession of a large quantity of gunpowder and could not explain why. Later it was discovered they were in league with the rebels. That will be enough to get a sympathetic jury to convict them of sedition and seal their fate.'

'Very neat.'

'Thank you. Yes, another thing. I would be grateful if you could persuade your friends and relatives to cure their natural tendency to boast of your prowess. If they spread the word about, our efforts will be in vain. Sadly, Bascom, keeping your involvement secret will also mean your principal reward must wait a little. It will come, I assure you, but only when it can be linked to something that will not suggest your true role. What, I have yet to work out.'

31

'I ALWAYS THINK THE OTHER ROOMS IN THIS PLACE ARE TOO LARGE for every day,' Lady Alice said. 'This is much better. Shall we take tea first? Afterwards, Dr Bascom can tell us everything we want to know.'

Lady Alice had invited everyone to her home to learn the final elements in the puzzle, so it was somehow fitting that the first journey Adam made from his home should be to Mossterton Hall. His broken arm had meant he had to bring William and let him drive, while he and Peter rode in style, but that was a minor point.

Her ladyship had wanted to invite Miss LaSalle too, but Charles offered instead to convey the details to Norwich himself. It was too far for her to come unaccompanied and Mrs Bascom was best kept away from learning any more than she must. Adam had already prepared a note for Charles to bear to his mother. While he trusted Miss LaSalle to be discrete, his mother was another matter. She had too many friends in the city who delighted in exchanging gossip. In his note, he had threatened her with the anger of Viscount Townsend and 'other persons highly placed at court' if she did not remain silent. That, he hoped, should be enough to prevent her revealing what little she knew about his involvement.

Thus, only five of them — Adam, Lady Alice, Peter, Charles and Ruth — were seated in this room their hostess had called the Small Parlour. A cosy room and not much bigger than any in Adam's house, which made it tiny by Mossterton standards. It lay on the south side of the house, where it caught the best of the light. Since it was close to noon, the sun was streaming in through the large windows and reflecting back off the pier mirrors between them. But what most dazzled Adam was the rich hue of the damask-hung walls contrasting with some of the finest furniture pieces he had ever seen. How could her ladyship bear to leave this behind?

She must have noticed where he was looking and guessed his thoughts. 'Much of the furniture in this room is around a hundred years old or more,' she said. 'Too old for Sir Daniel's nephew, who prides himself on his strict adherence to the latest fashion. It is all mahogany now, not the walnut and yew-wood that you see here. I was happy to agree to his suggestion I take the oldest pieces away with me.'

She was wearing much more homely clothes today than was usual for her, though fine enough, in all conscience. She would never consent to put on anything dowdy, but today's dress and petticoat were worsted and linen rather than cotton and silk. To Adam, admittedly biased, she could be no less beautiful however she was dressed.

The party exchanged small-talk while tea was being served as was the convention. Ruth and Peter began to discuss the best ways to tell certain families of plants apart, but Lady Alice told them all topics must remain of general interest. They could indulge themselves in specialisms later.

'All the paintings here go with the house, I'm afraid,' Lady Alice said. 'I do have a few of my own, which I keep in my bedroom and dressing room. Being a widow is quite disconcerting at times. When your husband is alive, the house and all the contents are yours because they are his. Afterwards, you become merely a caretaker, keeping all in good order for the next owner.'

'That's hardly fair, Aunt.' Ruth was determined to be peevish after being baulked of her botanical discussion. 'You know you could continue to enjoy it all for the rest of your life, if you wished to do so.'

'Which I do not, as you very well know, Ruth. It's no use trying to get onto that subject again. The Doctor and Mr Lassimer have no wish to suffer your pointless complaints.'

'Yes, be quiet, Sister,' Charles said. 'I'm longing to hear the full story of this affair.'

'It's all very well for you . . .'

Her aunt silenced Ruth with a look and turned to Adam. 'As I believe they say in certain theatres, Doctor, your audience awaits you with some impatience. Will you start? I suggest you begin by reminding us how this matter first arose.'

'When I was asked to keep my eyes and ears open for a missing professor from Switzerland, my lady.'

The beginning of Adam's tale owed a good deal to the one Wicken had told, leaving out the overt references to spying and 'our agent in . . .' Not until he reached the point where Mr Morris Dewmark, or Maurice Duparc, French spy, came to Melton Constable did he add his own discoveries.

'You say he was there to polish his command of our language, Doctor?'

'That is what I believe, my lady. Also, to find his feet in England. So far as I can understand it, he had not been in this country for many years. To be convincing in the role of Professor Panacea, he needed to be able to pass for an Englishman.'

'Why? Couldn't Panacea have been German, or Italian, or Swiss, or even Dutch? I can see French might be more difficult. Yet even that might have passed without too much notice?' With Ruth, you rarely got far through a tale without her wanting to argue.

'He must have been something of a perfectionist, Miss Scudamore. Most travelling quacks claim another nationality — it makes them seem exotic — but underneath the façade nearly all are English. To play an Englishman pretending to be, say, a Swiss, it helps to be able to pass for an Englishman first.'

Ruth subsided, though it was plain she wished to argue the

matter further. Adam hadn't caught the look her aunt had directed at her, but he knew it was there. That young woman must be the despair of many a hostess.

'Whatever the reason, Duparc — I ought to stick to one name for him, I suppose. It's difficult when I encountered him in so many different roles — Duparc wandered around talking to the local people and listening to their patterns of speech. That was when he made his first bad mistake. Sir Percival said the man was an inveterate womaniser. Betsy Wormald, by all accounts, was unusually beautiful, so it must have been like a moth finding a flame. Duparc never intended to marry her, of course. His proposal of matrimony was no more than his stock-in-trade script for seducing innocent girls —'

'How despicable! That's the trouble with men. They're all quite untrustworthy.'

'Even the Doctor and Mr Lassimer, Ruth?'

Despite the gentle tone, Lady Alice's eyes were signalling a final warning. This time Ruth realised her danger.

'Oh . . . no, of course I didn't mean . . . it's just . . . sorry . . .'

'One day you'll learn to keep your mouth closed.' Charles couldn't resist joining in too. 'Do what I do —'

'Which is generally nothing of any use. Be quiet, both of you. Save your squabbles for another time. Now, Doctor, please continue.'

'Yes, your ladyship. Duparc's action was indeed both reprehensible and unkind in the highest degree. If I call it a mistake it is because of what it led to. Betsy Wormald was feather-brained, but she was still an honest, wholesome girl, brought up in a Christian environment. Once she realised she was with child, her only wish was to marry the father in the proper way. That was the signal for Duparc to drop the role of Mr Morris Dewmark, disappear from Melton Constable and reappear in Norwich as Professor Panacea, Healer Extraordinaire — an entirely different person.'

'What I don't understand,' Peter said, 'is why he used a name in Melton Constable so like his own. Wasn't that bound to be dangerous?'

'Wicken thinks he was displaying typical French arrogance. I'm not convinced. It's hard to remember to be someone else the whole time. The role of Professor Panacea was different. He could put that on when he went on stage and set it aside afterwards. What he needed in Melton Constable was a name for every day. Something he would respond to without thinking, if it was called out in the street. The one he chose was exactly right for that purpose. I expect he assumed the village folk would be too rustic to see how odd it was for someone who said he was half French. Still, none of them would know a word of any language save English, I imagine. He could have called himself 'Helmut Vladimir Juan Busoni' and they would have seen nothing odd in it. The only thing that mattered was that there should be no link between the stranger in Melton Constable and Professor Panacea afterwards. Few, if any, would go to Norwich to see his lectures. Too expensive. None would expect to see him in a different guise. If you don't envisage seeing someone, you might well walk past without recognising him — unless you knew him very well.'

'Which Betsy Wormald did.'

'Yes. It was her ill fortune and his when she met him in the street. If she hadn't bumped into him, Duparc would have left her alone. It was even worse luck to find him walking with someone she knew. When he cut her dead, she had a way to reach him. Even though she never managed to get a message to Panacea via Peter Gort — that was the man with Duparc — the meeting proved her death sentence. Duparc knew the girl wanted to put things right in her life and was therefore desperate to force him into marriage. If he refused outright, or simply ignored her again, she might well tell people the truth. That risk was too great for Duparc to overlook. I'm sure he was well aware that Norwich is full of government spies and informers. If what Betsy knew about Panacea reached any of them, Duparc's mission was finished, so he had to silence her. He arranged a meeting in a private place and strangled her on the spot.'

'He killed her? Duparc did? Then did he kill the others too?' Charles was confused. 'What had they done to him?'

'Nothing. I'll get to them, but you've hit on my obvious mistake.

At the start, I assumed all three murders were the work of the same man. Even when I could not work out how this could be so, I persisted in that belief. The truth didn't occur to me until it was almost too late. There were two separate murderers, neither aware of what the other had done.'

'I knew from the start Panacea was a fraud, but I hadn't seen him as a killer.' Peter had been quiet for some time. 'I still don't understand why he had to kill Betsy. Couldn't he move away somewhere else, pick a new role and go on with what he was doing?'

'There wasn't time before the hoped-for invasion. He'd been instructed to base himself in Norwich to pass on all he could about suitable landing places to the north. He couldn't go anywhere else without failing in the main task he had been given. He also operated something like a post office for other French spies and informers in the area. They sent messages to him and he sent them on to France via the smugglers. It takes time to set up something like that. You can't wander off somewhere else and continue as if nothing had happened. I imagine pride came into it too.'

'He didn't want his masters to know he'd failed because of his womanising?' Peter said.

'Certainly not! I very much doubt his masters on the other side of the channel would show him any mercy if they knew.'

'He didn't want to dismantle the system he'd established?'

'It was more than either of those, I believe. Duparc was an actor and actors love to be on stage, enjoying the applause and the admiration. You yourself said he was a fine speaker, Lassimer.'

'He was. I'd say he adored being in front of that audience. I thought he was no more than a born performer in the field of selling imaginary cures. Now I understand he was more than that.'

'Much more. I suspect what I called the "post office" was in place before Duparc came. He added the role of Panacea. It wasn't only to make it easier for him to move about without suspicion. The main reason for that disguise was to put him back on the centre of a stage, playing a leading role and hearing the applause his performance generated. The man was delivering the performance of his life and he was too proud of his art to see it all ruined for the sake of a woman. Remember, she was nothing to him once her conquest had been achieved.'

Ruth made an inarticulate noise, the effort to stay silent proving almost too much for her.

'You said Duparc made two grave errors, Doctor,' Lady Alice said, trying to rescue her niece by moving the conversation on. 'What was the second?'

'Peter Gort. Panacea must have found him somehow, probably through a radical group in the city. He thought Gore would make a good assistant. Someone to fetch and carry. What he got was a 'true believer', a hot-head and a zealot. Gort knew Panacea was here to prepare for the invasion. What he wanted was someone to start his longed-for revolution. Neither understood the other. In time, Gort lost patience and decided to start the revolution on his own.'

Adam was about to explain the reason for Gort's hatred of the rich and powerful when Lady Alice asked him to pause. They all needed a break to stretch their legs and attend to other necessities. The servants also needed time to clear away the used tea things.

'You must stay to dinner,' she told Peter and Adam. 'I have had beds made ready for you, so you can spend the night here afterwards. Spring is not yet so far advanced that it is light far into the evening. The roads are too dangerous to travel after dark.'

Adam was mightily relieved. He was already tired and there was a good part of the story still to come. Would Peter agree? He would. The chance to tell his many customers — in a casual way, naturally — that he had recently been an overnight guest at Mossterton Hall was too great a prize to be turned down.

32

HALF-AN-HOUR LATER

WHEN THEY REASSEMBLED, ADAM CONTINUED HIS EXPLANATION. HIS audience was eager to disentangle the remaining parts of the mystery. However tired he felt, he could not disappoint them.

'Peter Gort,' he began. 'Duparc, now calling himself Professor Panacea, used him as an emissary to local radical groups and to Black Jack's smugglers. When Gort lost patience with Panacea's reluctance to start an immediate revolution, that role put him in an ideal position to set his own plan in motion. He simply couldn't wait to see the destruction of rank and privilege. These were the people he felt had caused his father's suicide and ruined his family. If Panacea was too cowardly or indolent to carry it out, he would take over. Both were fantasists. Duparc, the actor, relished the adulation and applause he earned as Professor Panacea and saw no reason to step aside from that role. It gave him the opportunity to carry out the tasks assigned to him, as well as feeding his vanity. Gort imagined himself as a revolutionary general, overthrowing all that he hated in English society.'

'Did neither know what the other was thinking?' Charles now took up the role of questioner. 'Didn't Panacea question what Gort was doing in his name? Didn't the French wonder what their spy was about when he asked for guns and gunpowder?'

'Panacea would have been fed reassuring lies by Gort. That is if he asked at all. Panacea — Duparc — struck me as arrogant and lazy, save in what most interested him. From his point of view things were proceeding well. I have no idea what his French masters thought. If I had been Gort, I would have concocted a story about needing to stockpile weapons and powder locally for use when the invasion came. I might even have suggested the local people who were expected to rise up and support their 'liberators' needed to be trained how to use muskets.'

'Would Gort have been clever enough to think of that?'

'I have no idea. He definitely showed a good deal of cunning and ability to organise.'

'So why would he need Panacea — I mean Duparc?'

'He didn't need him, but the Professor must have been useful, both as a way of screening his activities and to attract people who might be recruited to the cause. Following Duparc around also gave Gort the link to Bretherton and the smugglers.'

'But the rest of it was Gort alone?'

'Yes, I'm almost sure it was. Remember Gort had been in the army, before he deserted. He knew how to lead others to get the things he wanted done.'

'All these military matters seem to be taking us away from the point.' Lady Alice had been silent until now. Her sharp comment made Adam jump. 'You were going to tell us about the second two murders, Doctor, if you recall.'

'Indeed, your ladyship. The murder of the milk-seller's daughter and her young man were Gort's doing, I'm certain. The young man must have been drawn into one of the radical groups hereabouts. We know he was sharing revolutionary notions with his lady-love. He most likely knew about the plans for the gathering at Bacon-sthorpe Castle and couldn't resist dropping hints about the glittering future ahead. You'll recall he'd promised to marry the young woman and take her to start a new life in our former colonies in America. Unfortunately for him, she was a born gossip and couldn't keep it to herself. Word must have reached Gort that they were going to let the cat out of the bag. He was a fanatic, so two lives were nothing compared with the uncovering of his plans to transform Britain by revolution.'

'So, both Gort and Duparc — Panacea — were murderers?'

'That is how I see it, my lady. Both killed to keep their secrets safe.'

'Did they know the other had committed murder?'

'No. Gort could not know anything about Duparc's life before they met, save what he was told by Duparc himself and I don't imagine Duparc was proud of killing Miss Wormald. He may have thought it necessary, but there's no reason to believe he felt good about it. Only a madman enjoys committing murder.'

'Were either Duparc or Gort taken or killed at Baconsthorpe?'

'No, my lady. Duparc wasn't present. If I'm correct, he wouldn't even have known about it. If Gort was there, he got away in the confusion.'

'So, both murderers have escaped punishment?'

'One moment.' Charles had the orderly mind of a lawyer. 'You haven't explained about the plot to kill the Duke of York. Whose idea was that? Was Duparc party to it or not?'

Adam was growing more and more restless. He had been over all this with Wicken several times, before the great man had left to return to London. All he wanted now was to be able to forget the events of the past few weeks and get back to his proper business of doctoring.

'Gort's plan,' he said, '— remember all this is guesswork on my part — was to start a march on Norwich by disaffected rural artisans and labourers. They would meet at Baconsthorpe and head south, avoiding any places where they might meet real resistance. Along the way, they would pick up more adherents. At the same time, groups in Norwich would start the mob rioting there. Gort had convinced himself the poor would flock to join them, so, by the time they reached Norwich, they would be able to overwhelm what forces the mayor and city leaders could muster against them.'

'Numbers and confusion.' That was Peter.

'Exactly. Surprise too. Mob violence has a kind of momentum. The more it succeeds, the more people join in. If Norwich exploded into revolution, other cities would experience similar uprisings. Sheffield is known for its radicalism. Birmingham or Bristol might follow. The ultimate prize was London. It's not so long ago a single maniac, Lord George Gordon, started riots in London lasting several days.'

'Was that why Gort wanted to kill the Duke of York? To set off rioting against the King and his government?'

'That was opportunism. What Gort had envisaged, at first, as the signal for those bent on revolution in Norwich to start the riots, I don't know. When he heard the King's son was coming to review volunteers, he was quick to see the possibilities. He had gunpowder. If he could set off an explosion close to the royal party, maybe His Royal Highness would be killed or injured, along with many city dignitaries.'

'A large number of ordinary people as well.'

'You're right, of course, Scudamore. Yet I doubt that would have deflected Gort from his plan. Can you imagine a better signal to start a revolution than the death of a royal prince? Or anything calculated to produce more confusion than killing or maiming half the dignitaries of the county? Fortunately, General Gorras was able to warn the mayor and the gunpowder was discovered in time, along with the men who were to light the fuses.'

'All thanks to you,' Ruth said. 'You'll be a national hero, Doctor.'

'I won't, I'm very glad to say. Wicken says the government want to make as little of what has gone on here as they can. They'll portray the affray at Baconsthorpe as nothing more than local rioting against the price of grain or some such matter. There have been a good many of those recently and it'll be forgotten in a few days. An actual attack on His Royal Highness never took place and he insisted on going on with his engagements for the day. The discovery of the gunpowder will be put down to an amateurish attempt by one or two local malcontents to cause trouble. They'll be tried at the next assize and hung and it will all be over. In neither case will any mention be made of my involvement.

'Sir Percival also asked me to impress on you all the need to keep my name and involvement hidden. If word got about that I helped the government in this way, I would be of no more use to him.'

'You would also be in mortal danger,' Lady Alice added. 'Some of these radicals are violent men. None of us need to be told how Black Jack and his smugglers would deal with any threat to their safety.' She addressed her niece and nephew. 'If either of you breathe a hint of the doctor's actions to anyone else, you will answer to me.'

The look she gave them promised years of anguish as the reward for disobedience. Charles and Ruth swore to keep silent — and meant it.

'I'll make sure Miss LaSalle understands,' Charles said. 'Lassimer?'

'No one will learn of it from me, you can be sure.'

'Thank you all,' Adam said. 'I'm a physician, not a hero. All I want is to be allowed to get back to healing people as best I can.'

'You're a hero to us, Doctor.'

'Thank you, Miss Scudamore, but your praise isn't justified. As usual, I've stumbled through this problem by a mixture of luck and guesswork. Most of what I've told you I cannot prove. What I surmise is far more than what I can claim to know.'

Charles returned to tying up the loose ends. 'Do you know where Duparc and Gort are now, Doctor?'

'Gort is dead. Duparc escaped from Norwich and most likely headed for the coast to escape back to France.'

'I knew you hadn't finished the story!'

'Very well. Wicken told me his men discovered where Duparc had been lodging. They went there hoping to arrest him, but the bird had flown. However, they found the body of a young man, dead from stabs wounds.'

'Gort?'

'Peter Gort. Duparc must have realised at last how Gort had betrayed him to start his homespun revolution. Everything Duparc had set up was ruined. He would also know government men must be coming soon to drag him off to prison. I imagine he was furious, snatched up a knife and took his revenge at once on his treacherous subordinate. After that, he ran for it, using an escape route he had pre-planned in case of emergency. As I told Wicken and General Gorras, my guess would be this. He would have established a means of signalling to a pirate vessel or a privateer to come in close to shore so someone could row him out to the waiting ship. Weybourne seems the most likely place. There's deep water inshore there and it's a fishing village, where rowing boats or small skiffs would be plentiful.'

'Now, I suppose, he will have too great a start to catch.'

'That all depends on how soon he could contact a suitable ship to come to take him back to France. It's bound to be a matter of chance whether he's taken. Will our luck be better than his?'

'Will it?'

Adam sighed. 'You know, I'm so tired. Can't we leave this for another day?'

'Stop playing with us, Doctor.' Lady Alice shook her fist at him. 'You'll make me cross with you too.'

'But it's true!'

'When I was small . . .' she was not much over five feet tall now and slender as a lath, '. . . my brothers used to tease me without mercy. Until, that is, I climbed onto a chair one day and dared my eldest brother — that's the father of these two — to stand and face me.'

'My father is almost six feet tall,' Charles said, 'and very solid.'

'Fat,' Ruth corrected him.

'Not then,' Lady Alice said. 'Your father was athletic in his youth. Of course, he came up to me at once, grinning like a monkey and eager to continue the game. He forgot that a small, pointed fist like mine, driven hard into the right spot, would hurt a great deal.'

'He had a black eye for two weeks or more,' Charles said. 'He's still proud of it, as well as the sister who gave it to him. Be warned, Doctor. Our aunt's bite is even worse than her bark . . . and you rarely get a second warning.' They were all laughing now.

'Very well.' Adam held his hands up in a gesture of surrender.

'As soon as I mentioned my suspicion, General Gorras sent his aide de camp to Great Yarmouth at the gallop.'

'Have you heard the outcome?'

'A messenger arrived shortly before Lassimer came to drive me here. As luck would have it, a frigate, HMS Arcturus, brought His Royal Highness from London. He is travelling elsewhere after Norwich and will not have further use for it. It was still in harbour awaiting a contingent of extra crew members to be brought by a press gang. When he received the general's message, the commodore ordered it to sea on the next tide. The captain's orders were to sail north along the coast to try to intercept any ship which looked as if it ought not to be there.'

'Did they find one?'

'I am told they sighted a French privateer off the coast at Happisburgh. After a short fight, the privateer struck its colours and surrendered. No match for a frigate in speed or firepower. They found Duparc on board. I imagine he is now on his way to prison.'

'I hope they hang him for what he did to Betsy Wormald.' The nodding of heads showed Ruth spoke for them all. 'Callous brute!'

'He's murdered two people at least,' Adam said. 'He was a spy as well. I'm sure he'll deny any involvement in the attempted uprising and the botched assassination of the Duke of York, though I doubt it will do him any good. They'd hang him several times over if they could.'

They were all silent for a little after that. Then Lady Alice decided it was time to lighten their mood. 'Enough of death and gloom! My nephew has some happier news to give us.'

'Um . . . well . . . I suppose so . . . yes.' Charles didn't usually find himself lost for words. Now, with a ring of grinning faces about him and his face blushing almost scarlet, he was hardly able to speak at all. 'What I mean to say . . . Miss LaSalle has done me the very great honour of accepting my proposal of marriage. That's it!'

Murders and treason were forgotten on the instant, to be replaced by congratulations and laughter, and the rest of that evening passed in the atmosphere of happiness and good cheer, typical of such occasions. Even Peter joined in the general merriment at Charles' news.

The next morning, as he was driving Adam back to Aylsham, Peter's usual cynicism on the subject of marriage had returned.

'A most satisfactory outcome,' he told Adam. 'I mean the capture of Duparc, of course, not the other thing. It is as I said to you before, too many good men are falling prey to the plague of matrimony. You'll be next.'

Adam ignored that remark. 'It will come to you in the end, Lassimer, for all your brave words. One of your widows — perhaps that housekeeper of yours — will capture your heart. Then you'll be begging her to become your wife.'

'For your information, Bascom, my housekeeper has told me she is leaving.' Peter sounded smug. 'All thanks to your wise advice too. You told me to make it plain to her that she could not trap me into wedlock.'

'Now I must bear that on my conscience as well, I suppose. What did you do to the poor woman? Treat her like a servant?'

'She said she'd heard gossip that I'd been slipping into Fenner's barn with the blacksmith's eldest daughter, Nancy. I am also said to be paying court to Barbara Peck, the widow of the carpenter on the Blickling Estate. There's a fine figure of a woman for you, Bascom. Oh yes. She's well supplied with all that promises a lively time between the sheets. My housekeeper challenged me to deny the rumours. I refused — with dignity, of course. She has thus left my bed and announced she will go to live with her sister in Ipswich as soon as she may.'

'A pin for your denials, Lassimer! I expect the gossip is correct, isn't it?'

Peter winked. 'You know I never, never comment on idle gossip. It's true Nancy Richardson is somewhat free with her favours. Mrs Peck over at Blickling is a decidedly handsome woman with a generous figure, as I said. Aside from that, I have nothing to add.'

'You really should control yourself, Lassimer.'

'Why? There are some of the greatest in this land who are far more lascivious than I am.'

'That's no reason to emulate them.'

'Of course, by following your advice I must soon lack a house-keeper.' Peter on the hunt for information was more persistent than a terrier after a rat. 'When you and Lady Alice marry, there will be one housekeeper too many in your combined households. Might Mrs Brigstone come to work for me?'

'Listen well, Lassimer. I wish to hear no more speculation about my future relations with Lady Fouchard. Besides, Mrs Brigstone is a most respectable lady. She would have far more sense than to let herself be lured into your dubious household. Leave my servants alone and find your own — if anyone is still foolish enough to want to work for you!'

'I assure you I never have any problems in finding people, male or female, eager to take up employment with me. Now you are fit enough to walk abroad, you must come to my shop again. There you will meet a young woman who has newly taken up employment to help serve our many customers. I am also thinking of opening a second establishment in Holt, now I am free of unfair competition from foreign quacks.'

They both laughed at that.

33

29TH MAY, 1793

ADAM SAT LATE OVER HIS BREAKFAST THE FOLLOWING MONDAY. During the five — or was it six — days that had passed since they all met at Mossterton Hall, the weather had taken a turn for the worse; the sunshine and warmth of spring replaced by something close to a return to winter. The cold had kept him indoors, but also enabled him to spend time at last with young Dr Henshaw — and a nicer, more conscientious and more able physician you could not hope to meet. If Wicken believed Henshaw would learn a good deal from Adam, he should have realised the converse might also be true. Henshaw had only just left the university in Scotland and was familiar with the latest thinking and discoveries. Only the previous evening, the two had sat up until past midnight discussing various means of treating or preventing the commonest ailment of gentlemen — the gout.

Yet it was not going to bed late, or drinking too much brandy, that was to blame for Adam's lethargy. It was the discovery that this morning, the sun was shining once again, the air was warm and his list of appointments for the day was empty. It was an opportunity not to be missed to drink his fill of coffee, find an interesting book and retire to his garden to sit under his favourite tree.

At least, that was what he had promised himself. Now, looking again at the two letters Hannah had brought to him a moment ago, he feared his quiet morning was about to be set aside. He had no difficulty in recognising the handwriting on either. That one, which felt stiff enough to suggest several sheets of paper, was from Wicken. The other, almost certainly a single sheet, was addressed in Lady Alice's neat, feminine hand. Had they been grenades with smoking fuses, he could not have considered either with greater apprehension.

The long-case clock in the hall struck ten. Then he heard Hannah, or one of the other servants, step up to the door behind him, listen for a moment and open the door a crack to see if they might at last clear away the breakfast dishes. He must stop procrastinating, read what each contained and have done with it. If only he could decide which letter posed the lesser danger to his peace of mind. In the end, he chose Wicken's.

Whitehall, London

My Dear Doctor,

I was sorry to be forced to depart so swiftly once the danger was over, but I'm sure you will understand the many pressing duties I have to attend to in London at present. The threat of invasion is much too real for comfort and the uncertainty about where the attack will fall means that our forces must be spread more thinly than any would wish. Those who plan our response are therefore unremitting in their demands for fresh information from all possible sources.

I know General Gorras has acquainted you with the happy outcome to the advice you gave us to look for Duparc along the coast from Weybourne. It is true he was found many miles from that spot, and on the sea, but Weybourne was the place from which he had left. However, I must not spoil my tale by starting at the end. I am sure you are eager to learn the actual circumstances of his capture.

As I recall, you told us that whether Duparc would escape or be taken lay in the hands of fortune. All would depend on whose luck was better. As usual, you were right. This time, I thank the Lord, we were better served. The fortunate occurrences that allowed us to bring Duparc to justice began when His Royal Highness, The Duke of York, decided to shorten his journey to Norwich and Cambridge by travelling most of the way by sea. There are always some naval vessels in Yarmouth Roads, I imagine, but not often a 36-gun frigate with no duties but to wait for more crewmen.

The commodore took a severe risk, of course, in ordering it to sea on the next tide. He could not be sure his superiors would agree with his action; the more so because it was based only on a civilian's guesswork. Yet if he sent a smaller vessel, a well-armed privateer could well prevail if it came to a fight. Even some of the smugglers' cutters along that coast would present a challenge to the only other ship he had available, a smallish sloop-of-war. It had to be the decision of a moment. That he chose right was proved by the capture of the privateer. I imagine the poor man's relief was a sight to be seen. By now he will have received a letter of commendation from His Royal Highness, which should add further to his satisfaction.

The frigate, HMS Arcturus, came up with a privateer's ship off the coast near Happisburgh. Perhaps the French captain was unaware of the dangerous shoals that lie there, for he would have done better to take a route further out into open water. No matter, that was where it was, quite close inshore and flying the Swedish flag. The captain of our frigate guessed at once it could not be a merchantman, since it was the wrong build and rig. Quite unsuitable for carrying timber or iron, which are the usual goods sent from that country to other parts of Europe. A ship flying a false flag is always suspect, so he ordered a shot to be fired across its bows as a signal for it to heave-to and allow inspection. A second shot was also ignored and the other ship continued to make the best speed it could to the south. That was enough warning. Our captain wore his ship around to sail parallel and opened fire with a broadside. At that, the other ship fired back, hauled down the Swedish colours and hoisted those of France.

My naval colleagues agreed the French captain may have a been a brave man, but he was undoubtedly a fool. He had a faster and more powerful ship to windward, the tide running in upon a lee shore and dangerous shoals and reefs all about him. His cannon too were no match for the 24-pounder carronades carried by the Arcturus. He had but two choices. To have his ship pounded to *pieces by Arcturus' shot or wrecked on that notorious graveyard of ships known as Happisburgh Sands. As events turned out, the poor fellow came close to suffering both. Had our ship not, with its first broadside, brought down his mainmast and caused much of his rigging and sails to trail in the water, he would have driven full upon the shoal. Instead, the ship lost way during the remaining fierce exchange of cannon-fire, until it was lifted by the tide to ground gently, then fell over somewhat upon its side. Arcturus anchored at a safe distance and prepared to fire yet another broadside. At that point, the French captain, recognising the inevitable, struck his colours in token of surrender. If he had not, Arcturus would have fired into the bottom of his ship's hull and rendered it incapable of proceeding further anyway.*

When our men boarded, they found proof enough the ship was a privateer, though there were several Englishmen amongst the crew. All crew members who had survived were secured. It was not a large number. Thanks to the captain's bravery — or foolhardiness — the privateer had suffered more than 50 casualties, including 15 who were dead. At least the French survivors will suffer no further harm save imprisonment. The English on board will face the penalty for taking up arms against their lawful monarch. Among the French, our men found a man who answered to the description of Duparc. He claimed to be a common seaman, but this was easily disproved. Under questioning, he proved unable to name certain nearby elements of the rigging correctly or describe how to tie more than the simplest of knots. Our men therefore put him in chains and took him aboard Arcturus. Amongst those who serve me here are several who know Duparc by sight. Once the villain arrives in London, we will be able to confirm his identity beyond doubt. After that, since he is a double murderer to your knowledge and mine as well as a spy, his fate is obvious.

As I said before we parted, Gort's attempt at an uprising will be dismissed as yet another of the riots amongst poor folk that have taken place whenever the price of grain has risen too high. No mention will be made of radicalism or muskets brought from France. As regards the attempt on the life of The Duke of York, its swift discovery means His Royal Highness can be excluded from all reports of what happened. The mayor and I have agreed that the official account of the business will state the gunpowder was nothing more than a crude attempt by discontented artisans to imitate Guy Fawkes' plot of almost two hundred years ago. Two small barrels of powder were involved and they were of poor quality, probably taken from a store used for hunting and untouched for many years. If we face pressure to reveal the target, the mayor will say it was most likely himself, together with other members of the corporation of the city.

Your name, as I promised you, will not be mentioned under any circumstances. You are much too valuable to me to risk you becoming known as anything more than the excellent physician you are. However, you may be certain that a man who frustrates a seditious plot and saves the life of the King's son will not lack suitable reward. I am not the only one who thinks that way. His Royal Highness, The Duke of York, is fully aware of the debt he owes to you. It only waits for a suitable occasion, unconnected in the public mind with events of a political nature, for the proper action to be taken.

In the meantime, I am delighted to be able to tell you that the first instalments of that action will soon be communicated to you in a proper manner. They are these. You are to be appointed General Superintendent of Military Hospitals, with a yearly salary of £2,000.00. The duties are not onerous and I have no doubt you will be able to find a suitable deputy to discharge the bulk of them, especially those relating to several establishments overseas. The Duke of York is also minded to offer you the post of physician to his household. Such a prestigious role will doubtless ensure your practice becomes one of the most fashionable and sought-after in the country — in addition to the considerable increase in the fees you may demand.

I have also been consulted by the Mayor of Norwich on another matter, unofficially of course. There is a vacant position amongst the Directors of the Norfolk and Norwich Hospital, together with another as a Trustee of the Great Hospital. The latter appointment lies in the gift of the Lord Bishop, who most kindly deputed the mayor to sound me out on the subject of a suitable candidate. I had no hesitation in suggesting your name in both cases. You may expect to hear from the mayor and the bishop shortly. Both those roles also carry substantial annual stipends. From now on, I will not be the only person of influence dedicated to securing your best interests.

I have not overlooked those who assisted you either. Miss Ruth Scudamore will soon receive an unexpected series of commissions for her drawings from several prestigious London institutions. Mr Charles Scudamore will, I assure you, find no difficulty in establishing his legal practice and no shortage of suit-

able clients. As for Mr Lassimer, I believe the Society of Apothecaries is looking for someone to represent their interests throughout East Anglia.

This affair would have proved far more troublesome without your involvement. What I find even more surprising is that you were able to do all while confined to your house, recovering from a serious accident.

I remain, Doctor, your grateful and admiring friend and your most obedient servant,

Percival Wicken, K.B.

Adam put the letter aside. It had all ended so neatly for Wicken. An enemy spy uncovered, a plot against the state prevented and several potential traitors seized. That must surely have earned him a good deal of praise from men of the greatest influence. Was he in a similar position, as Wicken implied? He was to receive a raft of appointments, all carefully calculated to suggest solely medical reasons for awarding them to him. He could not decline any of them either, since to do so would give the gravest offence. It appeared he must say goodbye to the quiet life of an obscure country physician and accustom himself to moving in other circles.

He ought to be delighted. If he was not . . . was he the only one still mourning those useless killings? Neither Betsy Wormald nor the other two deserved to die. Their error had been to stand in the way of ruthless, heartless men. Well, not quite, he supposed. Betsy had been trapped as much by her own longing for a different life as by Duparc's deceitful promises. Better to say they were ordinary people caught up in extraordinary times. Might not the same be said of himself? None of us could be certain of our path through life. As a physician, he should know that better than most. He had seen enough of sudden, unmerited death to repose no faith in the idea of a beneficent Providence.

With that sobering thought, he took up Lady Alice's letter and broke the seal. He was right. A single sheet of paper. What he had not expected was to find was a single paragraph of writing.

My Dear Doctor,

Please come and see me, tomorrow if you can. I have been thinking deeply about my future and find I have much to say to you. I cannot make plans for work at Irmingland either, until I know your mind.

Your most devoted friend,

Alice Fouchard

Adam read it through three times. After that, he refolded both letters carefully, carried them through into his library and locked them in his desk. The implications of Wicken's letter were clear enough. Lady Alice's words might imply much or little. The fulfilment of his dearest hopes — or the end of them; or perhaps only a request for advice of a practical nature.

Turning to the nearest window, Adam stood for some time looking out into his garden. The sky was a cloudless sheet of blue, the sun bright and warm. Every leaf looked as if freshly washed and polished. There was even a splendid thrush, perched on one of the apple trees, singing its heart out. It was going to be a beautiful day.

His decision was soon made. He would go to Mossterton Hall first thing in the morning, as her ladyship asked. It was high time for him to talk with her about his future too. He had much he needed to say that he should have said long ago. And this time, damn it, nothing was going to stop him.

AUTHOR'S NOTE

I have taken a good many liberties with history in writing this story. While it is true that Norfolk at this time had a well-deserved reputation for radicalism, and many working men were caught up in organisations the government deemed seditious, the revolution planned by Peter Gort is entirely a figment of my imagination. There never was a 'Battle of Baconsthorpe'; nor any landing of French muskets at the Norfolk coast, at least to my knowledge. The attempted assassination in Norwich of the Duke of York is also a complete fiction. If it does not appear in any histories of the time, that is because it did not happen, not because of careful editing by government hands.

The smugglers are real enough, though not their leader, Black Jack Bretherton. The coast of Norfolk is a mass of shingle beaches, marshes, crumbling cliffs and muddy creeks even today. In the past, it was a smuggler's paradise.

There were naval ships anchored at Great Yarmouth in this period, though the 36-gun frigate *HMS Arcturus* is imaginary. Not so Happisburgh Sands, a jumble of reefs and sandbanks that have long been the graveyard of unwary ships. How you pronounce the name Happisburgh is up to you. In Norfolk, it is pronounced 'Hayes-bor-ough'.

Most of the other places mentioned can be found on any map of the area, though Mossterton Hall, Trundon Hall and Irmingland Abbey will defeat your search, since all are my inventions.

The Tory government of William Pitt the Younger in the early 1790s was continually on edge over the effect of the French Revolution on sentiment in Britain. Some members of the Whig opposition were openly appreciative of the notion of a republican form of government. More were supportive of the idea of asserting greater parliamentary power in the face of George III's attempts to revive royal influence and prerogatives. Not until fear of Napoleon's armies, and his revival of French imperial ambitions, peaked towards the end of that decade did the British people rally around their king. By then, government actions, some of dubious legality, had driven the radicals into hiding until after Napoleon's downfall in 1815.

Dr Bascom's political sentiments should be seen as typical of most wealthy men of the time, who had always seen the proper attitude towards the lower classes as paternal. The notion that ordinary people should have a share in deciding important issues was far too novel to win much support; nor did you need to be a government supporter to feel the status quo was preferable to the uncertainties of revolution. If you owned property, economic stability and security of ownership were always going to be preferable to the uncertainties of change. The 18th-century ruling class told everyone that Britain's forms of government after 1688 were very nearly perfect and no one in the rising middle classes saw any compelling reason to doubt what they said. The working classes generally believed what they were told by their masters and the poor were too focused on survival to care.

ABOUT THE AUTHOR

William Savage is an author of historical mysteries. All his books are set between 1760 and around 1800, a period of great turmoil in Britain, with constant wars, the revolutions in America and France and finally the titanic, 22-year struggle with Napoleon.

William graduated from Cambridge and spent his working life in various management and executive roles in Britain and the USA. He is now retired and lives in north Norfolk, England.

www.penandpension.com

ALSO BY WILLIAM SAVAGE

The Dr Adam Bascom Mysteries

- An Unlamented Death
- The Code for Killing
- A Shortcut to Murder
- A Tincture of Secrets and Lies

The Ashmole Foxe Mysteries

- The Fabric of Murder
- Dark Threads of Vengeance
- This Parody of Death

Printed in Great Britain
by Amazon

28527227R00148